MURDER
In The Winter Woods

BOOKS BY KATIE GAYLE

MURDER
In The Winter Woods

KATIE GAYLE

bookouture

Published by Bookouture in 2025

An imprint of Storyfire Ltd.
Carmelite House
50 Victoria Embankment
London EC4Y 0DZ

www.bookouture.com

The authorised representative in the EEA is Hachette Ireland
8 Castlecourt Centre
Dublin 15 D15 XTP3
Ireland
(email: info@hbgi.ie)

ISBN: 978-1-83525-884-2
eBook ISBN: 978-1-83525-883-5

To our editors, who make the books better, and save our bacon.

Sean and Julia followed the ringing of a handbell and the sound of a deep, full voice intoning: 'Hear ye, hear ye... All citizens of Hayfield and beyond are invited to gather in the town square...'

'That's the town crier you can hear,' said Sean.

'I thought town criers went out of business with the advent of the radio. If not the printing press.' Julia smiled, aware that she might be showing her age by even remembering radios and printing presses. No doubt the younger folk might roll their eyes at her, but Sean wouldn't.

'There are quite a few who do ceremonial sort of things, and big community events like this one.' His smile crinkled his face, in the way that made Julia want to hire a town crier of her own, to announce what a fine man she had found herself, so unexpectedly, this second time around.

'I must say, he's got the voice for it, and it's much nicer than an announcement over a loudspeaker.'

The town square was full to bursting with people and with good cheer. It seemed half of the inhabitants of the Cotswolds, as well as a good number of out-of-towners, had come to

Hayfield for the switching on of the village Christmas lights. Julia was pleased they'd decided against bringing the dogs.

They'd arranged to meet Sean's son Jono and his girlfriend, Laine, but Julia doubted whether they would ever find the young couple in the crush. She was just about to say as much to Sean, when they appeared in front of them. Jono was in his usual attire – black jeans, grey (perhaps previously black) pullover, large shapeless over-garment, boots – but Laine had dressed up for the occasion. She wore fitted green corduroy trousers and a thick, Christmas-themed jumper patterned with red reindeer leaping over a white background. The cuffs were ringed with green holly leaves. Silver baubles secured her dark hair in two high pigtails, and caught the last of the evening light. Julia had dressed somewhere between the two, in jeans and a Christmas-ish Fair Isle jersey, with a warm jacket over. The temperature was dropping, along with the sun, and she was pleased to have the layers.

'Isn't this fun?' said Laine. 'I do love Christmas. It's so cheerful, isn't it?'

'Is it always this busy?' Jono asked, sounding slightly anxious. It was Julia's first time at the event, too, and she'd wondered the same thing. Like Jono, she had limited capacity for crowds and hoped this one would thin out a bit once the formalities were over.

'I haven't been for a year or two,' said Sean. 'It was a much more modest affair last time I attended, but then again, that was around the time that I had a full head of hair and perfect eyesight.' Julia ruffled his hair which was, in fact, still quite thick and well-distributed. 'It used to be more of a local event, but these days people come from all over,' he said.

'Well, it's not every day you get to hear an actual town crier,' Julia said. She led the little group to the edge of the crowd, closer to the source of the calls, and stood on tiptoes to get a better look at the fellow who was ringing the bell and summoning the punters. Fortunately, he was standing on a small platform and thus easily visible. With him was the mayor for Hayfield, Colin Postlethwaite; a small woman in a sparkly dress; and a couple of other people who looked like local dignitaries or officials.

The town crier was perfect, just perfect. Rotund and bearded and red-cheeked, and all kitted out in a red and gold coat, breeches, boots. On his head, a tricorne hat. Julia was delighted: 'Oh, look at him! He's just the man for the job, isn't he? Isn't it lovely when something or someone exactly matches all your expectations?'

Before anyone could answer, the town crier began to announce the order of proceedings. There would be a brief introduction from the mayor of Hayfield, and then the main event – the turning on of the Christmas tree lights, followed by all the other lights in the village. Father Christmas would be in his grotto and looked forward to seeing any children who cared to visit.

Mayor Postlethwaite knew his audience well, and kept it snappy. After a few thank yous to the many worker elves who had made the event happen, he said, 'I am sure you are eager to see the Christmas lights go on and to get to the Christmas market and food stalls...' A small cheer went up. 'To help me, I've got a special celebrity guest...' A dramatic drumroll emitted from the speakers... 'Maggie Pringle from the hit television show, *Strictly Come Baking*!' At that, a louder cheer went up.

The tiny sparkly woman, who looked as if she'd never eaten a baked item in her life, advanced on the microphone. The mayor handed her something that looked like a television remote, which she waved around as she addressed the crowd.

'Well hello, Hayfield and surrounds, and merry Christmas season!' she said, in a voice that rivalled the town crier's in its volume. The sound system gave a shriek, as if in surprise, or perhaps pain. 'Oops, sorry,' she said, at more modest decibels. The crowd cheered again, good-naturedly.

'Maggie, please do the honours and turn on the festive lights!'

A little boy in front of Julia leapt up and down, the pointed elfin ears attached to his head bobbing in eager anticipation.

'Come on, everyone, count me down!'

The crowd didn't need further encouragement. Together, they roared:

'Three... Two...' And on the count of '... ONE!' Maggie hit the switch and the huge Christmas tree in the centre of the square lit up, to a communal, 'Oooooh!' Baubles and tinsel sparkled, and a big golden star flashed on top.

Moments later, she hit the switch again and the whole village was ablaze with twinkling light. Every shopfront was festooned with strings of fairy lights. More lights picked out the outlines of the little trees that lined the square. The roads leading into the square were strung across with lights and baubles.

The elf boy shrieked in astonishment and delight. 'Mamma, look!' His chubby little finger stabbed the air, pointing first at the reindeers pulling Father Christmas's sled, then at the snowmen outlined on the stationery shop, then towards the glittering curtain of lights hanging on the front of the church. Overwhelmed by the sheer number of magnificent things, he put his hand down and just sighed.

'What a sight. Oh, I do love Christmas,' said Laine, snuggling happily into Jono's shoulder. 'Don't you?'

'Ah, well, this is very nice,' Jono said. 'Let's go and have a look around.'

'Meet back here in an hour, shall we?' said Sean. 'We can find a place to sit and have something to eat. My treat.' His face was bathed in reflected light, red on one side, green on the other, and over it all was spread a gentle smile. Julia felt a stab of love for him, this kind man she'd fallen for so unexpectedly. She put her arm through his. 'Good idea. Come on, let's explore.'

Sean and Julia wound their way through the crowd, which had spread and thinned out, as people walked the village. The two of them were on no particular mission or schedule. They strolled arm in arm, stopping every now and then to admire a particular display. A fellow came by on stilts, which seemed very brave given the throng. 'That there's an orthopaedic disaster waiting to happen,' muttered Sean grimly.

'He looks steady enough. I reckon he's done it before.' The chap tipped his red bowler hat at Julia and loped on.

The smell of roasting chestnuts drew them to the market. 'Oh, that smell reminds me of my childhood,' said Julia. 'Every year, we would go into London for the Christmas pantomime, and Daddy would buy us a little paper bag of chestnuts from the seller.'

'Come on, I'll get you a bag,' said Sean.

They joined a short queue at the chestnut seller's brazier near the entrance to the market and watched as, with one efficient movement, he scooped up the nuts, deposited them into a packet and handed them over to the customer. The customer dropped two pounds in a bowl next to the brazier and went on their way. Next customer, likewise. And then a packet for Julia. Sean dropped a note in the bowl and wished the seller a merry Christmas.

The chestnuts hot in her hands, Julia strolled beside Sean along the lines of stalls selling festive treats and gifts, many of them handmade. Julia waved to her neighbours, Matthew and Hester, who were selling honey and honeycomb. She called a hello to Angela, from the florist shop, Blooming Marvels, who was selling beautiful Christmas wreaths made of silver-green leaves and tasteful red baubles. On they walked, the night darkening by the minute, with a million tiny lights like fireflies all around them.

They were stopped by the sight of a huge dappled Great Dane in a beautiful jumper, a fiery red embroidered with white and gold stars.

'Aren't you a glorious fellow?' said Julia.

'That he is,' the stallholder said, her hands on her hips and a proud smile on her face. The dog gazed modestly into the distance.

'Lovely jumper, too.'

'Thank you, I have all sizes, and lots of different designs. Like our logo says, "Stylish Togs for Every Dog!"'

'This one would look lovely on Leo, with his golden colouring,' Julia said, holding up a green coat with red edging. 'I think I'll get a Christmas gift for the dogs. What do you think would look nice on Jake? Come on, help me choose.'

Sean gave her a wry look, but went along with her mad idea. They rejected the outright ridiculous options – a Santa suit with a hat, which Jake would tear to shreds in seconds; an outfit with a hood and antlers for Leo – and opted for a nice red and black tartan for Jake, and the green edged with red for Leo.

Julia handed over her credit card. Dog clothing was surprisingly expensive, but fortunately, unlike humans, the animals didn't require an extensive wardrobe.

Jono was waiting for them. 'Come on,' he said, as soon as he saw them. 'By some miracle we got a spot in one of the pubs. Laine is keeping our seats.'

They squeezed through the crush at the Wig and Whistle, towards Laine's waving hand.

'I'm glad you're here!' she said. 'People were giving me the evil eye, taking up a whole table to myself. I was beginning to think I might have to fight off invaders.'

'I reckon I could take that fellow,' Jono said, jerking his head towards a huge man with a ruddy face atop a badly drawn neck tattoo of a dragon. Or perhaps it was an alligator.

'I'm off duty, so let's try not to give or receive any injuries, shall we?' said Sean.

'If we do, Dad, you could heal them and Julia could counsel them. It would all work out.'

Julia grinned. It was good to see Jono in fine spirits. He could barely be persuaded to say a word when he'd come down from London some months ago, and now here he was, joking and chatting, and with the lovely Laine by his side.

'Let's order quickly,' said Sean, catching the waitress's eye. 'We'll likely wait a bit for our food.'

When the waitress had taken their drinks and food orders, Julia spoke to Jono: 'How is work going? Are you still enjoying working at the vet's?'

'Oh yes. Dr Ryan is a good vet and a good boss. Of course, I love all the animals. And most of the humans are all right. It's interesting. There's never a dull moment. You won't believe the things we see. Goodness, just yesterday, a cat came in who'd swallowed a—'

'Eating,' Laine said, gesturing to the bread and butter the waitress had brought to the table. Clearly she'd already heard what the cat had swallowed, and the results thereof, and didn't judge it to be dinner table fare.

'Right,' said Jono, with a laugh. 'I tend to forget. Like you, Dad, and your surgery stories.' He turned to Laine. 'We'd be sitting down to a nice dinner and Dad would launch into some horrible story about someone's bunions...'

'He does like a good war story,' said Julia, putting her hand over Sean's. 'But it's wonderful that the work suits you so well, Jono.'

The waitress arrived with their drinks, and talk stopped while she handed them out. Beers for the passengers, sparkling water for Laine and Sean, the designated drivers.

When she left, Jono answered. 'Working at the vet does suit me. And now that I'm permanent, Dr Ryan is giving me more to do, training me up on the computer system, ordering the pet food stock and the medicines. He likes me to help him with the animals, too. Calm them down, hold them still, pass him things. It's nice to have more to do, more responsibility, more stimulation, and I do like working with the animals. In fact, I've been thinking that I might like to study veterinary science...'

Sean jumped in, all eager: 'Study? That's an excellent idea... Have you thought about where? I know a chap who works at the college...'

Julia could see that Sean's eagerness annoyed Jono. It reminded him of how at sea he'd been the past year or so, and how worried his father had been. He spoke a little sharply. 'I've thought about a lot of things, Dad, and I've done some investigation. First things first, if I've got any chance of getting in, I need to do A-level Biology, and to improve my maths grade. I can study online, and I can start in January.'

'Excellent!' Sean beamed. 'Well, I can probably remember enough to help you with the Biology.'

'Actually, Laine did Bio for A levels and at uni, so we're cool.'

Interesting. Clearly they anticipated this relationship continuing into the new year and beyond.

Julia felt a warmth that went beyond her snug winter coat at the thought of Laine and Jono staying in Berrywick, and staying together. There was something heartwarming about the idea of young people making a permanent home in the little village. And who could ask for a better and safer place to settle and, maybe one day, raise a family?

2

'These roads are ridiculously dark,' said Sean, leaning forward over the steering wheel and peering into the darkness. 'It's dangerous.'

'Especially this lane through the woods,' said Julia. She had suggested mildly that they should stick to the main roads going home from the Christmas market, but Sean had been insistent that the route through the woods would be beautiful at this time of year. He wasn't wrong – but it was terribly dark, and difficult to properly appreciate the beauty.

Sean laughed. 'I know, I know,' he said. 'You told me so.'

'I would never point that out myself,' said Julia, 'but yes, I did.' They both smiled. Julia thought how pleasant it was to be with a man like Sean, who could laugh at his own mistakes. Her ex-husband, Peter, would have gone into a bit of a sulk at this point.

'We should bring the dogs for a walk here again,' she said. 'During the day, obviously. But it is lovely.'

'I do love winter,' said Sean, carefully turning the wheel to follow the curve that took them into the depths of the wood. 'Hopefully we'll get some good snow, too.'

'Jake does love the snow.' Julia smiled at the thought of her chocolate Labrador, who was no doubt curled up next to the Aga and dreaming of walking as they spoke. She looked out of the window, trying to see if there were was any good holly to make a wreath. Perhaps she could bring Jake here and pick a bunch for the house. One of the joys of living in the country was the availability of seasonal wildflowers. But the sight that met her eyes on the side of the path was not at all what she had expected.

'Sean!' she yelled. 'Stop the car. Now!'

'What's wrong?' said Sean, carefully slowing down. He pulled over to the side of the road. 'This isn't a great place to stop, Julia. It's hard to see the car if you come around the bend at speed.'

Julia looked out of her window again. Yes, it was still there.

A dark shape, where only a footpath and bushes should be. A dark shape with a foot sticking out into the road.

'There's a person there,' said Julia. 'Lying on the side of the road. My side. I think that they've been hit!'

Sean put the hazard lights on and grabbed his medical bag from the back seat of the car. 'I hope we're not too late,' he said.

The two of them hurried over to where the person lay. Sean took a torch out of his bag, and knelt next to them, shining a light onto the face. 'Oh lord,' he said, 'it's Lewis Band.'

Lewis was the Berrywick taxi driver; the chap to call if you needed a local lift. His ageing Mercedes was a familiar sight along the Cotswolds roads.

Sean held his fingers to Lewis's throat, and shook his head sadly. 'I'm afraid that there's nothing I can do for him, Julia. We'd better call the police.'

As Sean spoke to the police, explaining exactly where they were and cautioning them against hitting his car as they came around the bend, Julia didn't know what to do with herself. It seemed disrespectful to just stand there, leaving Lewis's dead body lying on the side of the road, one foot still on the path. She remembered that Sean always kept a picnic blanket in the car, and she decided to fetch it. It made no sense – Lewis was past feeling the cold – but as she spread it over his body, she felt a bit better, like she'd given him some dignity. As she tucked the blanket around him, she realised that his shirt was muddy.

'Sean, pass me the torch, please.'

Finishing his call, Sean handed it over. 'What is it, Julia?'

'Look here. There are tyre marks all the way up to his body.' She shone the torch around. 'It's like they drove right over him. That can't be right.'

'Maybe it's old tyre marks,' said Sean. 'And he happened to land on them.'

'Maybe. And maybe that footprint is old, too,' she said, pointing to a footprint on the other side of the body. While Sean and Julia had left a fairly clear track of prints in the damp ground, this footprint was the only one on the other side of Lewis's body.

'Either way, let's try not to pollute the scene more than we already have,' said Julia. 'It might be that the tracks and that print will help the police find whoever hit Lewis.'

It was several hours later that Sean and Julia finally made it home. DC Walter Farmer had arrived with a colleague to cordon off the scene, and sighed deeply when he saw Julia. 'I'd just been about to go off duty, Mrs Bird,' he said. 'Amaryllis has a nice steak pie waiting for me at home.'

But when he'd seen the body, and when Julia pointed out the tracks and the footprint, Walter seemed to forget all about his pie, and his young wife, and focused entirely on the crime scene, calling for forensic backup and taking careful notes. His boss, Hayley Gibson, would be proud of him, Julia had thought, watching the young man work.

Sean and Julia let themselves in to Julia's house, where Jake greeted them as if they had abandoned him on an icy peninsula with no hope of future contact.

'A hit-and-run,' said Julia, patting Jake and putting on the kettle. 'What sort of person would do that?'

'It's hard to imagine,' said Sean. 'Perhaps a scared one. Or possibly a drunk one.'

'A coward, either way.'

'It would be tempting. Alone on that lane through the woods, no witnesses. You can see how it might cross their mind.'

'Sean O'Connor! You would never do something like that, and you know it.'

Sean sighed. 'You're right. I wouldn't. But it doesn't mean that I can't imagine someone else being tempted to just flee the scene.'

Julia handed him a cup of steaming tea, and they sat down at her table. Neither was quite ready to end the evening, after the trauma of finding Lewis's body.

'I'd hate to be the one having to phone his wife,' said Julia, sipping from her cup. 'Poor woman. And so close to Christmas.'

'It's a terrible shock. And a loss to the village.'

They both fell silent, each caught up in their own memories of rides with Lewis.

'I bet it will turn out to be a tourist,' said Julia. 'They really are a scourge at this time of year.'

'Spoken like a true local,' smiled Sean. 'But you're right. There's going to be a few people who agree with you on that one.'

This would, indeed, prove to be a most accurate prediction.

3

The meeting of the Berrywick Residents' Association was well attended. Julia hadn't done a head-count, but she suspected it was the biggest gathering of the Association since the referendum on whether to paint the park benches black or a very dark green. That was a year ago – black had won the day. The mood this time was a good deal more sombre, which was hardly surprising, given the circumstances.

Kevin Moore stood up. It was only his second meeting as Chairman of the Association, and he looked pale and serious, and somehow younger than his age, which Julia estimated to be about forty. His wife, Nicky, smiled encouragingly at him and whispered to Julia, 'Poor Kev, he's nervous. And I don't blame him. It's a sad time for Berrywick.'

It was indeed.

Kevin cleared his throat, and thanked them all for coming. He looked down at his hands and then raised his face to the room. His eyes seemed to glisten with unshed tears when he spoke: 'This is no ordinary meeting of the Residents' Association, because it comes in the wake of a terrible tragedy. First and foremost, I'd like to offer our sincere condolences to the family of Lewis Band. Lewis was a well-known and respected member of our community, a trusted driver for many of us, and a regular participant at these meetings. As you no doubt know, he was hit by a car on the road through the woods on Monday night, and died on the scene from his injuries.'

There followed a quiet chorus of tuts and clicks and sighs, reminiscent of spring rainfall on a shed roof. The quiet observations from the audience gathered force.

'Too sad.'

'Bless his soul, dear Lewis.'

'Ah, poor Coral, losing her husband like that. It's a tragedy.'

'It's a crime, is what it is.'

That last statement was issued firmly and loudly by Will Adamson, and it was addressed in the direction of DI Hayley Gibson and Walter Farmer, who were attending to represent the police. Hayley didn't respond.

Kevin interjected, trying to keep the meeting on course – and civil. 'Now, I know that we're all very distressed about what happened to Lewis, and concerned about road safety. And we will be looking at ways to—'

Another voice piped up from the back: 'Will's right. It's a crime, the way people drive around here.'

More voices joined in:

'Everyone in Berrywick knows that bend. We know to slow down as we go through those woods. It must have been someone from out of town.'

'Of course it was! It's those tourists.'

'True. You know what they're like. They don't know the roads, and they speed around like they own the place.'

'Some maniac in a Range Rover nearly ran over my Rover on Ranger Road,' said Yvonne. This statement confused Julia, until she remembered that Yvonne's Great Dane was indeed called Rover, and there was indeed a road in Berrywick called Ranger Road. 'Came round that sharp bend near the school and the bumper actually touched his tail. If I hadn't tugged him away, he wouldn't be here, poor dear Rover.' She looked so sad, it was almost as if she'd forgotten that Rover was alive and well and chasing ducks at the Big Pond, which was where he'd been that very afternoon when Julia had taken her Jake for his walk.

'Summer's the worst,' said Nicky. 'You expect a lot of cars, and you know to be careful. But there's been an influx this last couple of weeks, with the Christmas decorations and lights going up all over the region. It'll be busy for a bit, with people coming for the Christmas markets all over the Cotswolds. There's something on almost every day. We can expect a lot of visitors.'

'They're a menace, that's what they are,' came an angry voice from somewhere behind Julia.

Flo, the proprietor of the Buttered Scone, held up her hands in a 'hold on a moment' gesture. 'Well, not exactly. To be fair, the people that come to Berrywick are mostly very nice, and they do bring a lot of business into the village.' At least half of Flo's customers – the high-spending, salmon-eating half – were out-of-town visitors. Some cross faces turned towards her and a low grumble could be heard.

'I'm not supporting bad driving, and I'm not saying we do nothing about it,' Flo said quickly. 'We need to take action. We do. I'm just saying... let's not get ahead of ourselves. We need the tourists too.'

Without them, Julia knew Flo would be trying to make a living off the likes of Johnny Blunt occupying a prime table and eking out a coffee and a scone for two hours on a Tuesday morning. Many of the other shopkeepers, likewise. There were one or two heads bobbing in support of Flo's point. Kevin, whose job as manager of the Swan also depended in good part on the tourist pound (or dollar, or yen, or euro) stepped back into the fray. 'I am recommending that we form a sub-committee to look at road safety and what we can do to encourage better driving.'

His suggestion calmed the crowd somewhat, and drew some approving grunts. Kevin seized the moment and said, 'I'm suggesting we ask a small number of residents, and a liaison from the local police, to come up with some suggestions to keep Berrywick's roads safe. Now, if everyone's in agreement, I'll need some volunteers, or some recommendations for people to serve on the committee.'

Will Adamson's hand went up. This was no surprise. He was a man who sought power, status and influence, even in minor ways. 'I am familiar with the bylaws and regulations, of course, being in the property business,' he said. 'My schedule is very full, and my daughter will probably kill me for volunteering...' He gave a rueful smile, which drew some restrained tittering. 'But this is an important issue, a life-and-death issue, and if you think I might be useful, I would be glad to be of service.'

There was a muttering of thanks and one or two claps. Will beamed modestly.

It's not as if you're about to donate a kidney, thought Julia, and immediately felt ashamed of herself for her bad grace.

'Thank you, Will. I think I speak for everyone when I say you'd be very useful,' said Kevin.

Julia thought Flo should be on the committee. She was smart, she knew what was what, and she had an eye on the tourist market as well as the locals' welfare. Julia put up her hand to suggest it.

'Hello, I...'

'Thank you, Julia, we'd be pleased to have you on board.'

'Oh, no. Actually Kevin, I was going to put Flo's name forward.'

'Excellent idea. You and Flo and Will, that sounds like a good team.'

'Well, I meant *instead* of me...'

Julia's explanation went unheard, as Kevin continued, 'And DC Walter Farmer, will you be our police liaison?'

Walter nodded.

'And you, of course, Kevin,' said Will. 'You'll be on the sub-committee, I take it?'

Kevin agreed. 'Right you are, that's sorted. Thanks all. I have Tuesday off. Is Tuesday afternoon any good for you all for our first meeting? Shall we say three? We can meet at the Swan if you like. I can probably rustle us up a cup of tea.'

Murmurs of general assent rumbled from the other members of the road safety sub-committee. There was a brief moment when Julia might have cleared up the misunderstanding, and resisted more forcefully. She dithered. She did have the time and if she could be useful... But did she want another responsibility on her plate?

'Excellent. Now, let's move on to the next order of business.'

Julia took her little pocket diary from her handbag and removed the pencil from its holder. She turned to the page for Tuesday and, with a small internal sigh, wrote:

Road Safety Committee, 3 p.m.

4

Kevin had booked a small function room for the first meeting of the road safety committee, and was already there with a tray of tea, as promised, and a very nice-looking plate of sandwiches – egg and cress, cheese and tomato, and cucumber – cut into quarters. Julia's mouth watered at the sight of them. Why were little triangle sandwiches so much more delicious than regular sandwiches? Probably because everyone's mums had made them for childhood birthdays. The nostalgia was delectable.

Flo came in, followed a minute later by Will. Kevin was pouring the tea when DC Walter Farmer arrived, slightly pink and puffing. 'Sorry I'm late,' he said. 'A lot going on.'

'By less than two minutes,' said Kevin, consulting his watch. 'Don't worry, mate. Come and sit, catch your breath. Tea?'

'Yes, please, I'm parched. I had to rush to an appointment. Didn't even have time for lunch.' He eyed the sandwiches.

'Help yourself,' said Kevin, nudging the plate towards him. 'The Swan's finest sarnies.'

Walter reached over and took two. 'Oooh, just like my mum used to make. Plates of little sandwiches for every birthday party,' he said, neatly confirming Julia's hypothesis. He put one of the little triangles on a plate and the other straight into his mouth.

'Crusts or no crusts?' asked Flo. 'Your mum's sarnies, I mean.'

Walter swallowed and dabbed his mouth with a paper napkin. 'Crusts. We weren't *millionaires*, you know. Waste not, want not, was Mum's motto.'

Flo laughed. Julia, whose mother had cut off the crusts, kept her silence.

'Right then,' said Kevin. 'So, Walter, before we start, is there any update on the investigation? Have you found the culprit?'

'Not yet. Unfortunately, the incident happened in a place where there are no cameras. We're looking at the footage from the surrounding area.'

'That's a pity,' said Flo, shaking her head. 'I hope you catch him and make sure he faces the full might of the law. I can't believe anyone would be so cold-blooded. Imagine hitting another human being and not stopping to see if they're all right!'

'Actually, it seems like he did stop,' Walter said. 'The direction of the tyre marks and the footprint that Julia and Sean found indicate that he stopped, got out, and then drove off. It's our thinking that he saw that Lewis was dead and panicked. He decided to leg it.'

'Are there any leads?'

'We were hoping to get a good tyre print, which we might be able to match to the make of car and then cross check against the cameras, but there was a bit of rain that night, so it looks like that's not going to be possible. The same goes for the footprint. There's no detail on the tread, so we can't determine the type of shoe.' Walter Farmer looked thoroughly glum.

'Well, I'm sure you are doing everything you can,' said Kevin.

'We are, and we've got posters up everywhere, calling for

information from that night. Hopefully someone saw something. An erratic driver. Anything.'

'But for now, this road safety committee is looking forwards, right?' said Flo. 'To see what we can do to make sure Berrywick's roads are safer for everyone. So, what are your thoughts?'

It was inevitable that Will Adamson would be the first to give his suggestions, and that his suggestions would be punitive: 'We need a crackdown on bad driving and fast driving – more visible policing, more speed cameras, harsher fines.'

'I can look into the cameras,' said Walter. 'There's a procedure to request more. We'll have to make recommendations as to where they are placed.'

'I can do that,' said Will. 'I know where the problem areas are. I can get going on the application procedure, too. I have some experience navigating red tape.'

'That's very helpful, thank you. Perhaps someone can help you.'

Julia looked down at her hands. She didn't fancy being paired off with Will Adamson. 'I could do it,' said Flo, to Julia's relief.

Julia offered her own suggestion: 'I was thinking that it might help to communicate with drivers more. Put up some signs with messages that make them think, or slow down.'

'Like "Speed Kills",' said Will.

'Well, I did some research online, and there's quite some evidence that shows it's more effective to take a positive approach,' said Julia. 'Something like "Help us protect our wildlife", or "Our children use this road". Rather than "You're a terrible person".'

'That makes sense, actually,' said Flo.

Will made a snorting, huffing noise. 'You've got to soft-soap everything these days, haven't you? Don't want to hurt anyone's feelings. Couldn't have that.'

'Well, I suppose it makes sense to do what works best,'

Kevin said mildly. 'Julia, how about you and I come up with some ideas for the signs?' Julia nodded. 'Will and Flo will look at where cameras might go. Walter can help with that, and investigate where the speeding and accidents take place. Then we'll see about permissions.'

'That sounds good,' said Julia, pleased to be paired with Kevin, who was a decent chap. The others nodded in agreement.

'I will get right onto it,' said Walter, determinedly. 'This should never happen again in our village.'

'I'll make a group and we can use that to share ideas,' said Kevin.

'Good work, everyone,' said Flo. 'Now if that's all, I'd best be getting back. Tea time's always busy with the school-run crowd. Hungry little footballers and their mums.'

Will looked at his watch and stood up. 'Me too. I've got a site meeting to get to.'

Flo and Will left, but Walter didn't budge. 'Do you mind?' he asked, gesturing towards the plate with the remaining sandwiches.

'Not at all, help yourself!' Kevin slapped him on the shoulder on his way out. 'I've got a few things to see to, but you finish them off!'

Julia, who had nothing more pressing than a dog walk ahead of her for the rest of the afternoon, stayed with Walter.

'Want one?' he asked.

'No thanks. I had lunch just before I came.'

Walter picked up a cucumber sandwich and bit it in half. 'I didn't. I was at a meeting. A doctor's appointment actually, with Amaryllis.'

'Oh, I hope she's all right.'

'Yes, yes, she's fine. More than fine, actually.' Walter hesitated, and then leaned in towards Julia with a funny smile on his face. 'The thing is...' He lowered his voice, although there was no one else in the room. 'The thing is, we're expecting.'

'A baby?' asked Julia, redundantly. 'Amaryllis is pregnant? Oh, how wonderful, Walter!'

'We haven't told anyone yet. We will be visiting her mum and dad this weekend to give them the good news. We wanted them to be the first to hear. But I just wanted to say it, out loud. We're pregnant! I'm going to be a dad.' He looked proud of himself.

'Oh, Walter, how lovely. And of course I won't say a word to anyone until you've announced the news to the family. And what good news it is! You are a good man and I'm certain that you'll be a marvellous dad. And Amaryllis will be a lovely mum. That's one lucky baby.'

Walter beamed. 'Really? Do you think so? I really want to be a good dad...'

'No doubt in my mind.'

'Thank you. It's just...' A series of microexpressions chased each other across his face – Julia thought she saw delight, confusion, fear. 'I mean, it's a lot, isn't it? Being a parent. Like, it's huge. I mean, it's everything... And the world, it's so unpredictable... So dangerous.'

'Well, there are dangers, of course, but it's also a good and kind place, Walter.'

'I suppose that, being a policeman, I see all sorts of things. Difficult things.'

'That's true. I felt the same as a social worker. It's hard to come face-to-face with the dark side of humanity, and even just the random awful things that can upend people's lives.'

'Like this hit-and-run accident with Lewis. It's so horrible and sad, and so random. I mean, at least it's an accident, but still: the man was walking through the woods in the evening, minding his own business, just getting a breath of fresh air after a good day's work and dinner with his wife. Just taking an evening stroll before turning in, and the next thing he knows, BAM! A car hits him and he's dead. And Coral is a widow.'

'I hear you, Walter. It was a horrible, tragic accident.'

Walter hesitated, and then said, 'And there's something else, Julia. Something I can't get out of my mind.'

Julia waited.

'The car that hit Lewis? It reversed back over him.'

'What? My God, I didn't know that.' Julia felt slightly sick thinking about this. Perhaps Lewis might have lived if the car had only hit him once.

'We didn't release that yet; it's still part of the confidential information. It looks like the driver hit Lewis, felt the impact and reversed to see what he'd hit. He didn't see Lewis lying on the ground, stunned. The post-mortem says that's what killed him.'

'How utterly appalling.'

'You see what I mean? The world, Julia. It's just... so dangerous. So random. And you never know what's coming your way. And soon I'll have a kid. I don't know how I'll sleep at night. Or go to work and leave him. Or her. And then they'll want to go and play with friends. And go swimming. And ride bicycles...' Walter shuddered at the very mention of bicycles.

'I know that feeling. When I had Jess I felt so vulnerable in the world; I didn't know how I would survive having something so precious. But I knew I had to try to manage that anxiety, if I was going to bring up a child who felt safe and independent. All you can do is love your child, and prepare them for the world, Walter. And, if you can, try to make the world a little bit of a better, safer place.'

He nodded, solemnly. 'That's good advice. I'll try to do what you say, to manage my worries. As for the world...' He stood up, and straightened his shoulders. 'Well, I am going to do my bit to make the woods and lanes of Berrywick safer, for a start.'

5

Wilma pulled a dusty box from the depths of the storeroom at Second Chances. *XMAS!* was written on the top in large capital letters in green felt-tip pen. Someone had sketched a Christmas tree underneath the word.

'Brace yourselves ladies, it's that time of year again,' she said, dragging the box across the floor.

'Time for decking the halls, is it?' Julia bent down to help her. The box slid more easily with two.

'Fa-la-la-la-la, la la la la,' said Diane. She gave a little jump and made jazz hands, for reasons that were inexplicable to Julia.

Wilma straightened up with a big smile. 'I want to have a look at what we've got, and start our Christmas display,' she said. 'I do love Christmas.' This was not news to her colleagues. They had both had first-hand experience of Wilma's Christmas Fever. It had taken Julia until March to get rid of the Christmas carol earworms, and to find and remove the last bits of glitter from about her clothes and person. 'It's so cheerful,' Wilma continued. 'So good-spirited.'

'Also, there's cake,' said Diane. 'And mince pies.'

'Oooh, here's an idea. How about we give the first three

customers of the day a free mince pie?' said Wilma. 'I'll supply them. My treat.'

Diane's eyebrows raised imperceptibly, along with Julia's own. Wilma didn't eat sweet things, on account of always watching her figure, and she was not known to give something for nothing. She had clearly been touched by the Christmas spirit.

'I love that. I've got another idea,' said Diane. 'How about we curate a special arrangement of Christmas gifts for different categories of people? Presents for kids. For dads. For teachers. For foodies. And so on. To help people do their Christmas shopping.'

Wilma looked delighted. 'Excellent idea. We can get working on that this week. It's only five weeks until Christmas. People are shopping already.'

'Nice idea, Diane,' said Julia. 'I was thinking we could spread the message that pre-loved gifts from places like Second Chances are the most cost-effective and environmentally responsible gifts you can buy. Buying used means cutting down on packaging waste, and the money they spend in the shop goes to the charity.'

'That's a very good idea. But how do we spread the message?' said Diane. 'We could just tell people, of course. But maybe put up a notice outside the shop?'

'We could call it "Feel-Good Christmas",' said Julia, who was getting very enthused by her idea.

'Excellent idea!' said Wilma. 'Why don't we see if one of the local papers or radio stations can run something for us?'

'I could ask Jim McEnroe from the *Southern Times*. He'd be a good place to start.'

Their planning chatter was interrupted by the tinkle of the bell on the front door of the shop. They turned to look, and all three women started to laugh.

'What's up?' said Jim, looking rather unnerved to find himself the unwitting provider of such mirth.

'Speak of the devil,' said Wilma.

'We were just talking about you,' said Julia. 'Literally, before you walked in.'

'Uh-oh, that doesn't sound good.'

'Don't worry, there was no scurrilous gossip, Jim,' Julia reassured him. 'I was wondering if you might be interested in writing something about having a greener Christmas? Buying pre-used gifts, and so on. We've got some ideas, and it would help us too.'

'Actually, that's not a bad idea. To be honest, it's a slow time of year news-wise. Other than the accident, of course. Every year, I interview the fellow who plays Father Christmas in the village. Every year. Same bloke. Bill Jenkins. Same questions.' He held out his hand as if clutching a microphone, '"So, tell me, Bill. How did you get started as Father Christmas...?" "Well, it was back in 2003. Ho ho ho..."' He made a sound somewhere between a sigh and a laugh. 'So yeah. I'm always keen to talk if you've got an idea for something different at this time of year.'

'Julia's the one to talk to; it was her idea,' said Wilma.

'Actually, there's something I wanted to talk to you about too, Julia,' said Jim. 'Can you take a break? Coffee at the Buttered Scone? We can kill two birds with one stone.'

'Now?' Julia looked at Wilma. There was a lot to do in the shop.

'Go, go,' said Wilma, making shooing motions with her hands. 'Diane and I can hold the fort.'

'Well, if you're sure...' Julia said, already lifting her handbag to her shoulder.

Ten minutes later they were seated at a table with a coffee, waiting for their cheese toasties. 'Might as well. It's pretty much lunchtime,' Julia had said, not entirely accurately. It was 11.15, but Jim seemed quite happy to go along with the toastie plan.

Jim sipped his coffee while Julia told him her Feel-Good Christmas idea – the pre-loved presents, the environmental advantages, the money saved, and the proceeds going to good causes.

'So Jim, what do you think?'

'Well, it's a win-win for sure,' said Jim. 'Great idea.'

'Would you be able to help us promote the idea? Not just for Second Chances. The principles apply everywhere.'

'I like it. As I said, we're always on the lookout for seasonal stories at *Southern Times*. Second Chances would have to be the focus though, being local. We'd interview you and take some pics of you in the store.'

'Wilma would be the one to take a picture of – she's the boss,' said Julia quickly. She didn't fancy the idea of having her face splashed all over the media, even if it was just a regional newspaper.

'Whoever. We'll take some pics. Human interest stuff, you know.'

'Perfect! Thanks, Jim.'

With impeccable timing, Flo arrived with their toasties, which were golden and glistening and oozing with cheese.

Jim beckoned dramatically: 'Come to me, best toastie in all the Cotswolds!'

Flo laughed, putting the plates down first in front of Julia, then Jim. 'Ah well, you're not the first to say it, I won't lie. It's all in the cheese, you know. We use only the finest local Double Gloucester. Well, and the butter, of course. You have to butter both sides of the bread. Inside and out. Don't skimp! That's how you get that lovely crispy toast.'

Julia felt fleetingly worried about how much dairy fat she'd be ingesting with all that cheese and butter, but she wasn't one to let such thoughts ruin a good lunch.

'They are absolutely the best,' she said, taking up her knife and fork.

'While we're here, maybe you can help me with something,' Jim said, when Flo was out of earshot.

'With pleasure. What do you need?'

'I'm writing a piece about Lewis Band, the taxi driver who was killed in the hit-and-run.'

'Poor Lewis. Terrible story.'

'It is. Did you know him?'

'Just a little. I'd used his services once or twice, and saw him about the village. He was very reliable. He seemed like a good chap. Are you doing a news story about the circumstances of his death?'

'No. There's another piece going in about the standard of driving on the country roads – which, as you know, is an issue.'

Julia nodded.

'News-wise there's not much to say, other than the fact that some bastard hit a pedestrian and drove off without stopping.'

Julia noted that he didn't seem to know that the driver *had* stopped, and in fact, got out of the car. After accidentally reversing over him. Interesting that the police hadn't released that piece of information. Jim also didn't seem to know that Julia herself had found the body. She knew he would love that detail, and her first-hand account, but she decided to keep it to herself.

Jim continued: 'I'm looking at a soft piece. More of a longish obituary, giving a sense of the man, him being well-known in these parts. I'm gathering anecdotes and quotes from people who knew him.'

'I'd be happy to help, but I'm sure there are better people to speak to than me. As I said, we didn't have much to do with each other.'

'Right, well. No worries. I've asked a few people and I've got a few quotes. It's probably enough. I was just hoping for something meatier, more specific. And I know that you're good at noticing things about people.'

Jim turned his attention back to his lunch. He seemed lost in thought, sawing through the sandwich with a great deal more concentration than one would have thought was required to create a bite-sized triangle. He popped the piece into his mouth and chewed contemplatively. Julia was about to enquire after Moxy, Jim's Schnauzer-poodle cross, when he spoke. 'There was actually a bit of a funny vibe when I asked some people about him.'

Julia frowned. 'About Lewis?'

'Yes.'

'Really?' She waited for Jim to say more.

'Yes. Look, there's no doubt, he was a popular guy. Lots of people knew him and used his services. They sang his praises. But I've had a couple of weirdly lukewarm responses to my inquiries.'

'That's surprising. From who?'

'Dora, for one.'

'Dora from the sweet shop?' Dora looked like an illustration from a children's book about a perfect sweet shop owner or an ideal granny. It was hard to imagine her saying anything lukewarm about anybody.

'Yes. She'd known him her whole life. Her grandfather and his father were second cousins or something, I believe.'

'She's a sweetheart – I can't imagine her being mean about anyone, let alone the recently deceased. What did she say?'

'It's more what she didn't say. It was as if she was holding something back. Reticent, might be the word. She said she knew him better when they were younger, but it was long ago, and she didn't remember much about him and they'd rather lost touch, and she'd prefer not to be quoted about "that man". That's what she called him – *that man*.'

'Slightly odd, seeing as they lived in the same village their whole lives,' Julia mused. She took a bite of her oozing toastie, and chewed it while she thought. 'It sounds to me like they had some kind of falling out. Not uncommon in families, is it? Or in small villages. People have their disagreements.'

'I suppose so. Who knows, maybe he stole her parking space in 1985.'

'Trod on her toe at the school dance.'

They laughed, and stopped talking to pay due attention to the best toasties in the Cotswolds. After a few more bites, Jim said: 'Ah well, I guess it could be that he just wasn't such a great chap.'

'Well, nobody's perfect, Jim.'

'You're right, no one is universally adored and admired, are they? I suppose I'm just irritated because it's made my life difficult. I thought I'd whip the article together in an afternoon, but I'm a bit short. I can't use the lukewarm comments for this sort of piece. All I've got really is a lot of people saying he was a good chap, never late to fetch you, and he didn't talk too much in the taxi or play the radio loudly or smoke or anything. That's why I asked you when I saw you. Thought you might have an anecdote or some such. No worries, though, I'll ask around, see what I can find out about old Lewis.'

Flo arrived soundlessly and made them both jump, saying: 'Poor Lewis. He was a good chap.'

Jim looked up with a grin. 'Tell me more, Flo. Tell me more.' Julia had to bite back a laugh. Flo never had to be encouraged to tell anyone more about anything.

'Well, I met him, what, ten or fifteen years ago, I'd say? I had a bad ankle sprain and couldn't drive. Quite reliable he was, and gave me a special rate. Now, who's for something sweet?'

They demurred and waved her away, having each eaten sufficient calories to sustain them on an Everest ascent. Julia leaned back in her chair. 'That was fantastic.'

'I could do with another one,' said Jim. 'Like, next week maybe.'

Their laughter was interrupted by the arrival of Pippa at the table next to them.

'Hello, Pippa. No puppies today?' said Julia. She thought Pippa actually looked slightly strange without them. Herself but not herself, in a way that reminded Julia of the time Peter had shaved his moustache off after ten years of facial hair. When he'd come home, she'd known there was something wrong, but it had taken her a good few minutes to see what it was.

'Sadly not. I am on my way back from a visit to my Aunt Margaret, who's not well. I left them at home. I didn't think it sensible to bring a brace of wild half-grown Labradors to visit a frail older lady.'

'I'm sorry to hear about your aunt, Pippa.'

'Ah well, it's sad. It's not easy. She's not even that old, but she has a brain tumour and they're not sure what they can do. Inoperable, is what the specialist said. I suppose it comes to us all eventually.'

The two women sat silent for a moment, contemplating their own brisk forward march in that direction. Julia, herself, was, inexplicably, in her sixties. And not sixty-one, either. Pippa was a good deal younger, but not so young that she could be oblivious as to what lay ahead.

Jim, who was decades away from his sixties, had no such worries. In fact, he had his own, more immediate, agenda. 'Now, Pippa,' he said, leaning across to her. 'Tell me. Did you know Lewis Band?'

6

Julia was showered and dressed and standing in front of the bathroom mirror applying a dash of lipstick – the final task of her minimalist morning routine – when the doorbell rang. She looked at her watch. Nine thirty exactly. One thing about Brendan Blunt, he was as punctual as the sunrise.

Julia smacked her lips together in front of the mirror, tossed the lipstick down and shouted: 'Coming!' Not that Brendan would be able to hear her above Jake's excited, high-pitched barking.

'Jake, be quiet!' she instructed, to no avail. It was a wonder she had two intact eardrums, frankly.

Jake was out of the door the second it cracked open, hurtling around Brendan's ankles, smacking his legs with his tail.

The young man patted him, trying to calm him down. 'There's a good chap. There you go, Jakey. I'm pleased to see you too.'

When the dog had calmed down sufficiently for them to have a conversation, Brendan said, 'Shall I get busy then, Mrs Bird? Johnny told me what needs doing, and I think I've got all the materials in the van.'

Brendan was the grandson of Johnny Blunt, who had been the handyman in the village as long as anyone could remember. Possibly longer. Between the two Blunts, they maintained the fiction that Johnny was still in charge and he was training Brendan up to take over 'one day, when I'm getting too old for it'. In fact, Johnny was no longer nimble enough for a ladder. When he was on site, he issued instructions from ground level. He wasn't often on site. In fact, he spent a large portion of the day in the Buttered Scone. Brendan, who had been working as Johnny's apprentice on weekends and holidays since his school days, and full-time for the two years since, did almost all of the work. Julia suspected he took Johnny's instructions more from kindness than necessity. He had, to all intents and purposes, taken over, but you wouldn't say as much to Johnny Blunt, not if you knew what was good for you.

Julia and Brendan walked over to the chicken run. The day was mild and there was no rain forecast – good DIY weather, fortunately. The chicken run was being 'winterised'. This, Julia considered an awful term, but it seemed to have entered the modern lexicon and there was nothing to be done.

'The water's getting in, and it's not good for them,' she explained to the young handyman.

'I'll make a little gutter there,' Brendan said, pointing. 'Just to drain the rainwater away so it doesn't make a lot of mud around the chooks.'

'Good. Chickens can stand a bit of cold, what with their nice warm feathers, but they don't like to be soggy. And the roof?'

'Johnny's given me something to give them some more insulation.'

'Lovely, thank you, Brendan. Will you check the nesting boxes while you're here? Make sure they are sturdy?'

'Will do, Mrs B. With that and some fresh warm bedding, they'll be as snug as anything.'

'I'll leave you to it. You know where to find me if you want to chat about anything, or if you fancy a cup of tea.'

Julia fed the animals and, to the not-unpleasant sound of Brendan's hammering, ate her own breakfast of oats topped with farm yoghurt, banana and the honey given to her by Matthew and Hester, her beekeeping neighbours. It always made her smile to know that her breakfast honey was made by bees who had undoubtedly buzzed happily in her own poppies and hollyhocks, collecting pollen.

Julia had never been what one might call 'a morning person'. Getting the morning chores done, Jess off to school in time for the first bell and herself to work had always felt like a challenge that she managed to complete imperfectly, in a rush and just in the nick of time. But to her surprise and delight, Berrywick had brought out the early bird in her (either that or it was some mysterious post-sixty development – there were certainly enough of those). She enjoyed the industrious mornings in the country – feeding Jake, Chaplin the cat and the chickens; applying her fresh brain to the morning's word games; answering calls and emails; making lists and plans; and lingering over the newspaper and breakfast.

Today, her mind was on her conversation with Jim the day before. She had quite a clear day ahead, and decided to start doing some preparatory work on the Feel-Good Christmas message. No time like the present. Jim would probably have finished the obituary by now – assuming he'd found a few more contributors – and would be ready to get onto the next story.

It was surprising that he'd encountered such muted enthusiasm for Lewis. In Julia's experience, the opposite effect usually came into play when someone died. People couldn't say enough nice things about them, producing glowing reports and cherished memories, even if the real live person had been less than a saint. Many was the obituary or eulogy that was met with raised eyebrows and surprised expressions. But when it came to Lewis, even sweet old Dora from the sweet shop hadn't been able to drum up a reasonably sincere compliment.

She was turning this over in her head when Brendan knocked on the door. 'Sorry to disturb, Mrs B, but could you keep Jake inside? He's a lovely boy but he's making it a tad difficult to get my work done.'

'Oh dear, what's he doing?'

'He wants to play. He's trying to help me with the gutter, and he gets weird when I go near the chickens, especially the big one.'

'That would be Henny Penny. They have a thing going. I'll come and get him.'

Outside, she found Jake scratching enthusiastically at the area where Brendan had been digging a channel. Henny Penny sat close by, watching with her beady little eyes. When Jake saw the humans, he leapt up and turned in circles.

'I'll take him for a walk,' said Julia, who was familiar with this mad excitement and knew that it wouldn't settle until she gave him a distraction. 'It'll give you some peace and quiet, and hopefully tire him out. Come on, Jake.'

He was reluctant to leave the site of so much entertainment, but when she took his lead from its hook by the door, the faintest clink of the chain summoned him instantly. He skidded to a halt at her feet. She clipped on the lead.

'We're off,' she called to Brendan. 'I've left the door open, help yourself to tea and biscuits.'

Julia had no particular route in mind. She let her feet and her dog lead the way, turning right out of the gate in the direction of the river. They followed the path along the water, away from the village. The early-morning joggers and dog walkers had finished their exercise and moved on to their daytime pursuits, and there were few people out enjoying the crisp winter air. They passed a mum with a tiny baby attached to her in a sling, its head – the size of an orange – just visible in a soft yellow beanie. They passed old Aunt Edna, who didn't return Julia's greeting, but gave Jake a stern look and a raised eyebrow. He hung back to ensure that Julia was positioned between him and the old woman.

It was so pleasant out, and she had so much buzzing around her head, that Julia walked further than she'd intended. It was only when she spotted Dora's little sweet shop that she realised quite how far they'd come. She stopped and surveyed the little shop, hardly bigger than a caravan, with a red and white sign saying simply SWEETIES. How odd that she'd been thinking about Dora, after what Jim had said, and she'd found herself right outside her shop. It almost seemed – Julia wasn't a super-stitious woman, and not one to see signs in tea leaves or faces in clouds – but it almost seemed like she was *meant* to find herself here. Perhaps she was *meant* to have a sweet little treat. And if that led to an interesting chat, well, there was nothing that Julia could do about that.

'You know what, Jake?' she said. 'I think I might fancy a humbug.'

She left Jake outside, with strict instructions to sit. He watched her through the open door. The shop was so tiny that he was only a few steps away from her. Once inside, Julia marvelled as always at the sheer comprehensiveness of the sweetie offering in the minute space. They were all there – mint humbugs, sherbet lemons, pear drops, acid drops, jelly babies and dolly mixtures, even the rhubarb and custard sweets you hardly ever saw these days. And then there were the chocolates, and the crisps. Dora had, of course, decorated the shop for Christmas, with a Christmas tree so large in proportion to the shop that Julia didn't know quite how it fit. It was hung with classic candy canes and ribbons, entirely in keeping with the old-fashioned beauty of the shop.

Dora was at the counter. She peered round the tree, and her friendly, pink-cheeked face broke into a smile when she saw Julia.

'Well, this is a nice surprise,' she said. 'Where are you off to, on a Thursday morning?'

'Jake and I are just out for a walk. And I thought, you know what? I could gobble up a humbug.'

'Well, you've come to the right place for humbugs.'

Dora took a little packet and scooped sweets into it until Julia held up her hand and said, 'Enough! I shouldn't be having too much sugar.'

'I know they say it's not good for you,' Dora said, 'but I think, well, life is short, you might as well enjoy yourself.' Dora's short, round figure and cheerful demeanour attested to this position, and it had to be said she looked very well with her healthy colour and her halo of white curls.

'You are so right, Dora. Who knows what tomorrow brings? I mean, look at Lewis Band, walking along the lane in the woods and a car hits him out of the blue. Tragic.'

Julia popped a humbug into her mouth and waited.

'Yes, an unfortunate thing that was,' said Dora, not looking especially upset. But then she frowned and added, 'Poor Coral.'

'Did you know them?' Julia asked, casually.

'A little. I knew him quite well when he was younger. He was the same age as my little sister, Janice. That was a long time ago. And people change, don't they?'

This struck Julia as a rather odd observation, although a true one. 'They certainly do. What was he like?'

Dora glanced down at her hands, and then looked at Julia, her blue eyes wide. 'If I have to be honest, Julia, I didn't like him back in the day. He didn't do right by Janice. In fact, he did her wrong. But I don't like to speak ill of the dead, and it was a long time ago. And things change, don't they?'

'They do indeed... What sort of things do you mean?'

'Ah, well. Men and women. Boys and girls. If a chap got a bit handsy, a bit pushy, you didn't make a thing of it back then. Not like today, with all the #MeToo.'

'Well, I'd say it's probably better these days, wouldn't you? Hopefully people have learned to behave with kindness and respect. And face the consequences when they don't.' Julia wondered if the wrong that Lewis had done Janice was of the face-the-consequences variety, or of the things-were-different-then variety. Admittedly, it was often one and the same.

'Oh, yes. Back then, you'd warn off your girlfriends if a chap wasn't good with being told no. Make sure you weren't caught in a tricky situation alone. But you didn't say anything, not in public.'

Dora looked uncharacteristically pensive – sad, even – and then she said: 'Ah, well, he was thirty-five years with Coral, a good husband, an upstanding member of the community. So he did all right, I suppose. Everyone deserves a chance to change and to do better.'

'Yes, yes they do.' Julia spotted the Walnut Whips on the shelf behind Dora. 'Could I have two of those, please?' she said, pointing. 'You don't often see them these days, and they're Sean's favourite.'

'A classic,' Dora said, reaching for them.

'We're going to see a film this weekend. In an actual cinema, if you can believe it. I'll bring these along as a treat,' said Julia. 'Now, what do I owe you?'

7

'You look lovely,' said Sean, giving Julia a good old up-and-down look. 'I like that dress.'

She blushed. She didn't have a lot of call for smart clothes, living in Berrywick, and she hadn't worn this dress in a year or two. When she'd put it on, she'd wondered whether it was too smart, or too tight. But the look on Sean's face told her it was all right. More than all right.

'Why, thank you. I seem to have been in my gardening clothes all week. All the winter chores, the hen house, the wood pile – you know what it's like this time of year. I felt like dressing up for a change when I finally left the house.'

'Tights, too! I don't think I've ever seen you in tights.'

'Hmm, maybe once or twice. At Peter and Christopher's wedding, for instance. It's chilly in a dress at this time of year, though. I needed the warmth.'

'Well, you certainly do scrub up nicely, Ms Bird.' He took her arm, and they steadied each other along the garden path on their way to his car. 'Laine told me to enjoy "date night".' He made little air quotes with his fingers to emphasise the ridiculousness of the term. 'Date night! Have you ever? I must say, that's not a term I expected to hear applied to myself,' he said in a tone somewhere between grumpy and amused.

'Whatever you call it, it is very nice to be going out, just the two of us.' She squeezed his hand, marvelling again at her good luck in having met him.

Sean cleared his throat awkwardly and said, 'Things have been different the last few months, with Jono living with me. I know it's not as easy for us to be as spontaneous, or get time alone. I'm sorry.'

'Oh, Sean, no!' said Julia hastily. 'I didn't mean it like that at all! I think it's very good for you and Jono that he's here with you, and he's so much happier. And I like having him and Laine around, I really do.'

'Ah, okay. Well, I like it too.' Sean looked relieved. He opened the passenger door for her, and she slid into the passenger seat, noting again how neat and clean he kept his car. It helped that Leo lay down obediently on a blanket in the back seat and went to sleep, unlike certain other canines.

They left early enough to get to Hayfield with time for a drink and a snacky supper at the little bar in the cinema where they would be watching a screening of Ian McKellen in a National Theatre Live production. Julia was in an excellent mood – she'd been wanting to go to the Hayfield Electric Picture House since she'd read about it in the *Southern Times* ages ago. And now here they were, heading out of Berrywick at an easy pace, enjoying the sun setting over the village, the way the stone of the walls and the houses glowed golden. The light dropped suddenly when the road cut through the woods, entering the long shadows of the trees. Sean put his headlights on. Julia felt a shiver, remembering that this was the stretch of road where they had found Lewis's body. She was about to mention it, and remind Sean to drive cautiously, but she thought better of it. No point in spoiling 'date night' with a gloomy topic. And besides, he was a good and careful driver.

But when they reached the curve in the road, Julia found herself compelled to speak. Perhaps, she thought somewhat cynically, she was looking for closure.

'Sean,' she said, 'could we stop at the accident site?'

Sean was not the type of man to ask too many questions, or object. He slowed down even more. As they reached the woody bend, something fluttered on the side of the road, catching the edge of the headlight's beam. A thin flash of yellow, flapping in the breeze.

'It's the police tape,' said Julia. 'That bit must have been left behind when the police cleared the scene.'

Sean rolled to a stop on the broad roadside between the tar and the start of the vegetation, just behind where Lewis's body had been.

Next to the short length of tape, an informal memorial shrine had been set up – a bouquet of a few wilted flowers, a small stuffed teddy bear, a photograph. They stared through the windscreen at the poignant display.

Julia reached for the door handle. 'I just feel like I need to pay my respects. Do we have time?'

Sean nodded.

She got out of the car and walked slowly towards the little memorial. Bending down, she looked at the photograph, which showed Lewis leaning against his car and smiling. It had been printed on a home printer and slipped into a plastic sleeve, but it was already damp and the ink was fading.

Sean came up behind her and she straightened.

'Sad, isn't it?' he said, taking her hand. 'The little memorial.'

'It is. And so awful to think that someone lost their life right here. Took his last breath.'

'That car must have hit him hard and fast,' said Sean. 'At least it was quick. That's something to be grateful for, I suppose.'

'I just can't picture it. Why someone would hit a person

walking along the side of the lane. I wonder if the tyre had a blowout or something?'

Sean frowned. 'There could have been something mechanical like that – except that they drove off just fine. And besides, it would have shown up in the forensics. There might have been something in the road, and they swerved to avoid it?'

'More likely, the driver had been drinking. That's probably why they didn't stop. Scared of being breathalysed.' Julia paused, and then decided to share the other piece of information she had. 'Walter Farmer told me – confidentially, so don't repeat it – that the driver reversed back into Lewis after he'd hit him.'

Sean winced. 'Good lord.'

'It seems Lewis was already down, and the driver looked in the rear-view mirror but didn't see him. He reversed to see what he'd hit. The police reckon he got out and saw what he'd done, then drove off in a panic. It would tie in with the alcohol theory. He'd know he'd be in even more trouble if he was drink-driving.'

'Good God. How appalling. I hope whoever did this is found and faces the full might of the law. It's a disgrace.' Sean looked quite pale and angry.

Julia paced slowly round the scene. If she was a religious woman, she might have said a prayer, but instead she stood still and thought about Lewis and his wife Coral, and in some vague kind of way wished them peace. It felt ineffectual, but the best she could do, under the circumstances.

'Shall we go?' Sean asked, after a minute or two had passed. He had already moved back to stand by the car. 'We're cutting it a little fine if we want to eat something.'

His voice shook Julia out of her musing. 'Yes, I'm ready. Thanks for stopping.'

Sean got in the car and turned on the engine. It was getting dark, and he switched on the headlights to light her way. Julia was about to turn to make her way back to the car, when she noticed that the low beam had caught something glinting in the undergrowth a couple of feet beyond the little shrine. She stepped closer to look. If it was a tin can or some other piece of rubbish, she'd take it home and put it in the bin. She peered into the undergrowth, but from her position on the road she couldn't see what it was. She had half a mind to leave it – she wasn't exactly dressed for nature, in her nice dress and tights and shoes – but once you've had the thought of picking something up, it's hard to just leave it there.

Resigning herself, she waded into the undergrowth. Now she was closer, she could see it was a chain of some sort with something hanging off it. She reached for it, trying to keep her tights away from the spikes and sticks that would rip them in an instant. To her relief, she managed to grab it and extricated herself and her tights without incident.

Julia turned the object to the light. It was a short chain with a round pendant attached. The pendant was etched with something, perhaps a figure, but it was difficult to see under the dirt it was caked in. She turned back towards the car, squinting to try and make out the details. As she stepped out of the undergrowth onto the road, she felt a pull on her tights, and a scratch on her calf.

'Exactly why I haven't worn tights or stockings for about three years,' she said darkly into the undergrowth, in the direction of what she deemed to be the offending branch. 'And this is the last time, for sure.'

The Hayfield Electric Picture House was everything Julia had hoped. It was festooned in Christmas decorations, with a towering tree in the foyer. They got there in time for a drink and snacks at the bar. Sean went in while Julia popped to the loo, removed her shredded tights and threw them in the bin. 'Last time,' she muttered in their direction, hoping that she wouldn't feel too cold in the theatre.

Sean was at the polished wooden bar counter, mulling over a cocktail menu. 'What do you fancy? I think I'll have a martini,' he said, and handed the menu to her.

'How very James Bond of you.' She took the menu from him with a smile. There was a dizzying selection of classic cocktails and more experimental combinations of alcohol and sweetness. Julia opted for the seasonal special – eggnog. The barman – a man of about Jono's age, with slicked-back black hair – worked the cocktail shaker with wiry tattooed arms, and an understated flourish.

From a tempting menu of bar snacks, they chose roasted nuts with rosemary, tuna carpaccio with shaved fennel and red onion, and a basket of sourdough with fancy butters. The hot roasted nuts were so rich and delicious, she felt she could toss the whole bowl into her mouth in one go. But she restrained herself, picking them one at a time, sipping her drink in between.

She took the silver chain out of her pocket and laid it on the bar.

'What do you think it is?' Sean asked.

She picked up a paper napkin and rubbed at the disc to reveal the etched figure more clearly. 'Oh! It's a St Christopher.'

'The patron saint of travellers?'

'That's him.'

'Well, if it was Lewis's lucky charm, it didn't work,' said Sean. Julia was surprised at the unfeeling comment, and Sean was too, it seemed, because he added quickly: 'Sorry, that came out somewhat harsher than I meant it to.'

'You're not wrong, though.' She looked at the St Christopher again. 'You can see the link is broken. I think it must have been attached to something, like a bunch of keys or a necklace. Oh, well...'

Julia popped it into her handbag and they moved on to a happier topic – the possibility of a seaside holiday in Cornwall in the spring. It felt good being out in the world, somewhere new, in a stylish bar with Sean's knee pressed against her thigh. The rest of the snacks arrived, plated on flat black slate.

A bell rang, and the barman announced, 'Ten minutes to curtain up.' Julia popped a sliver of fennel-topped tuna into her mouth. It had a sharp, lemony dressing, and a crack of black pepper. 'My God, that's good. A perfect little morsel,' she said. 'Try it.'

Together with the bread, and a complimentary bowl of Spanish olives, the snacks proved sufficient to prevent hollow tummy rumbles from competing with Sir Ian McKellen for the audience's attention.

'Last call…' came the barman's voice.

Sean stood and took Julia's hand. Into the cinema they went.

8

Sunday morning started with a gift, personally delivered to Julia in her own bed.

The gift, unfortunately, was a mouse, and the delivery man was Chaplin. Julia had been dozing when he jumped onto the bed with a loud *prooowww* sound, and nudged her with his hard forehead.

'Hello, kitty cat,' she muttered sleepily, keeping her eyes determinedly closed. She reached out a hand to give him a stroke and push him gently away. He was all the more insistent, coming right up into her face, so that when she opened her own eyes, she was looking straight into his yellow ones, directly above the dangling figure of the dead mouse.

'Bloody hell, Chaplin,' she said, practically levitating into a sitting position, while flapping her hands about without a clear purpose. 'Get off.'

Chaplin retreated to the end of the bed, proudly holding the little brown corpse in his mouth.

'Oh God, take that thing away, will you?'

Julia tried to disentangle herself from the bedclothes without making contact with the cat or the mouse. Chaplin seemed bemused by the commotion and, frankly, disappointed by the lack of gratitude for his fine present. He stood his ground, the grisly gift hanging from his jaws. Julia got up crossly, slapping her feet down on the cold floor and stomping off to the bathroom for the loo roll.

She'd feared having to wrestle the victim from Chaplin's jaws, but by the time she got back he'd dropped it onto her duvet. The poor little thing. It was tiny, and really rather cute with its little round ears and its whiskers. Fortunately it was in one piece, and not torn to shreds or bleeding all over the place. She wondered if it had died of fright. Chaplin's stare was pretty alarming; that might have done it.

Julia pulled off a wodge of loo paper and used it to pick up the mouse without making contact. She set off down the passage to the kitchen, where she found a plastic bag. Dropping the mouse and the paper into the bag, she slipped her feet into her gardening shoes and opened the kitchen door so she could put the bag in the outside bin. Jake delayed matters with an enthusiastic morning welcome, dashing in and out of the door, turning circles this way and then that, yapping excitedly for his breakfast.

'In a minute,' Julia said, trying to make her way past him without her shins being bashed by his hard head or his whipping tail.

The cold air hit her, cutting straight through her pyjamas. She considered going back for another layer of clothing, but opted to hurry to the bin.

Picking up the bin lid, she tossed in the small rodent. She had a momentary urge to say a short blessing, but instead said, 'Bye, little chap. Sorry it had to end this way.' Closing the lid, she hurried back inside.

There was no going back to sleep. The cold had braced her fully awake, and besides, Jake was now convinced that breakfast was imminent. She went back to the coat hooks and took the long shapeless cardigan she used for gardening in the chill.

'Ah, the glamorous life of the Cotswold retiree,' she said out loud, looking down at her slip-on rubber waterproof shoes and her flannel pyjamas. She pushed her arms into the sleeves of the cardigan. 'All that Burberry. The cashmere jumpers. The fine tweeds. The shooting jackets. What even is a shooting jacket, come to think of it? Or a gun dog?'

At the word 'dog', Jake looked at her worriedly. What on earth was she on about, and what did it mean for him?

'There's nothing to worry about, Jake. I'm just out in the garden in the freezing cold in my pyjamas, tossing out dead rodents and talking to myself. Breakfast's on its way.'

She fed the dog and the chickens. There were no eggs to collect. The girls' laying had slowed down to next to nothing in the shorter days and colder weather, even with Brendan's winterising efforts.

Back in the kitchen Julia turned on the kettle, shed her stylish garden-wear and went back to her bedroom to fetch her book and her handbag. She would hit restart on Sunday morning, first with the full suite of word games, and then with the new prize-shortlisted novel Tabitha had pressed on her with glowing recommendations.

Ten minutes later, she was dressed and sitting at the kitchen table with a tray of tea. She'd made herself a generous pot of Earl Grey, the first cup already poured and just cool enough for sipping. On a plate next to her were two slices of wholemeal seed loaf, generously spread with butter – one topped with marmalade made by Pippa, and the other with Matthew and Hester's honey.

Yes indeed, Sunday was looking up. Julia had nothing specific planned. Sean had dropped her home after the cinema and gone back to his house to sleep. He had Sunday plans with Jono – something that involved going to a very large shop to purchase some very specific electrical item for a speaker or some other music-related thing that Jono had requested as his Christmas gift. She was pleased not to have such an errand herself, nor to have been roped into theirs.

She wiped her hands and got going on her games. She always started with Wordle, which she knew was probably more luck than skill, but she persisted in thinking she was rather good at it. She got the word in three goes, which was satisfactory. She went on to Connections, and then the crossword puzzle, followed by Sudoku. She considered topping up the teapot and making a third piece of toast, and taking to Facebook to lurk, spying on friends and acquaintances, but her inner goodie-goodie won out.

'Okay, that's enough,' she told herself sternly. 'It's time to do something more useful.'

With a determined flourish, she dropped her phone into her handbag to seal the deal, even though she hadn't quite decided what the 'something more useful' might be. There was a small metallic sound, and at once she remembered the St Christopher pendant she'd picked up yesterday. She felt around in her bag and pulled it out, turning it over idly. It made a certain kind of sense that Lewis might have carried an image of the patron saint of travellers. After all, he'd spent his life on the roads. It was likely a precious lucky charm, a talisman.

There and then, Julia knew what the 'something more useful' would be.

Julia had never visited Lewis Band at home, but she knew where he'd lived. His taxi, when not in use, was to be seen parked outside a pleasant, modern little house in Wood Grouse Lane. Julia had often noticed the car, and the magnificent magnolia beside it that looked like any old, rather boring, tree until spring came, and then it was filled with an astonishing number of glossy pale blooms, seemingly overnight. Passers-by stopped to admire it, or to pose for photographs or take selfies in front of it.

It would be months before the famous magnolia blooms would arrive, and the whole place had a gloomy, wintery air. Julia slowed her walking pace as she neared the front gate, suddenly reluctant to engage with the house's sadness, or with its owner, Lewis's wife, Coral. Julia didn't know Coral beyond occasional superficial encounters at Second Chances, or the library, or at village meetings or get-togethers. Standing in front of the gate now, looking at the front door with its cheerful holly wreath, she began to second-guess her decision to come over with the St Christopher. Perhaps it was too soon to call on a new widow, whom she knew only in passing. However, in the moment of Julia's dithering, the door opened and Coral appeared in the doorway.

Although it was Sunday morning, Coral was smartly dressed in a rather formal, old-fashioned style, in what used to be called a trouser suit. The matching top and bottom were a dark tan colour, and she wore a cream polo neck underneath. Pearls adorned her throat and studded her ears. Her face was made up and her golden-blonde hair looked as if it had been highlighted, and recently liberated from a set of hot rollers. It had to be said that she looked remarkably good for a recently widowed woman. But Julia recognised her type – some people fall apart in their grief, but others try to protect themselves with an armour of coping skills. Coral Lewis was clearly one of the latter.

'Hello?'

Coral voiced it as a question, and frowned as if trying to make out who was at the gate, or perhaps why they were there.

'Coral, hello. It's Julia Bird.'

'Oh, Julia Bird. Hello.'

'I'm here to...' The conversation was awkward, conducted in raised voices across the little front garden. 'Could I come in?'

There was a moment's hesitation. Julia sensed some reluctance, but then Coral said, 'Yes, of course.'

Julia opened the gate and made her way up the neat little path towards the front door. 'I'm very sorry for your loss, Coral,' she said, as she drew closer. 'It's a terrible, shocking thing.'

'It is that,' said Coral. 'I don't know what's become of the world, I really don't.'

'I have something...'

'Please, come inside.'

Carol had an odd, stiff manner which, together with the pointedly put-together outfit, seemed an attempt to ward off the uncertainty of life. In Julia's experience, life's uncertainty was guaranteed, and not to be deterred by matching two-piece outfits, or by pearls, or by a proper manner.

Julia followed her into the house, past numerous flower arrangements, some still with cards attached, and into the kitchen.

'Tea? The kettle has just boiled.'

'Only if you're having one. I won't stay.'

Coral took that as a 'yes' and took two cups and saucers from the cupboard. 'Carrot cake, scones, mince pies?' she asked, waving to a pile of tins and Tupperwares and packets at the end of the counter. 'I've got just about anything you fancy. And there's more in the fridge. Tomato soup? Quiche Lorraine? Lasagne? People have been very kind.'

'Carrot cake would be lovely,' said Julia, noticing that it was close at hand and already cut.

'Do sit.'

Julia did as she was told, taking a seat at the kitchen table. 'Thank you. I won't stay long. I wanted to bring you something that I found. Something I think might be Lewis's.'

'How would you have something of Lewis's?' Coral asked

sharply. 'I didn't know you knew him.' She sounded almost suspicious.

'I didn't know him, really, although he did drive me once or twice. He was a very good driver, and seemed like a friendly chap.'

'Oh yes, he was that, very friendly. Everyone liked him. The ladies especially.'

'Well, you felt you could trust him, I always thought. And people do worry about getting into a car with a stranger. Women especially; they like to have someone they know and trust.'

'Oh, they liked Lewis all right,' Coral said, sniffily. 'It was always like that, especially when we were younger. No end of trouble, it was.'

It seemed rather an odd thing to say, under the circumstances, and Julia wasn't sure how to respond. She was saved, mercifully, by the shrieking of the kettle, which drew Coral's attention. Julia watched as she set about making tea – properly, with leaves, and a pot and a milk jug, none of your 'swirl the bag around' nonsense.

While Coral was slicing and plating the cake, Julia opened her handbag and took out the short chain with its dangling saint. 'I came to bring this,' she said, putting it on the table in front of her. 'I was walking near the site of the accident and I found this St Christopher. I thought Lewis might have dropped it. And that it might have sentimental value for you.'

Coral sat down, putting the cake plate in front of Julia. She picked up the charm. 'This is not Lewis's. I've never seen it before.' She put it down with some distaste, and brushed her hands together as if to remove dust.

'Oh, well, it seems I jumped to the wrong conclusion, what with his job... St Christopher is meant to guard travellers, you know.'

'Oh, Lewis wasn't superstitious like that. He believed in

keeping your wits about you on the road. Not that that helped him in the end...' Coral's rather formal manner cracked and her eyes teared up.

'I'm so sorry, Coral,' said Julia, stricken. 'The last thing I wanted to do was to come here and upset you. I thought it might be something special or personal... But it's obviously not.' She slipped the offending item back into her bag, and put her palm over the widow's shaking hand. 'Now, you take a minute and I'll pour us some tea.'

Coral nodded meekly, while Julia bustled with the tea things. By the time she'd poured their second cup of tea, and they'd started on a second slice of cake – 'Just a sliver, now' – Coral had a better colour. She seemed to have warmed to Julia, after her initial suspicious manner, and had started telling her about their son, who was married to a dentist, and had twin baby boys and twin Airedales.

When they'd finished their tea and cake, and Julia had a full picture of the family tree, along with considerable insight into the twins' similarities and differences, she stood up to go.

'I'd better let you get on with your day, Coral. I'm sure you have lots to do. I'm sorry to have disturbed you.'

'Not at all. I appreciate you coming. It was kind of you to bring the saint,' Coral said. 'And it was nice to meet you properly.'

'You too, Coral. Thank you for the delicious tea. Now you take good care of yourself, and remember I'm here if you need to chat.'

Back at home, Julia allowed herself a bit of Facebook lurking. It was slim pickings, frankly. A lot of memes. The 'I Love Berry-wick' page had the usual notices about upcoming events and things to do – everything from a Tuesday morning knitting circle called Knits & Wits, to a volunteer bat counting project, to the Christmas market.

There were the usual things for sale, and a few lost-and-found notices. Scrolling through them, Julia had a thought. She took out the St Christopher, placed it on her desk and snapped a picture. She put up the photograph, together with a caption: *St Christopher. Found on Maple Road. DM me if it's yours.*

Scrolling through some more, she saw that someone had shared Jim McEnroe's *Southern Times* tribute to Lewis – *Life of local taxi man killed in hit-and-run*– which had attracted scores of comments. Lots of people expressed shock and sadness and sympathy. A good many expressed their outrage at the kind of driving that had killed him. Which reminded Julia of her other intended task for the day – to work on the ideas and messages that would inspire visitors to drive better and slower in Berrywick.

9

Julia rang the intercom and Hayley buzzed the door open without even waiting to hear who was there, which didn't seem like excellent security practice from a police person. In the little foyer, Sean picked up a few scattered flyers and letters that had been pushed through the letterbox and put them on the table against the wall. Julia walked to the front door of the flat on the left of the staircase, and knocked. The door had recently been painted a bright peacock blue, she noted, and the gleaming brass knocker looked brand new. She suspected this welcoming combination was Sylvia's influence.

Hayley's voice came from within: 'It's open, come in!'

Julia opened the door to see Hayley's sister Rosie bustling towards her, wiping her hands on her apron, which was printed with silhouettes of birds, stamped in green.

'Julia! Sean! How lovely to see you again,' she said. 'And under *much* happier circumstances.'

The circumstances under which Julia had first met Rosie a year or so ago, had indeed not been pleasant. Rosie had come to stay with Hayley, who had been signed off work and confined to her home with a badly broken leg after a hit-and-run that had turned out to be an attempted murder. Rosie – bless her – had had the unenviable task of tending to the grumpy, frustrated, housebound detective until she was able to hobble back to work.

Rosie hung up their coats. The weather had turned positively chilly, but Hayley's flat was pleasantly warm, a fire glowing in the corner.

'I can't wait to meet Hayley's Sylvia.' Rosie rubbed her hands together and spoke in an eager stage whisper which was easily loud enough to carry into the kitchen, where Hayley could be heard clunking pots and pans around. 'She'll be here any moment, I expect. She's on her way over, doing a few last bits of shopping on the way. I am sure she's lovely. She sounds lovely. Is she lovely?'

'She certainly does seem so, and they seem happy together,' said Julia.

Some months after they'd become 'an item', Hayley was finally ready to introduce her new girlfriend to her sister. Hence the early midweek supper. Sean and Julia were there for moral support, and to smooth over any awkward silences or tricky moments.

Rosie was such a cheery, pleasant creature, however, it seemed unlikely that any smoothing would be necessary. Her appearance matched her personality to a pleasing degree. She had a creamy complexion, and her face had a soft plumpness, as if she were made of clouds and sugar and cherubs.

Hayley came through from the kitchen, and Julia was once again struck by how different she was from her sister, not only physically – the detective inspector was darker, more angular – but in personality. Rosie was a guileless, open-hearted sort, while Hayley Gibson had a more cynical view of the world, as you would expect from someone who investigated crimes for a living.

Julia gave Hayley a sort of hug and presented her with a bunch of dahlias which she'd picked up from Blooming Marvels on her way home from working at Second Chances. Sean gave her the bottle of wine that he had brought. 'Shall I take the apple pie into the kitchen?' Julia asked.

Hayley nodded. 'Yes please. I hope you can find a spot for it.'

Indeed, it looked as if every item from every drawer and cupboard had been used in preparing the meal, and was now scattered about the countertops. Julia piled a few plates on top of the dishwasher and put the pie down in the little space she'd created. She looked at it with satisfaction, proud of the job she'd done on the lattice pastry.

Hayley came into the kitchen and filled a vase with water, dropping the bunch of dahlias in. Rosie followed, in conversation with Sean. '... so I thought I'd come up and visit Hayley before I start my new job. It's going to be full-on, getting settled, and then I'll be off to New York for a conference, so who knows when next I'll get three or four days to myself.'

'A new job?' asked Julia. 'Congratulations. What is it you'll be doing?'

'Ah well, it's a lovely job. I'll be in charge of a team of data analysts for the security department of a big bank,' Rosie said in her cheerful, lilting voice. 'Can't tell you which bank, I'd have to kill you...' she added, and gave a tinkling laugh.

'It's a big job, very important and demanding. Rosie is terribly clever,' Hayley said proudly. Julia felt guilty that she'd underestimated the younger sister, based entirely on her sweet manner and her pink-cheeked appearance. She'd known only that Rosie did 'something with computers', a large and mysterious category of occupations that seemed to encompass everything from typing to launching space rockets. She'd had no idea Rosie had such a high-powered career.

'Ah well, so are you,' said Rosie, taking the vase of flowers from Hayley. 'Just clever in different ways, aren't we? I could never do what you do.'

'Likewise,' said Hayley, watching as, with a couple of swift hand movements, her sister fluffed up the dahlias into an attractive shape. 'That, for example. You're a genius with flowers.'

'Oh, go on, it's nothing,' Rosie handed the vase back. 'Do you want to put those on the table?'

They all went through to the sitting room where the dining table had been set, and in the centre of which Hayley put the vase.

'The table looks lovely,' Julia said, noting the pretty plates, white with a blue trim, the elegant wine glasses, the heavy white cotton table napkins with a blue stripe.

'It looks all right doesn't it?,' said Hayley. 'I tossed out the non-matching stuff I'd had since whenever, and bought a few new things. A new set of crockery, new glasses.'

Julia remembered the sparsely equipped kitchen from her visits to Hayley-the-invalid. It had been the sad mish-mash belonging to someone who spent too much time at work and ate too many takeaways. She again suspected the hand of Sylvia in this new arrangement.

As Julia thought of her, so Sylvia appeared, opening the door and struggling through with a shopping bag in each hand.

'Hello, hello, sorry I'm late.'

'Not at all,' Hayley said, taking the bags from her with a warm smile. 'Thanks for getting these. I can't believe I forgot to buy the drinks!'

Sylvia gave her a grin. 'Well, you're a busy woman with a lot on your mind! And we've got plenty now. Sparkling water, orange juice, some new kombucha sort of thing with apple...'

'Sounds perfect. Please, everyone, help yourselves,' said Hayley, putting the bottles on the sideboard. 'The chicken needs about fifteen minutes more.' They sat down, filling every chair in Hayley's little sitting room.

Hayley did the introductions. Sylvia and Rosie were, in fact, cut from similar cloth. Golden, pink-hued cloth. Sylvia was a little taller and slimmer and blonder, and had a direct and playful manner. Rosie had curlier hair, a fuller face and figure, and was generally a little softer in her ways. But if a stranger had to guess which two women at this little gathering were sisters, they would pick these two.

'It's mayhem on the roads,' said Sylvia. 'People have come from all over for the Wednesday Christmas market. I nearly got taken out on the pedestrian crossing by someone on a bicycle. Missed me by inches.'

'That's terrible,' Hayley said. 'Did you get a description? What sort of bike was he riding?'

Sylvia laughed. 'Put away the handcuffs, Detective. It was just a kid. He made a mistake and, as you see, I lived to tell the tale. Much as I appreciate your concern, you don't need to track him down and have him put away for life.' She gave her girl-friend a hug to show that the teasing was with no malice.

'We're all touchy about bad driving since Lewis Band got run over,' Julia said to Sylvia, by way of explanation.

'Of course you are. What a terrible thing.'

'We drove past where the accident happened at the week-end,' said Sean. 'We stopped to look at the place again and, honestly, I don't know how the driver managed to swerve like that right there. I reckon he must have been drunk and going much too fast.'

Julia was about to mention the St Christopher when Hayley said something that stopped her in her tracks. 'Well, we're not so sure it was a him. We think it might have been a woman, based on the very little evidence we've got from the footprints. The only thing we can say for sure is that the person who got out of the car was small and light.'

'Nothing useful from the street cameras?' Julia asked.

'Not so far. We don't have much information to go on – we don't have good tyre tread impressions, so we don't know the make of the vehicle involved. And the cameras aren't everywhere, as you know.'

'The road safety committee hopes to get more cameras,' Julia said. 'That, and to encourage people to be extra careful. I'm working on the communication side – signage, flyers, that sort of thing. Our aim is for everyone to feel committed to keeping our roads and our road users safe.'

'I really think that's where change has to start,' said Sean. 'With education, and with people deciding to change their behaviour. Whether it's smoking or driving or anything else.'

'I agree one hundred per cent. And you can't start too young!' said Sylvia. As a nursery school teacher, she was a great believer in the power of early influences.

A buzzer went off in the kitchen, and Hayley jumped to her feet. 'Chicken's ready. Fill up your glasses and get to the table!'

In all the excitement of dinner's arrival, the little St Christopher drifted out of Julia's mind once again. It stayed buried in her bag, keeping its secrets. For now.

10

'Oh, Sean, look – the Christmas night market is still open!'

The evening at Hayley's had been a great success, and by the time they said their goodbyes, Julia would have sworn that she had no energy left for anything and just wanted to go home. But the sight of the little field near the village centre, strung with lights, called to her.

'Let's stop and get some bread and cheese, please,' she said.

'You'll do anything to go to another market,' teased Sean, but he turned the car into the little parking area next to the main field. 'You won't let it stop you that it's the middle of the night and most of the stalls will be closing up.'

'It's not *quite* the middle of the night.' Julia smiled at him, then looked around the little car park. 'Although perhaps you're right; there aren't a lot of people left.'

'We're parked now,' said Sean. 'Might as well pop in and see if we can get your bread and cheese. And no doubt jam and eggs and perhaps a strange knitted thing that you swear will make someone a perfect gift.'

Julia could not deny it – she had bought more than a reasonable number of strange knitted objects this festive season, at markets much like this one.

'A good point,' she said. 'I haven't yet found the perfect knitted object for your stocking.'

'In that case, let's hurry, all the good ones might be gone.'

The two of them were laughing as they walked across the boggy parking area towards the little gate that led to the market. They almost collided with Matthew, Julia's next-door neighbour, carrying a box of honey.

'Julia, Sean,' he said happily, immediately stopping and putting the box down. The thing about Matthew Shepherd was that he liked a chat. His wife, Hester, was much shyer, and Julia knew her far less well. But Matthew was one of the characters of Berrywick, known for his ability to make a short story long, and a boring story funny. When you saw his white hair and bright blue eyes bobbing down the road in your direction, you knew to add a good ten minutes to your expected arrival time. If they had a chat with Matthew now, there would be no chance of any of the stalls still being open by the time they got there.

'Isn't this a fine Christmas season?' Matthew said, as his opener. He was wearing a bright yellow shirt that Julia knew was his favourite for attending the markets. 'Makes people think of honey,' he'd once told her. 'It's all in the psychology.'

'Indeed,' agreed Sean now. 'I take it from this that you've had a good day at the market?'

'Ah yes, we've had plenty of orders. We'll be busy with deliveries the next few days, that I can tell you. People know where to come for the best honey in the Cotswolds.'

'In the whole of England,' said Julia, loyally.

'There's a good operation in Yorkshire,' said Matthew, taking her somewhat literally. 'They make a fine, fine honey. I think they might be as good as us.'

'I'll keep that in mind if I'm ever in Yorkshire,' said Julia. 'But tonight, it's cheese I'm after.'

'You'd better hurry, then,' said Matthew, making no move to shift out of the path. 'The cheese stall has done a roaring trade. And how are things in the doctoring business, Sean?'

'Lots of seasonal colds,' said Sean. 'Keeps me busy.'

'Well, I'm glad you've had a successful evening, Matthew,' said Julia, wondering if she could just step around him. 'I'd best be getting to the cheese.'

'I've just got to pack up and then I'm off back to Hester,' said Matthew. 'She'll be starting to worry. And wanting to know what the sales have been like.' He sighed. 'I can't wait for the time that the honey isn't our only source of income. That'll be a fine day.'

Julia was wondering how to respond to this, given that Matthew and Hester were hardly of an age to expect another career opportunity to come knocking, when Matthew bent down and lifted his box. 'Well now, I can't be standing here chatting. Best I be on my way. Have a good night, then.'

'You too, Matthew.'

'He's a good man,' said Sean, once they were out of sight. 'Always leaves me with a smile on my face.'

The market had mostly wound down, but twenty minutes later, they had managed to find some soft goat's cheese, a strong brie, and the last of the loaves. Julia had also bought a bunch of early snowdrops – the last that the flower seller had.

'It's late, but that was worth it,' she observed, as they walked through the now almost completely deserted market. The last of the stalls were packing up. Sean opened the small gate between the field and the parking area and Julia stepped through. A light drizzle had started and Julia looked up, wondering if it would turn to snow. As she looked around, her eye caught a flash of yellow on the far side of the parking area.

'There's something on the ground over there,' she said to Sean, pointing.

Sean squinted through the rain, and then suddenly started running. 'Julia, I think it's a person!'

'Who could it be?' said Julia, following him quickly.

But she'd already seen the yellow, and she knew the answer to her own question.

Sean pulled up outside Julia's house. She'd left a couple of lights on when she had gone out, and they glowed softly behind the curtains. The house looked cosy and welcoming, and she knew that Jake and Chaplin would be waiting for her and delighted to see her. The home she had made in Berrywick was a place she was always pleased to come home to. But tonight, she was weighed down with what had just happened, and what she knew would be next.

As she stepped out onto the pavement, Julia was startled to see a figure lurking in the shadows just a few steps away.

'Hello?' she called sharply. 'Who's there?'

'It's me, Hester.' Julia's neighbour stepped out of the shadows, so that Julia could now see her better.

'Oh, Hester! Gosh, I couldn't see you properly in the dark.' Hester looked so cheerful that it broke Julia's heart to think of what she now had to tell her.

'Hello, Julia. Sorry. I didn't mean to give you a fright. I heard your car and I thought it was Matthew coming home from the Christmas market and came out to have a look.'

Julia didn't know what to say. When they'd left the crime scene, Hayley had told Julia and Sean that she would be immediately behind them, to come and speak to Hester.

'Hester…' started Julia. 'I think maybe we should all go in and sit down.'

Sean had climbed out of the car too. 'Maybe we can put a kettle on while we wait,' he said to Julia.

'Wait?' said Hester, looking from Sean to Julia. 'For

Matthew? Do you think he'll need a cup of tea?' She smiled and then immediately frowned. 'I mean no disrespect, but Matthew will be tired when he gets back. Maybe this isn't quite the time for a midnight tea party. He never stays at the market this late.'

'Hester, something's happened.' Julia gently touched Hester's arm. 'To Matthew.'

'Did you see him?'

Julia wasn't quite sure how to answer this question. 'We did, yes, but...'

'Oh well then, he'll be on his way shortly, won't he? Thanks, Julia. Thanks, Sean. I was worrying for nothing. Silly me.' Hester turned to go away, and Julia felt like the whole situation was slipping out of her control.

'Hester,' she said, slightly more loudly than she intended. 'Matthew was in an accident.'

'In the van?'

'In the car park at the market. He was hit by a car.'

'Oh, lord.' Hester gave a weak smile. 'Okay, I'll just go in and pack him a bag. Then I'll get a taxi to the hospital; I'll just call... Oh no, I can't call Lewis. How awful, I forgot. I guess I'll have to find another taxi driver. Or maybe, Julia, you and Sean would be so good as to take me?'

'Hester, there's no need for you to go to the hospital.'

'Oh, is he on his way back? Oh good. For a moment there, you had me worried!'

Julia took a deep breath. There was never an easy way to break this type of news to a person, and experience had taught Julia that sometimes the only way was to rip the plaster off. Certainly, she couldn't let Hester carry on in this state of confusion one moment longer.

'Hester, I'm so sorry. Matthew was killed at the scene. He was run over.'

It was at this pivotal moment that Hayley's car came screeching up the lane. Julia was dimly aware of Hayley parking and jumping out of the car while Hester stared at her blankly.

Hester finally spoke as Hayley walked up to them. 'Killed at the scene? Run over?' she said, before gently crumpling into a heap on the path.

Hayley looked down at the unconscious woman. 'I see you told her, then,' she said with a sigh.

11

Julia was dressed and breakfasted, having fed the cat, dog and chickens, and was about to embark on her morning Wordle, when there was a knock on the door. She had not slept at all well, thinking of poor Matthew, the state they had found him in, and the fact that this was the second hit-and-run accident that she had almost witnessed in a matter of weeks. Mostly, she felt a deep sadness that the world, and Hester, had lost a gentle and kind man.

At the sound of the knock, Jake started hurling himself about in such a fit of excitement you'd have sworn a delivery of warm pork sausages was waiting for him on the doorstep. Julia managed to circumvent him with her shins intact. When she opened the door, she saw Hayley Gibson.

'Can I come in?'

'Of course,' Julia said, stepping aside to let the inspector in and Jake out.

'Sorry to drop in unannounced, but I was next door.'

'How is she?'

'Not well,' said Hayley, shaking her head. 'She's taken it very hard. Unsurprisingly, I suppose.'

'Matthew was a lovely man. It's a terrible loss to all of us who knew him.'

'Well, that's why I stopped in. I wanted to ask, how well did you know Matthew?'

'Quite well. He was a good man. Solid. Down-to-earth. Gentle. Very kind. He'd always give me a jar of the new season's honey. When the tree in their garden toppled onto the fence in that big storm, he was the one who cut it up and then mended the fence. He said I could have half the wood for my fireplace, even though it was their tree. He even brought over the logs for me and stacked them up neatly in the woodpile. A thoroughly decent man.'

Julia got up and fetched a teapot from the kitchen counter. She added teabags and boiled water. She poured the tea into two mugs and handed one to Hayley, who dosed it liberally with what Julia considered far too much milk.

'Heaven knows, we could do with more thoroughly decent men in this world,' said the detective grimly. 'What do you know about his friends and family?'

'He and Hester kept to themselves. They were quiet people who doted on each other. Hester, in particular, was cheerful but very shy, but Matthew did like a chat.' Julia paused, her eyes filling with tears as she thought of that last chat with Matthew. If only she'd shown more patience, and spoken to him for a while longer, maybe none of this would have happened.

'Is there family?'

'There's a daughter, Violet, who comes by with a sweet little toddler. I can't remember the child's name.' Julia tapped her forehead in frustration, which did nothing to dislodge the name.

'Not to worry. It's not relevant.'

This was true, but still, Julia would like it if her brain was better at retrieving proper nouns.

'Their bees kept them busy. There always seemed to be something going on – getting the honeycomb out, and what have you, I don't know what exactly. And then pouring it into jars and selling the honey, of course.'

It was incredibly sad. Hester and Matthew had been so close. When Julia thought of one, she thought of the other. Hester holding the ladder while Matthew sawed a branch off the tree. Matthew handing over a jar of honey while Hester took the money from a customer. The two of them checking on the hives together in the early morning.

Poor Hester would be lost without him.

Hayley Gibson's phone rang, interrupting Julia's thoughts. When Hayley answered, a voice could be heard indistinctly on the other side of the phone – it sounded like a man, but Julia couldn't be certain. On this side, Hayley spoke in brusque monosyllables, questions and acknowledgements: 'Yes... Mmm... Mmm... Time?... How many?... Right. Okay.'

She ended the call and drained her tea, placing the mug down with a heavy clunk and standing up like a determined drunk finally leaving a bar. 'I'm off. Bob Jones from forensics says the results are starting to come in.'

'Good luck with it. I hope you find whoever did this.'

'Oh, we'll find him all right. I hope the tyre prints are more helpful this time. Nice and clear.'

'This time? You don't think... I mean, do you imagine that the two accidents might be connected? Or...'

'I'm not in the business of imagining, fortunately,' Hayley said. 'I'm in the business of evidence. Which I'm going to examine now. Thanks for the tea, Julia.'

After Hayley left, Julia sat alone at the kitchen table, draining her second cup of tea. It was cold and unpleasant, but it did the job that was required of it, which was that of delaying her visit to Hester. Julia had made many difficult visits, under difficult circumstances, to many different people, but today she was thinking of the first one.

She had been nine years old when her friend Gladys

Painter's father had died. The families lived on the same road, and the two girls had played together all of their young lives. And then Gladys's father had died of a heart attack. This in itself was unimaginable. A grown-up, one who Julia knew well, one who wasn't someone's grandfather or great-grandmother, had died.

'Get your coat,' Julia's mother had said, when the news came through from the neighbourhood. 'We're going to pay our respects to the Painters.'

Her mother put on her hat and waited while Julia stood rooted to the spot. 'I can't go.'

'It has to be done.' Her mother spoke firmly, but not unkindly.

'What will I say?'

'You will say that you are sorry for their loss.'

'Please don't make me go.'

Julia knew that she couldn't possibly go, just as she knew that she would have to.

'Julia, the Painters are our neighbours. Gladys is your friend. We have to visit her, because seeing a friend might make her feel just a little bit better.'

With trembling hands and tears welling behind her eyes, Julia nodded. She put on her coat.

'Good girl. We have to do a hard thing because someone else has a much harder thing to bear. It's what we do. We do what must be done.'

And so it was now, more than five decades later, with trembling hands and tears welling behind her eyes, Julia put on her coat. She walked across her lawn, out of her little gate, into Hester's little gate, and across the neighbour's lawn.

12

Hester was outside at the beehives, wandering around in a slow, vague sort of way, talking to herself. The morning was chilly, and she was wearing an ancient olive green winter coat and fleece-lined boots over pale blue pyjamas dotted with little cartoon daisies.

Julia felt awkward, disturbing her grieving neighbour in such an undignified outfit, and seemingly absorbed in whatever odd thing it was that she was doing. Julia hesitated, wondering if she should return to her own house and come back later. But in her moment of hesitation, Hester turned towards her and beckoned.

Julia walked over the damp grass. Hester put a finger to her lips and whispered: 'Shhhh. I'm telling the bees.' She turned back to the closest hive and laid her hands on its top, muttering in a low drone. Julia stood still, and in the morning quiet she could hear a soft hum from inside the bee box. Hester took what looked like a large black handkerchief or serviette from the pocket of her coat and draped it over the hive.

'Bees, bees...' came her droning voice, a little louder. 'I come to you with sad news.'

Her voice dropped again, and Julia could no longer hear what she was saying, just the soothing, solemn tones. She felt as if she were witnessing a spell being cast, or some ancient ritual enacted. Something that shouldn't be disturbed or questioned. Unless, perhaps, Hester had gone mad with grief, which seemed not impossible.

Minutes passed, her voice a low monotone. and Hester turned away from the boxes, leaving the black handkerchief in its place atop the hive. She walked slowly towards the house, Julia falling into step beside her.

'You have to tell the bees when there's important news in the family. Births and deaths particularly.' Hester's voice had lost its mystical crooning quality and now sounded quite matter-of-fact.

Julia nodded, uncharacteristically at a loss for words.

'Bees are part of the family, you know. They must be informed. I remember when my mum told them Dad had passed, she went out and broke the news. She was from the old school, Mum, she sang her message. And when my Violet was born, oh my, but weren't the bees all a-buzz when I told them! Such a joyous occasion, and the honey that year was the richest and sweetest I've known. You can't imagine.' Hester's eyes shone at the happy recollection, but only for a moment. Her face softened and sagged. 'And now poor Matthew. The bees won't be happy at all. *I* won't be happy. It's... It's...'

'It's so awful Hester, just tragic,' Julia said. 'I'm so very sorry for your terrible loss.'

Hester stopped and wrung her hands together in a gesture of hopelessness and said simply: 'I don't know what to do.'

Julia put a hand on her shoulder. 'Of course you don't. You have experienced a life-changing, earth-shattering event. Nothing feels right, or real.'

'That's exactly it. I keep thinking I made a mistake. It can't be right. He'll walk in here, muttering about the latest argument he had with the vegans.'

Julia was struck dumb by the bizarre turn the conversation had taken. After a moment, she managed to ask, 'The vegans?'

'The vegans at the market. The ones selling the nut butters. They call themselves the Butter Nuts. They've been going on at us about the bees.'

'The bees?'

Julia, it seemed, could only parrot the last two words of Hester's sentences.

Hester frowned at Julia as if she was the one being obtuse. 'The vegans at the market have been shouting at us about the bees. They say we're exploiting them. *Exploiting them!* I've never heard such nonsense. We *love* the bees. We look after them.'

'Ah, well. People do have some funny ideas, don't they? But they shouldn't shout at you, that's not nice.'

'The Butter Nuts are not nice people,' Hester said. 'They're very shouty. One of them especially. Poppy, her name is. *Poppy.* I ask you. Such a pretty name for such an ugly person. She was always shouting and yelling and badgering us. It was likely her that did it.'

The conversation seemed to be veering in a strange direction, a direction Julia didn't want to prolong, but she couldn't help but ask: 'Did what?'

'Killed Matthew,' said Hester, and she walked through the kitchen door, into her house.

Julia had only been inside Hester's house once or twice, and each time she had found the experience distinctly odd. Their houses were two of three identical houses built in a short row, Julia's at the end of the row, on the far right as viewed from the road, and Hester's next door. They had once been the outbuildings of a big house, accommodation for servants or workers. Each house had a small front garden onto the road, and a bigger garden behind, with a door out from the kitchen. The floorplan of each house was exactly the same – Hester's front door was where Julia's front door was, with Hester's kitchen window overlooking her back garden just as Julia's did hers – but the overall impression was completely different. Hester's door was painted yellow, and through the window the four beehives could be spotted. Julia's door was varnished wood, and her kitchen window looked onto her vegetable patch and her chicken run. Hester's house was more rustic, Julia's a little tidier. Their fridges were in different corners, but their kitchen tables were positioned in the same place.

It was there at Hester's kitchen table that the two women were seated now, drinking big hot mugs of elderflower tea, generously sweetened with honey from the hives outside the window.

'I don't mean they *killed* him, killed him,' Hester now explained. 'Not on purpose. But they upset him with all their harassment. They put signs up and gave out little pamphlets about the bees and the honey. They shouted the most awful things – "You people should die like the bees..." Things like that. "Humans like you should be going extinct." I tried to ignore them, the idiots, but they really got to Matthew. And in the Christmas season, we have been at the same markets, so we have had to put up with their harassment every week. It drove him mad, because it was so unfair and untrue. Beekeeping is actually benefitting both bees and wildlife in general and there are studies to prove it. Matthew was a devoted beekeeper.'

'That must have been very upsetting.'

'The sad thing is, the last phone call we had, on the night he died, he told me that that Poppy woman had been at him again. Shouting, accusing, disturbing the customers. I keep thinking how horrible his last market session was. And wondering if he was so upset and distracted by the Butter Nuts, that he didn't see the car that was coming towards him. That they caused his death in some way.'

'Did you tell the police about them? About the things they said?' Julia asked.

'No, I didn't. It's not as if they ever *did* anything to us. They are just rude and unkind and shouty. And, frankly, Poppy did seem a little mad.' Hester sighed and said, 'I've got myself rather worked up. I'm just being silly. I will never know what Matthew was thinking when he went out to his car to drive home. Probably nothing much: he would have had a long day at the market, and was carrying the crates back to the car. I doubt he had a thought for the silly Butter Nuts. He was probably just thinking about coming home to me.' Hester's eyes filled up with tears.

'Sean and I saw him, Hester,' Julia said gently. 'We spoke to him. He *was* thinking about coming home to you – he said so. He knew that you would be worrying.'

'He was always worrying about me.' Hester paused. 'You found him, I believe.'

'Yes.' Julia wasn't sure what else to say, so she reached across and squeezed Hester's hand.

'Could you tell me how you think this could have happened?'

Julia took a deep breath. 'It was quite dark in the car park. There was no moon last night and all the Christmas lights were turned off already. There were just a few lights left on at the market for the stallholders who were still packing up their wares, but the parking was very gloomy. I suppose whoever hit Matthew just didn't see him. And if he saw them, he didn't get out of the way in time. Everyone was eager to get home, they might have been driving too fast. It was a horrible accident.'

But as she said this, Julia was imagining the scene. Anyone leaving a dark car park would presumably have their headlights on, Julia thought. In which case, Matthew would have been able to see them, and they would have seen him. She didn't mention this to Hester. There was no sense in upsetting the grieving widow further with her questions and theories. DI Hayley Gibson and her team would look into all of that.

'The thing I don't understand,' said Hester sadly, 'is how they could have just driven off and left him there.'

'It's unimaginable,' said Julia. 'Absolutely unimaginable. I can only think that they panicked. They got scared.'

'Especially if they'd been drinking.'

'That could have been a factor.' This conversation had a horrible sense of déjà vu. Just a week ago, she'd been having an eerily similar one about Lewis's accident.

'But to hit someone, and drive off...' said Hester with a shudder. 'And leave that person to...' She hesitated, as if she couldn't bear to say the words.

Julia looked at her expectantly.

Hester just shook her head, and reached for the teapot: 'More tea?'

13

It was later that day, and Julia was on her way back from the supermarket, from her monthly 'big shop' of items too heavy or cumbersome to carry home, when the car in front of her slowed unexpectedly. There seemed to be something going on the side of the main road, between the school and the police station. A small knot of people held up signs, the writing of which was illegible at this distance. Julia drove slowly and looked at the little group, trying to see what was going on. As she got closer, she recognised Diane, her colleague from Second Chances, among the small gathering. A few metres closer, and she could read Diane's sign: *Citizens for Safer Roads – Action Now!*

Julia pulled up alongside the pavement to get a better look at the protesters. It was hardly a crowd. In fact, there were only three of them. Well, five if you counted the two young kids sitting in a large double-seater pram, pushed by a young woman with a sign saying *Keep Our Children Safe*. The third adult was an old man in a voluminous red puffer jacket. He had daubed: *BERRYWICK POLICE! Wake up!* in red paint on a flattened-out cardboard box. The letters got smaller and smaller towards the right-hand edge of the sign as its maker had struggled to fit them in. The words 'Wake up!' proceeded up the edge of the cardboard, with the last word running along the vertical in rather smaller letters. Julia was jolted by a moment of instant recognition from the projects of her school days – 'THE PYRAmids' sprang to mind – and compassion for the man's artistic challenges.

Berrywick police had indeed woken up, it seemed, because DI Hayley Gibson was coming through the glass door of the station and walking towards the protesters. DC Walter Farmer trotted behind her. The detectives stopped right next to Julia's car, facing the protesters.

'Hello, Hayley,' Diane said, her voice clearly audible through Julia's open window. She removed one hand from her sign to tuck her hair awkwardly behind her ear. In a small village, where everyone knew everyone, this sort of awkwardness was fairly common. A police officer wasn't only a police officer, she might also be a Padel opponent, or your next-door neighbour, or an old girlfriend of your brother's. Diane and Hayley were of an age – Hayley perhaps a few years older – and had likely been at the same school at the same time.

'Hello, Diane. What's going on?' Hayley spoke perfectly pleasantly and casually, but Julia knew her well enough to notice the tiny pulse in her jaw that signalled stress, even from this distance.

'Well, Hayley, we are all quite upset about the bad driving. About the two deaths.'

'That's understandable, Diane,' Hayley said. 'I am too.'

'We all think there needs to be swift action taken to make our roads safer.'

'Yes, Diane, I hear you, and I'm of the same view.'

Julia was paralysed with inaction. She could hardly swing the door open and emerge right into the middle of the little gathering. Nor could she drive away, with Walter Farmer positioned three inches from the car's bumper.

'We want action by the police,' said the man in the red puffer. 'It seems you people are doing nothing!'

'Good morning, Fred,' said Hayley. 'Now, it's not true that nothing is being done. We have taken the situation extremely seriously and are actively investigating both deaths.'

'Ah, what exactly are you civil servants doing besides sitting at your comfy desks writing a few *emails?*' He spat out the word.

'Now, Fred, you know I can't share the details of the investigations.'

'Meanwhile, all over the village, people are being mowed down by maniacs from *London*.' Fred's face had taken on a hue to match his jacket. He looked like a furious strawberry. 'Monsters who don't even bother to stop their car...'

'Fred...'

'I have *grandchildren*!' He spoke with such anguish that Julia realised that his fury was really an expression of fear, as was so often the case.

'And I have children,' said the woman with the double pram. 'All the mums are in a state. People are too scared to walk around the village. Something must be done.'

'I hear your concerns, really I do,' Hayley said gently. 'And I promise you that I will do everything in my power to find the people who killed Lewis and Matthew.' She looked down, and for the first time saw Julia seated in her car. 'And we're working with a committee of concerned Berrywick citizens to communicate safer driving practices, and to get more cameras and speed bumps on our lanes.'

Walter followed Hayley's gaze, and looked down at Julia, trapped there in her car. He stepped out of her way.

'I'm sure you are doing what you can, Detective Inspector Gibson,' Diane said. 'But until you have someone behind bars for these awful hit-and-run crimes, you can expect to see us here.'

'I'll join you,' said an elderly lady, who had been moving down the pavement towards them at a glacial place with the help of a walking aid with four rubber feet, and was now standing firmly at Diane's side. 'I don't like the idea of all these madmen on the roads.'

'You'd be very welcome, Mrs Evans,' the young mum said. 'I'm Barbie Lincoln, by the way. Nancy Lincoln is my nan.'

Mrs Evans pulled up a pair of spectacles dangling round her neck on a chain and peered through them into the younger woman's face. 'Heavens, but you look just like her! Dear Nancy, she's a good woman. Well, pleased to meet you, young Barbie.'

'And you, Mrs Evans.'

'Call me Lorraine. My, isn't this fun? I used to love a good protest, back in the day. Not much call for it these days, but I should think I still remember a few of the songs...'

Walter Farmer addressed the little gathering. 'We've heard you. And speaking for myself, I will do everything possible to keep Berrywick citizens and all road users safe. Obviously you can stay and protest as long as you like, that's your right in terms of the law, but we're going to be going back to work now.'

'Thank you, Walter,' said Barbie, the young mum. 'My best to Amaryllis. Feeling all right, is she?'

'Well, you know. A bit queasy.'

'Poor girl. The first trimester is the worst for that; it should ease up soon. Get her some ginger biscuits. They sometimes help with the nausea.'

'Thanks, Barbie, we'll give that a try.' Walter smiled, and Julia could see that this whole exchange had filled him with a sense of pride that he was the father of the pregnancy under discussion. Walter and Amaryllis had clearly decided to spread the news wider than their families.

'I should be getting the little ones home for their tea,' said Barbie with a sigh. 'Fancy a cuppa, Lorraine? Our house is just down the street and round the next corner.'

'Lovely, you can tell me all about your nan, it's been a while since I've seen her...'

With that, the protest broke up peacefully.

'Same time tomorrow!' shouted Fred as they dispersed.

'Right you are,' said Diane.

Julia was about to drive away when Hayley leaned down and said, through the open window, 'Everything all right, Julia?'

'Oh, yes, I was passing and I saw the signs. Just being nosy really...' Julia smiled.

'That, I can believe,' said Hayley with a smirk. She knew that Julia was what might be politely termed 'curious' by nature.

It was a friendly smirk, which emboldened Julia to say: 'On that subject. Have you got a moment? It's about Hester and Matthew.'

Hayley opened the passenger door and got in. 'It's chilly out!' she said. 'Right then, what is it?'

Julia relayed the information about the Butter Nuts and the bees.

Hayley looked sceptical. 'Vegans object to bees making honey?'

'They object to people harvesting the honey. Well, some of them do, at least. They think it's cruel to the bees. Look, Hayley, I'm sure there's no connection between the vegans and Matthew's death, but Hester was pretty upset by them. She said they hounded her and Matthew, and they were on at him at the market the night he died. She worried they had distracted him, and that's why he was run over.'

Hayley didn't respond. She wore the serious almost-frown that meant she was processing facts and factors.

When Julia could stand it no longer, she said, 'It's probably nothing, but I thought I'd mention...'

'It's not necessarily nothing.'

Julia waited.

'People with passionate political beliefs can get very carried away. Even violent. It sounds like this lot are pretty convinced of their position. And they were certainly angry.'

'That's true, but it's not as if Hester thinks they *killed* Matthew. I mean, on *purpose*.'

'Even so, I'll have Walter look into those Butter Nutters.'

'Butter Nuts.'

'Whatever. They might have harassed Matthew. They might have hit him with a car by mistake. We don't know.' Hayley was using her official voice, which was slightly but significantly different from her friendly voice.

'But even so, an accident...'

'Leaving the scene of a car accident is an offence that carries a fine and possibly even time in prison. If they knew that someone was injured or dead as a result of the accident, that's even more serious.'

'Yes, of course. It would be.'

'Between you and me, Julia...' Hayley paused. Julia leaned in attentively. 'And I mean *really*, you and me...'

'Yes.'

'Both Lewis and Matthew were hit and then driven over again.'

Julia, of course, already knew about Lewis from Walter, but she didn't want Hayley to be angry with him for telling her. She didn't have to fake her horror though – it was terrible and ominous that the same thing had happened to Matthew.

'God, how awful.' Julia had to fight to stop herself picturing the situation.

'Again, it was dark both times. Now I don't like to jump to conclusions, but it does make me wonder...'

'Do you think it might have been... deliberate?'

'I can't imagine why. It makes no sense... But I can't discount the possibility. Despite what some members of the public seem to think, we are taking these two motor incidents very seriously. I intend to bring the guilty parties to book and get convictions. We must set an example to all road users.'

'I know you're doing everything you can, Hayley. People are just upset.'

'Understandably. The people of Berrywick demand and deserve safe roads. It's our job to make sure they get them. Now, thanks for the info. I'd better get back. There's a ton of forensic information and paperwork coming my way today. Some of it useful, I hope. And please will you do me a favour and message me the name of the butter company and any of the people's names you have. I'll get Walter onto it.'

'Right you are.'

'And Julia, what I said about similarities...'

'Not a word, I promise.'

Julia had packed away the groceries, household cleaning products and pet food, and was ready to put her feet up. It had been all go, go, go that morning, first with Hayley Gibson's arrival, then the visit to Hester, and then the shopping and unpacking. Not to mention swinging by the protest. She hadn't even had time to do her word games. She got out her phone to remedy that oversight, when she remembered her promise to send Hayley information about the Butter Nuts. She googled them – 'the Butter Nuts, Cotswolds' – hoping to find contact details and save Hayley at least a little bit of research. They were surprisingly ubiquitous on social media. There was an Instagram account and a Facebook page. On both, their products were colourfully displayed, and described in cheerful, wholesome prose. It was neither controversial nor combative. There was no evidence of it being a company of psycho bullies, or vehicular murderers. In fact, Julia fancied trying the macadamia nut butter. With a little digging, she found an email address and a phone number, which she shared with Hayley, and carried on clicking aimlessly through the content.

Poppy's name popped up. Curious to see the woman behind Hester's horror stories, Julia decided to do a bit of nosing around. She clicked through to Poppy's personal social media accounts, which bore out what Hester had related. Here was the controversial and combative side! Poppy had gotten into quite a number of beefs – if that term could be applied to vegans – largely, but not exclusively, to do with the bees. She felt very strongly about a number of issues, and she didn't mince her words.

The blood of the bees is on your hands! she'd told a woman who had proudly posted a picture of her homemade honey cake on Facebook. Julia wondered if bees actually *had* blood. But the point was clear, either way.

Poppy also posted regular pictures of what she labelled her 'yoga practice' and shared classes offered by the studio that she attended. She probably needed the yoga to calm her down after all the stress of arguing on social media. Julia knew the Hayfield studio in question – she had visited it on one of her previous amateur sleuthing missions, and remembered the lovely, lithe young lady who had run the place.

'Long black hair. Boyfriend worked at the garden centre. What was her name again?' she asked herself impatiently. Proper nouns were quite tardy in arriving at her conscious brain these days. 'Milly!' she said, relieved, when the name dawdled in.

She rolled her stiff shoulders, enjoying the clicks and the easing of stress. 'I really should do yoga more regularly. Tomorrow is as good a time to start as any.'

14

Jake looked up eagerly at the clinking of the car keys. His eyes bored into Julia's, and she could almost hear the whirring of his brain trying to interpret the signs. What did this mean? Was it good for the dog? What larks might be on offer? Was there a morning walk in his future? Or at least a trip in the car? Or was he to be abandoned? Bereft?

'No, not now, Jake, we'll go out later,' said Julia. She had learned not to use the word 'walk' in his presence, as it only got him excited, even with a 'no' in front of it. Her body language and the word 'no' were enough to convey the bad news. Not only was there no walk, but he wasn't invited on the outing Julia had planned for the morning, which was to a 10 a.m. yoga class in Hayfield.

Julia had found, in her online investigation, that Milly's yoga studio, the one that Poppy frequented, offered a free trial lesson to new students. She had messaged Milly the previous evening to enquire, and now here she was in tracksuit trousers and a rather shapeless long-sleeved T-shirt, which would have to pass for yoga gear.

Jake put his head on his paws and sighed dejectedly. Chaplin, who frankly couldn't give a toss about Julia's plans for the day, stared fixedly at his bowl. As long as his tummy was filled, and there was a comfortable and warm spot to sit, he was fine. Julia put down her bag and car keys, topped up the bowl with fresh biscuits, stroked his head, and went on her way.

At the far end of the Hayfield main road, just past the last of the shops, was Milly's small yoga studio. Julia opened the front door and stepped into a little area fitted with shelves for shoes and bags. She stowed her things and went into the studio itself, a calm and restful place, with pale wooden floors and white walls. With her characteristic punctuality, Julia had arrived twelve minutes before the scheduled time for the class to begin. The studio was empty, except for Milly, who was straightening a pile of yoga blocks.

She turned when she heard the door. 'Julia!' she said, and reached out to take both Julia's hands in her own. 'I was so happy to hear from you, and I'm pleased you are here.'

'And I'm pleased to be here, finally. I've been meaning to come for ages.'

'You never regret the time and energy you put into your physical and emotional health,' said Milly, reminding Julia how sweet and earnest she was. One of those trusting, kindly sort of people. Which made Julia feel bad about being less than entirely honest with her about the motive behind her sudden interest in yoga.

'Well, I'm sure you're right about that. The other day I saw something about your studio on Facebook and I thought, well, that's a sign! So here I am.'

'Really? What did you see? I'm not very good at all that online marketing.'

'It was on someone else's page. Poppy, her name is. You know how these things mysteriously come up on your screen.'

'It's the algorithm,' Milly said, as if that explained everything.

'Poppy makes all those nice nut butters. I saw them at one of the markets and I googled them. And the next thing I was on their page and it showed me her profile, and I saw she was somehow connected to you.'

'Yes, Poppy is a regular here.' There was a slight reserve in Milly's voice. 'In fact, she'll be here any minute. She lives down the street and she always comes to this class.'

'Ah, well, that's nice. She did seem a little stressed in her Facebook posts. Angry, even. I'm sure the yoga helps her relax.'

'Yes, poor Poppy *does* struggle with her anger. It's such a destructive emotion. Poisonous to the body and soul. It comes from a good place, it really does – she cares so much about the animals. She just gets worked up.'

'She certainly seems very committed.'

'I'm vegetarian – I have been since childhood. So I understand her position and her passion. But you can't expect everyone to be where you are. And shouting at them doesn't generally help them come over to your views.'

'You catch more bees with honey than with vinegar, as my mum used to say.'

'That's so true, Julia. Your mother was a wise woman, by the sound of things. But I wouldn't be mentioning honey around Poppy. Or bees. She gets very angry about that, too.'

Julia was about to enquire further, when Milly's phone rang. 'Excuse me,' she said, and answered it. A series of short, non-committal comments: 'Yes... The old Mercedes...? Gosh... That sounds horrible... I hope you're all right... Yes... See you soon... Poor you, do try and do some deep breathing, and if you can manage a few stretches... Okay. Bye, Poppy.'

Milly ended the call. 'Well, it looks like Poppy won't be here after all. She has to take her car to the panel beater in the next village. She's getting a dent fixed.'

'Oh dear, that doesn't sound good.' It didn't sound good for

Poppy, thought Julia, especially if she had come by that dent in the way that Julia was thinking.

'She's fine, apparently. It was just a bump, and it's a big, solid old car. It belonged to her gran.'

'Hello!' came a call from the door. Two more women came in, followed quickly by another. They were clearly regulars, judging by the chummy way they greeted each other. They welcomed Julia, and took up their positions on the mats.

'It's okay, Gill, you can move forward into this space,' Milly said, indicating a big gap that had been left open in the front centre.

'What about Poppy? That's where she likes to stand.'

'She's not coming today.'

'Go on Gilly, it's safe,' said one of the others, and they all laughed. The laugh of shared understanding of something ridiculous and annoying – doubtless, in this case, Poppy's territorial behaviour.

The class was more pleasant and less humiliating than Julia had feared. She'd done some yoga and Pilates on YouTube, and between what she'd learned, and keeping a close eye on Milly, she managed to approximate most of the poses. Of course, Milly was small-boned and delicate and deceptively strong, and instead of old tracksuit trousers and T-shirt, wore matching sage green leggings and a crop top, with her shiny black hair plaited and hanging down her back. She made everything look graceful and effortless, but in a way that was soothing, rather than intimidating.

Julia was surprised to find how well she was able to focus on the instructions and give herself over to the moment. She was determined to wait until the class was finished to think about what she'd heard about Poppy's car.

She left the class walking on air. 'I will definitely be back!' she said to Milly. 'It was wonderful, thank you!' She felt great! Her hamstrings felt soft and pliable. Her stiff neck had eased.

The oxygen was flowing through her veins. This was the new Julia, a supple, calm and happy yogi! She would definitely keep it up.

Once in her car, she turned her attention to the matter of Poppy's accident. There wasn't much to think about, actually. She would simply tell Hayley Gibson, and the police would follow it up. No time like the present, she thought, taking her mobile from her bag. She phoned Hayley's number, but the detective didn't answer. Knowing how Hayley disliked listening to messages, Julia didn't leave one, but sent her a text message to call when she could.

With that behind her, she drove home, enjoying the feeling of cruising through the countryside, with the fresh-released endorphins and yoga-oxygenated blood pulsing through her body. The trees were bare, but beautiful, and today the sky was an icy blue, but clear. She decided to take a different, slightly longer route home, for a change of scene through a different village. She kept her wits about her – it was Friday, and the weekend traffic was already building – but enjoyed the views, singing along to the music playing through the sound system.

The traffic slowed suddenly as she entered the next village, and she soon saw why. Traffic cones lined the road to accommodate a crew working on the grassy verge, narrowing the road considerably.

'That'll teach me to take a pleasant detour to stop and smell the roses,' she said to herself, out loud. It didn't matter though; she had nothing pressing to get back to. Julia looked about her as she crawled through the outskirts of the village. From this approach, at least, it seemed bigger than Berrywick, more modern and less charming. There was a small industrial strip with a few workshops, a hardware store and a panel beater.

Julia almost slammed on her brakes when she saw it. A car, a big old Mercedes, parked in the panel beater's yard. And a sticker on the car, a sticker saying: *The Butter Nuts*. It had to be Poppy's car.

Julia pulled in behind the Mercedes and got out.

A thin, balding man in blue overalls emerged from the workshop. 'Can I help you with something?' he asked, looking at her car. 'I could fix that up in a jiffy.' He pointed to a scratch that Julia had made a few months ago, when a shopping trolley had slipped from her grasp in the wind and made a desperate bid for escape. Every time she looked at it, it annoyed her.

'Oh, hello,' she said. 'That would be super. Can you do it while I wait?'

'If you can wait five or ten minutes, then that would be a yes.'

'I can definitely wait ten minutes.'

'Glad to hear it. Everyone seems to be so busy and impatient these days.'

'Not me,' she said. 'I'm taking the slow road home.'

'That's the way. I'm Geoff.'

'Julia. Pleased to meet you.'

Geoff wandered back into the workshop and emerged with a couple of cloths and an aerosol tin of something.

'Isn't that Poppy's car?' Julia said casually, looking at the Mercedes.

'It is indeed. She just brought it in for that dent on the bumper. It'll be here for a couple of days, so it makes no difference if I sort out your scratch first.'

Geoff sprayed a foam onto Julia's car and set about rubbing it with hard, circular movements.

Julia stepped closer. There was indeed a dent on Poppy's car's bumper.

'It doesn't look too bad. I wonder what she hit.'

'Ah, she didn't say. Poor thing was quite upset, though. Stressed. Some people get like that about their cars. I always say, as long as no one's hurt, everything else can be fixed. She's gone to get a sip of water, to settle her nerves.'

Julia squatted down. There was something dark on the bumper. She took a hankie out of her pocket and touched the dark patch gently with the corner. The fabric came back with a tiny, dark red spot on it.

Unless Julia was very much mistaken, it was blood.

15

'Is there a tap or a bathroom where I can wash the dust off my hands?' Julia asked, rubbing her perfectly clean hands together.

'The bathroom is inside, on your right,' said Geoff, without looking up from the scratch which he was attending to with vigour.

Julia walked into the workshop, past the little office area on the left, and was about to open the bathroom door when a woman walked out. It was Poppy. Julia recognised her from her social media. Her bright red hair – dyed to match her name? Julia wondered – made her instantly recognisable.

Julia stepped back and held the door to let Poppy pass. The woman looked distracted, and walked past Julia without even making eye contact, let alone saying thank you. It was as if she didn't even see her. Julia had become accustomed to her invisibility as a woman of a certain age. On a good day, she even appreciated it. It had its uses, on occasion – like now, for instance, when she was engaged in amateur snooping.

A man's voice came from the workshop: 'There you are, Poppy. Are you all right?'

Julia glanced behind to see a man coming towards the redhead. He took her in his arms.

Julia stepped into the little bathroom, leaving the door slightly ajar. She stood by the door, her ear to the gap, to catch their conversation.

'Thanks for coming to fetch me, Ollie.'

'It's no problem. But what's going on? Why didn't you tell me about the accident?

'I was confused. Upset. I didn't want you to think...' Poppy gasped between the words. 'There was this horrible sound. I'll never forget it.'

'It was an accident, darling.'

'I took a life... I killed a living being.'

'It was an accident, Poppy. You wouldn't even kill a mosquito, everyone knows that.'

'Well, now I've killed something, and not a mosquito. A sentient being. I've committed a crime. A soul is dead.'

'You need to go to the police, tell them everything.'

'No, I can't tell them... It'll draw attention to us.'

'They'll find out.'

'I can't go to prison, Ollie. They eat *meat* there.'

Julia shut the bathroom door, her blood pounding in her ears. A confession! She needed to tell Hayley immediately. She washed her hands, shook off the drips, and dried them on the paper towel. She reached for her phone and dialled.

Hayley answered in two rings, rather to Julia's surprise.

'What's up?' she asked, with her usual brusqueness.

Julia described what she'd seen and heard. She told her about the blood, and was only halfway through relating the results of her bathroom eavesdropping when the detective cut her short.

'Got it. Thanks. Tell the mechanic not to touch that car. The police will be impounding it. Can you come by the station, give DC Farmer your statement? And I'll get onto this Poppy person.'

The protesters were outside the police station again. There were eight of them now. The old chap, Fred, was there, still in his voluminous red puffer jacket. The woman with the double pram wasn't present. Presumably, two small kids kept her too busy to be protesting every day. Diane and the older hippy lady – Lorraine, that was her name – were bossing around the new recruits.

'Oh, hello, Julia,' Diane said. 'Have you come to join us?'

'Ah, no, although I support your cause. I've got other business today.'

'Well, we're here from twelve until one every day.'

'I see, well, I might see you on another occasion. Right now, I've got an appointment at the police station.'

'Ah, and what would that be...?'

Diane didn't finish her question – which Julia was thankful for – because more reinforcements had arrived in the person of a middle-aged couple, one of them wearing a *No to nuclear!* button badge which he'd presumably had in a drawer for thirty years. His partner had a homemade sign saying *Safe streets!* on one side, and *Mind children, crossing!* on the other, which was a little confusing thanks to the comma placement. It did remind Julia that she had promised the road safety committee that she would have her slogans to them this evening, so that the signs could be printed.

'Right,' said Fred, looking at his watch. 'It's twelve. Everyone ready?'

As they took up position along the pavement, hoisting their signs to their shoulders, Julia crossed the road to the station.

'Thanks for coming in,' said DC Walter Farmer.

'No problem, Walter, anything I can do to help. How are you?'

The question was more than just a formality. Walter was looking particularly harassed this morning. His eyes darted about in his pale face, and a small rash of pimples stood out on his chin. 'Ah, well, I'm all right,' Walter said, not very convincingly. 'There's a lot going on with the two motor vehicle accidents... or, well, I should say, deaths.'

This was interesting. Had the police formally opened this as a murder investigation? Before Julia could formulate the question, Walter had moved on. 'And Amaryllis isn't sleeping, on account of the pregnancy. Her back hurts. And she's up and down like a jack-in-the-box, which means I am too. If I got four hours last night, it was a miracle.'

The sound of what seemed to be singing floated in an open window. Someone must be driving by with their car windows open and the music on full.

'Ah, that's hard when you've got a busy day at work.'

'Busy it is, Julia. Busy it is. Speaking of, I should get going on the job, shouldn't I? DI Gibson is busy with the car and the forensics. She wants me to take your statement. Everything you know about the car at the panel beaters. And what you saw or heard.'

Julia recounted what she'd seen on the car. Walter scribbled furiously in his notebook. She then handed over her handkerchief, dropping it straight into the evidence bag Walter held open.

'It certainly looks like blood,' he said, peering at it through the clear plastic.

'That's what I thought.'

He placed the bag carefully on his desk, picked up his pen and notebook, and said, 'Please, go on.'

When Julia started on the conversation she overheard from the bathroom, Walter squinted at her, his lips twitching with a smile for the first time since she had sat down. 'Overheard, hey? That was a lucky coincidence.' Like Hayley, Walter knew Julia well.

'Yes. Right place at the right time, I suppose,' said Julia.

The singing was still going on, and it seemed louder now. It couldn't be coming from a car.

'Well, thanks for coming in, Julia. I'll give this to the boss, see if she needs anything else.'

'Walter,' Julia said, hesitantly. 'You don't think these two deaths were an accident, do you?'

There must have been half a minute's silence, before he said, 'It seems like too much of a coincidence. The same manner of death, in the space of a couple of weeks, within five miles of each other.'

'And the forensics?'

'Nothing substantial: just that very indistinct, quite small footprint.'

Julia tried to remember Poppy's feet, but couldn't. She wasn't a big person, that much Julia knew. 'Do you think it was the same print at both scenes?'

Walter's phone rang. He held up his hand. 'Julia, I have to get going. This is DI Gibson on the phone. She'll be needing me, I'm sure. If you think of anything else, phone me.'

He took the call.

Julia left his office deep in thought. As she drew closer to the front door, the indistinct singing got louder. Through the glass in the door to the police station, she saw Poppy and Ollie pause outside, as if putting off their moment of entry. They stepped to the side, close together, their heads down.

Julia opened the door, keeping her head turned away from them. She didn't have anything to hide, exactly, but they might think it an odd coincidence, the same strange woman popping up at the panel beater and the police station. She needn't have worried, though: they were completely engrossed in their own world. She walked slowly, trying to listen in. It wasn't easy. Lorraine was leading the motley crew of protesters in a tuneless version of 'We Shall Overcome'. They seemed a little unclear on the lyrics, and there was quite a lot of mumbling.

Ollie kissed Poppy tenderly, and said, 'Now you go in. Just remember, tell them it was a fox. Just because they have called you in doesn't mean that they know everything.'

'I wish you could come in with me.' Julia could hear the tears in her voice.

'You'll be fine. I'll go and get rid of the evidence. This whole thing will be over by teatime. Now go.'

Julia quickened her step to avoid being seen by Poppy. She heard the station door open and close, followed by the sound of footsteps coming quickly behind her. As she got to her car, Ollie walked past her and got into the car parked two or three ahead. The blue Renault pulled out, into the main road.

Lorraine had moved on to 'Imagine', which was an improvement (off a very low base), because the singers had a better handle on the lyrics this time. Fred, in particular, gave it a proper go.

As she got into her car, Julia wondered what John Lennon would think of his song being used by a grandad in the Cotswolds, protesting for safer roads. She reckoned he'd be quite pleased.

Julia slammed the door, muffling the sound of the singing, and phoned Walter's number, to tell him about Ollie saying he would hide evidence. The phone call went straight to voicemail. Walter must be in with Poppy. Julia left a message for him to phone her back as soon as he got the message. She tried Hayley, with the same result. She dithered for a moment, wondering whether she should go back into the police station. It didn't seem worth it, she decided. Presumably they would both be talking to Poppy and she'd be hanging around for ages waiting for them. It had been a busy day, and the idea of hanging around for half an hour on those hard plastic chairs, reading the same old posters, didn't appeal. She'd go on home to her nice comfy sofa and her library book. They would call when they could. She indicated, and pulled out of her parking spot.

As she joined the road, she found herself driving behind Ollie's little blue car.

'Ah well,' she said. 'Might as well see where he's going.'

It was easy enough following Ollie. He was a cautious driver, who drove on the speed limit, and indicated in good time, giving her plenty of notice of his intentions. There weren't many cars on the road, but it was just busy enough that she didn't think he would notice her behind him. Julia wondered what evidence Ollie could possibly be on his way to destroy. There wouldn't be a weapon of any kind, given that the murder weapon of choice was a car. Perhaps something like a letter – a threatening letter? Or some incriminating personal item of one of the victims? Or the shoes that had made that print, perhaps?

Julia was still mulling this over, not very successfully, when Ollie indicated left and pulled off the road. She slowed, and saw an untarred lane leading into the woods. She drove on a little way, parked well off the road, and walked back to the start of the lane. Keeping to the tree line, she got close enough to see where Ollie had stopped the car. He'd got out, walked to the boot, and opened it. She couldn't see what he was doing at that angle, but he reappeared in front of the car, walking into the woods, with a spade over his shoulder. The brambles were too high for her to see much, and she dared not go closer.

The harsh metallic sound of a spade hitting the ground pierced the silent wood, and startled Julia. She inhaled sharply. An insect or a piece of dust flew into her lungs. She stifled the cough and edged away with her hand over her mouth. Her lungs felt like they might explode. Staggering further into the woods until she was well out of sight of Ollie, she leaned against a tree, and allowed herself a big cough into her elbow. Whatever had been causing the trouble was ejected, and she took a few welcome deep breaths. Her heart slowed and steadied.

Julia started towards the main road, and her car, eager to phone the detectives. What would she tell them? She realised she would have to give them directions. Stopping in the lane, she looked back to where Ollie's car was still visible. A telephone wire crossed a few yards beyond it. Across the road from the car was a dead pine tree. She made a mental note. At least she'd have markers for the police.

Back at her car, she phoned DI Hayley Gibson and told her what she'd seen.

16

'I'm sorry, Hayley, it seems I was wrong about everything. The dent on the car, the blood... I thought it was important, but it turns out I wasted everyone's time. All those forensics people...'

Julia shuddered at the memory of them all swooping into the lane in their vans, donning their white booties and their gloves, unrolling their spools of crime scene tape. She'd watched them start with the careful digging and bagging of the earth where Ollie had been digging not an hour before.

Julia had left then, and was grateful not to have been at the scene for the discovery of the buried evidence. It was a corpse – not a human corpse, but that of a large white swan, she heard later from DC Walter Farmer. She felt a fresh flush of horror, imagining the bird's long floppy neck and orange beak emerging muddied from the hole Ollie had dug, and a flush of shame for all the trouble she'd put everyone to. Jake padded across the kitchen floor and sat next to her, leaning his big brown self against her thigh in a supportive sort of way. She stroked his silky head and did feel a little calmer.

Hayley put down the mug of tea Julia had made her and

reached across the table to pat her hand. 'That's what forensics are for – to determine what, if anything, the evidence means.'

'Which turned out to be nothing, in this case.'

'Not at all, Julia. We got new information and discounted a potential suspect. Based on what you'd heard and seen, you did the right thing, telling the police. You heard Poppy and Ollie talk about hiding evidence of a crime, and you saw him furtively digging in a secluded area.'

Julia had expected a proper talking-to, after her interference. The fact that Hayley was being so nice and understanding made Julia feel, if anything, worse.

'How were you to know,' Hayley continued, 'that it was nothing to do with the two motor-vehicle-related deaths? That she'd killed a swan?'

'Poor swan. And poor Poppy,' said Julia. 'She is so devoted to animals; she must have felt terrible hitting that swan with her car.'

'She did. Her story, when we called her in, was that she had hit a hare. As soon as they found the swan, I told her what we'd discovered. She did feel awfully guilty and sad. And she was scared. She'd heard – like most of us have heard – that all swans belong to the king.'

'I looked it up,' Julia said. 'Apparently the monarch has the right to claim ownership to any white swan in the open waters of Britain, but doesn't generally exercise that right.'

'Well, Poppy seemed to think that killing one was some sort of crime against the monarchy, which was why Ollie was burying it. Heaven knows what they thought was going to happen to her.'

'Probably thought you'd march her off to the Tower of London or something.'

Hayley gave a weak chuckle at Julia's little joke. 'Maybe a few days in the stocks.'

'A public flogging.'

Hayley drained her tea, and put the cup down. It was a gesture that spoke of finality. Hayley had stopped at Julia's house on her way back from the crime scene. She'd accepted a cuppa and a piece of toast, having missed both breakfast and lunch. Having hoovered them down efficiently, and updated Julia on the swan discovery, she was no doubt impatient to go.

'I should get to the station,' she said. 'Walter will be wondering where I've got to. And there will be the usual avalanche of paperwork.'

'Sorry if I added to it.'

'Look,' said Hayley, 'I shouldn't say this, but we were actually in the process of checking all the panel beaters in the area in any event. Your lead was, if anything, the best result that we had. I guess people don't really take their cars to be fixed if they got dented committing murder.'

'So it's official. You think Lewis and Matthew were killed?' Julia hesitated, and added, for clarity, 'On purpose? By the same person?'

Hayley considered her answer. 'I am now working on the assumption that the deaths were deliberate, and connected.'

'I agree. It's too much of a coincidence, the two of them dying like that, in such a similar manner. But why? And who?'

The detective stood up and hoisted her bag over her shoulder. 'That, Julia Bird, is what I aim to find out.'

With Hayley gone, Julia squeezed the last half-cup of tea out of the pot and put a second slice of bread in the toaster. It was a surprise to discover it was only 3.45 p.m. She'd been up early to get to the yoga class, and had been running around ever since. Jake was wandering around looking at her in an expectant sort of way as he did when he was hoping for a walk. It was that time of day, after all.

'Give me a minute,' she said. 'We'll do a short trot around the block when I've finished my tea.'

She felt like nothing more than an hour or two on the sofa with the cosy mystery story she had downloaded onto her Kindle, but she knew a short walk would do her the world of good. There would be time for reading later.

Julia was as good as her word. Ten minutes later, she was walking down the lane with Jake trotting happily at her side. They made fairly slow progress, because the world was full of fallen leaves that required urgent investigation by a shiny brown nose. Once they got to the river path, Julia let him off the lead. She dawdled while he raced up and down the path. She was in no hurry. Her mind was still mulling over today's developments, and one thing in particular – that DI Hayley Gibson believed that the deaths of Lewis and Matthew were not horrible accidents, coincidentally occurring within weeks of each other. On the contrary, they were deliberate, and somehow connected. But how?

Julia wondered if the two men had known each other and, if so, how well. They lived in the same village and were roughly the same age, so it was very likely that they were acquainted, but to the best of Julia's knowledge, Matthew and Lewis had lived in quite different worlds. Matthew was quiet, gentle; a maker and doer and grower of things. He was a homebody who spent most of his time with his wife and his bees, when he wasn't working the markets. Lewis was personable and chatty, always on the road, always in the know, a favourite of the elderly neighbourhood ladies who he drove to the bigger towns for theatre or shopping.

'Come in, Jake,' Julia called, spotting the emaciated figure of Aunt Edna coming towards them. The woman had a distinctive listing, tottering sort of gait, but she kept up a fair pace, given her advanced years (her exact age was unknown, but apparently

Edna had already been ancient and mad when Tabitha had moved to Berrywick well over a decade ago).

Jake came in and Julia clipped on his lead.

'A short leash makes for a good dog,' said Edna. Her pronouncement had a profound sort of truth to it, and Julia wondered if she'd made it up on the spot, or if it was an ancient adage. 'A short dog is no good though. Too close to the ground, is a short hound,' said Edna, rather undermining the profundity of her first statement.

'How are you today, Edna?' asked Julia.

'As well as can be expected, given, you know...'

Julia didn't know. She raised her eyebrows in an encouraging, quizzical sort of look.

'The war, of course!' the old woman said, crossly. 'Goodness, you young people.'

'Ah yes, well, war is terrible, of course.' Julia wondered which particular war Edna was referring to. One of the World Wars? The Gulf War? The war on drugs? It could have been the American Civil War, for all the sense Edna made.

'Mostly, trouble is closer to home,' said the old woman, cheerfully. 'Right on your doorstep. Right next door, even. Old wounds, old wounds.'

She turned her pale, watery eyes to Jake and wagged a bony forefinger: 'You mark my words, and I'll mark your birds.'

Edna tottered off without a goodbye, leaving a nervous-looking Jake and a pensive Julia on the river path, watching her go.

'Right next door?' Julia said out loud to herself. 'That reminds me, I'd better pop over to Hester and see how she's doing.'

Hester was sitting at her kitchen table, staring at three bunches of flowers that were lying on the table, slowly dying.

'Why do people even send flowers?' she said to Julia, who had let herself in after calling out a few times. 'All it does is remind us that everything dies.'

'Well,' said Julia. 'Let me put these in vases for you, and then perhaps the reminder will be less immediate.' She wasn't one hundred per cent sure, but she thought she saw a small twitch of humour at the corner of Hester's mouth.

'It's Christmas that I'm dreading most,' said Hester, as Julia put the flowers in three vases that she found in a cupboard under the sink. She tried to arrange them artfully, hoping that some beauty might bring Hester a small comfort. But flower arranging had never been Julia's strongest skill, and after a few useless moments fluffing up and rearranging the blooms, she put the vases to the side, and opted instead for making tea. She felt on decidedly firmer ground with tea, and she could see that someone had dropped off some fresh mince pies.

'I suppose this way, at least Violet will now come for Christmas. She wasn't going to. But she has to come now, doesn't she?'

Julia put a cup of tea and a mince pie down in front of Hester, feeling sad at how difficult relationships with adult children could sometimes be.

'I'm sure it will help you to have her here,' she said gently.

'She's devastated. A real daddy's girl.' Hester said this fondly, a small smile on her face. 'Of course, we need to let Lewis be buried first. Two such deaths so close. I can't believe it.'

'Two men who didn't know each other in life, joined in death,' said Julia. She felt this was quite a profound observation. The sort that Aunt Edna might make, on a good day.

'Has someone else died?' asked Hester, horrified.

'Well, yes. Lewis.' Julia felt confused. Hester herself had just referred to it.

'Lewis and who else?'

Good lord, was the woman going insane from her grief? 'Matthew,' Julia said, in her gentlest, most therapeutic voice.

'Yes, but who is the other one?' Hester was getting quite het up.

'The other who?'

'The man who didn't know them?'

'Each other,' said Julia, enunciating slowly. 'They didn't know each other.'

'Well, of course they knew each other!' said Hester. 'They went to school together. Goodness, they even had a band together! How we used to laugh – Lewis Band, your friend from the band, I used to say.'

'A band?' Julia felt as if this conversation was rapidly hurtling away from her, and she needed to get it firmly back on track.

'It would have been, what, the mid-eighties?' said Hester, her eyes narrowed, as if she were squinting into the past. 'They were in a band together when they were youngsters, but it had split up by the time Matthew and I met.'

'Did they still see each other, the band members?'

'Not as a group, no. There had been some bad blood between them at the end. They'd been doing quite well, apparently. They'd got a big London manager, who had got them in with a record company. They were going to make a record, but something happened, Matthew was never clear exactly what and it used to upset him talking about it. Anyway, at the last minute they weren't signed up. Before my time, that was, but the breakup was quite fresh when Matthew and I got together. A few months before, if I remember. I just know that there had been a lot of blame and bitterness, and a lot of fighting. The band fell apart. Bands, you know. Matthew and Lewis were the only ones who stayed in the area; the others moved off.'

'Were Matthew and Lewis friends later on in life?'

'They weren't enemies, but they weren't friends, particularly. I suppose they just didn't have much in common, other than the band. But they'd say hello when they saw each other in the village. They were friendly enough, but they didn't make plans, or get together.'

Hester got up to poke at the fire that she had lit just before Julia arrived.

'What was the band called, Hester?'

'Oh, now you're asking. Gosh, I should know. I *do* know. It's on the tip of my tongue...' She tapped impatiently at her forehead, as if trying to dislodge that sticky piece of information.

Julia was all too familiar with the tip-of-your-tongue feeling, and the anxiety it engendered in the sixty-something mind. She also knew that the head tap didn't work. 'Not to worry, Hester, I was just curious.'

'Well, it's going to bother me all night if I don't remember it. Wait a mo, I'll get Matthew's photo album. He's got one specially for the band. It's got lots of pictures from the gigs they played, and a little tour they did around the area. Gosh, I haven't looked at that in years.'

Hester got up and walked over to a big wooden dresser. A matching set of stoneware was on the upper shelves. She opened the lower cupboards to reveal a stack of albums. Julia felt pleased that she seemed at least more energetic than she had been.

'This is it,' she said, pulling a big red-covered book from the bottom of the pile. It was fat, and crumpled papers peeped from between the leaves. She opened the book at a random page, and pulled out the flyer. 'The Red Berries! Of course, how could I have forgotten? The Red Berries because they were from Berrywick. God, I hope I'm not going dilly.'

'You're not going dilly. Stress affects memory recall, you know. Stress and grief, both.'

'Well, there's enough of that about,' Hester said sadly, turning the pages of the book slowly, as if lost in thought. 'It's funny,' she said, 'their most popular song was a Christmas one.'

She started singing softly:

> '*As white as the snow*
> *The Christmas trees glow*
> *And now I must go*
> *Hoooooooommmeee.*'

It was ghastly. But Julia smiled.

> '*As red as the holly*
> *The holly is jolly*
> *And now I must go*
> *Hoooooommmeeee.*'

Julia wasn't sure she could stand it if Hester moved on to the next colour, but she was saved by Hester finding the picture that she was looking for. She turned the book to face Julia, handed it to her and pointed: 'Here he is, look at him. He was a fine-looking fellow, was Matthew.'

There he was, her elderly beekeeping neighbour, forty-odd years younger, in slim-fitting blue jeans and a neon shirt, his hair in a shaggy eighties mullet, a shy grin on his face, and a bass guitar slung around his neck. Julia found herself smiling as she thought back to her own shaggy eighties hairdo, and accompanying neon clothes. Matthew certainly had been a good-looking chap. A blonde girl and two other young men stood, similarly attired, similarly smiling into their glorious futures. Julia recognised one of them: the shortest and stockiest of the men, with the biggest grin, sitting behind a drum kit.

'That's Lewis Band!' she said.

'So it is. Lewis was the drummer. Look how young they both were. And now... Still, it makes me happy to see Matthew.'

'He looks great there. Handsome and happy.'

'I couldn't believe it when he took a shine to me,' said Hester with a laugh. 'A chap like that? A girl like me? Heavens.'

'Oh, I can see why he fancied you,' said Julia. 'You're a natural beauty, with a kind heart.'

'Ah, what a sweet thing to say. Funnily enough, that's sort of what he said too. It didn't hurt that he'd just come out of a relationship. He liked to joke that I was a rebound fling that lasted forty years.' Hester's laugh turned into a sort of strangled sob. She put on a 'buck up' voice and said, 'You know what? I think it's time for a slice of our homemade honey apple cake.'

'Gosh, that sounds delicious.'

'It is delicious, made with our own apples and our own honey,' Hester said, getting to her feet. 'Back in a jiffy.'

While Hester went off to fetch the cake, Julia held the heavy album in her lap, turning the pages slowly. Another photograph of the band caught her eye: in this one, they were squashed up on a long sofa with a few girls. It seemed to be a celebration. They each had a champagne glass – the old-fashioned bubble glasses, not the flutes – and they were larking about. The pretty blonde from the band sat on Matthew's knee, her mouth open in what looked like laughter. Lewis was turned towards them, toasting them. Another girl with a halter top and spectacular afro stood behind, holding her glass towards the camera. A waif in a mini skirt stood with a foot up on the arm of the sofa, and her arms up. A few other men, who Julia took to be the other band members, or perhaps producers or some such, were caught in similarly celebratory poses.

Julia noticed the caption, the ink pale from all the years, but still legible. *Jupiter Records!!!! London, May 1986*, it said. Below was a string of names – some of them, like Lewis, so familiar that they were identified just by their initials or a nickname, all in a tiny, illegible scrawl. Julia leaned in and peered through her glasses at something like: *M... Egg... L, Dom, M, K...*

It was a lovely photograph, so happy and optimistic. Clearly, it had been taken before their record deal fell apart, with recriminations all round. Poor innocent young things.

Julia couldn't imagine that a shared experience in an eighties rock band might connect two men killed in hit-and-run incidents in a Cotswolds village, but she reached into her bag for her phone, and took a photograph of the photograph. Because you never knew, did you?

17

It felt strange to be driving on the motorway, with a stream of other cars, all travelling at speed into London on a Saturday morning. Julia had once been used to whizzing along the motorways and around the city streets, dashing about to meetings and clients and courts all over town, but she'd become rather out of practice after her years tootling slowly around Berrywick and the neighbouring villages. They had debated taking the train, but both liked the freedom of having a car with them, and the ability to pack as much luggage as one wished. Julia concentrated hard and held the wheel firmly. She flicked her eyes between the road and the rear-view mirror. She kept a good following distance and indicated well in advance of any movement.

Sean, in the seat next to her, did most of the talking. 'The last time I was on this road, it was to fetch Jono when he was chucked out of his London flat,' he said, staring pensively out of the window. 'It feels like a lifetime ago. So much has happened since.'

'That it has. He was a very troubled chap when you brought

him to Berrywick, but his time here, and being with you and Leo – and then with Laine – has really settled him.'

'You've played a part too,' Sean said. 'He likes you and looks up to you. And you're the one who suggested him for the job at the vet, which has been brilliant for him.'

'You know what they say, it takes a village to raise a troubled young adult,' Julia said, lightly. 'And look, it's paid off handsomely – we've got someone to look after all the animals this weekend while we're in London for the party.'

Christopher, Julia's ex-husband's current husband, was turning fifty. Christopher had dithered about a celebration, torn between his horror at the clocking up of another decade, and his deep and abiding love of a party. The indecision had gone on for quite some time, driving poor Peter completely mad, but Christopher's party-loving side had won out and an event had been hastily planned. ('As if there was ever going to be any other outcome,' Peter had said, in loving exasperation.)

As a result, on quite short notice, Julia and Sean had booked a night in the city, and Jono and Leo had agreed to move into Julia's house with Jake, Chaplin and the chickens. Julia was used to managing the animals' various schedules, diets and foibles, but when she wrote out the list of who did what, and ate what, when, and where they slept and played, and so on, she realised what a complex arrangement it all was. Jono had seemed completely unfazed and assured her it would all be fine.

The road got busier, and the countryside more built-up as they neared the outskirts of the city. 'You'd better ask The Lady for directions now,' Julia said to Sean. 'We are getting close to the off-ramp.'

'The Lady' was the voice inside the map app. Sean had put in the address of their B&B earlier, and now he turned it on

'In one mile, take the next exit,' The Lady said, in the cool, plummy voice that inspired confidence and calm in Julia. The Lady deftly directed them, but failed to warn them of a double-decker bus stuck across the road, where traffic officers were directing them around a detour, much to The Lady's distress. She similarly failed to mention a closed road, and she certainly knew nothing of the many cyclists who came weaving in and out of the traffic. Julia was sure that the cycling population of London had increased exponentially since she had left – soon it would be like Amsterdam, but without the convenience of cycle lanes. Somewhat late, and somewhat stressed, they arrived at the B&B, which was in walking distance of the hotel where Christopher was hosting his 'little get-together' that evening. Knowing Christopher, and having seen his event planning in action at his Cotswolds wedding to Peter, Julia fully anticipated a stylish affair, not so 'little', with good eats and the champagne flowing.

She wasn't wrong. The space, simply called Eye, was on the fifteenth floor of a building in the City, with dizzying views of some of London's most famous landmarks. The Gherkin glowed outside the window, and Christopher's friends glowed inside. Julia was pleased that she had rather overdressed, and broken out her grandmother's amethyst necklace. She was even wearing heels.

'Quite a trendy crowd,' she remarked to Sean.

'And young,' he said. Of course, most of Christopher's friends were quite a bit younger than her and Sean. And younger than Peter too, for that matter. Julia noted that fifty seemed both terribly young (it had been a decade and then some since her own fiftieth) and, somehow, too old (how could the ever-youthful Christopher be half a hundred years old?).

'They are. You look beautiful and elegant in that frock.'

'Frock?' she laughed.

'Dress then, if you prefer. Either way, you look lovely.'

'Thank you, kind sir. You look quite dashing yourself. In fact, I'd say we've scrubbed up okay for a couple of sixty-something villagers, up from the country.'

'More than okay. Just wait till they see us dance!'

They both laughed heartily at that, because Sean – a man of many talents – was a truly terrible dancer.

'Julia, darling! And Sean!' Christopher cried, bustling towards them. 'Thank you for coming all this way. What will you have? They do a mean cocktail. I'm drinking a Paloma – heaven knows what's in it, but it's delicious.'

Julia and Sean helped themselves to champagne flutes from a tray by the door. They were old enough and wise enough to know to avoid cocktails of mysterious ingredients. At least with wine and bubbles, you knew what you were getting.

A name tag at each place distributed guests across two long tables. Julia had Sean on her one side and on the other, a slim older man with a shock of white hair and a narrow, angular face with trendy facial hair. He wore a black polo neck and round, black-rimmed glasses. He looked vaguely familiar, and she wondered if he was Someone Famous. Christopher swooped down to introduce them. 'Julia, this is David, my second cousin. Second cousin, but first favourite family member...' he dropped his voice dramatically and put a finger to his lips. 'Sssshh-hh... Don't tell the others. David, Julia is Peter's first spouse, and a dear friend. I think the two of you will get on swimmingly. You're both wonderful, and you have so much in common.'

Christopher swanned off to continue his hosting duties, and David turned to Julia with a grin. A golden hoop glimmered in his ear. 'Pleased to meet you, Julia. With a glowing introduction from Christopher.'

'Likewise. I wonder what it is that we have in common.'

'Do you like to cycle? I am a keen cyclist.'

'I'm more of a walker. I have a chocolate Labrador who insists upon it, daily. Or twice a day, for preference. Do you like dogs?'

'I'm more of a cat man. Do you have cats?'

'One, who I adopted by mistake in a moment of weakness. He has an imperious nature and a peculiar moustache.'

'I have three cats. And a peculiar moustache.' He stroked it, with an exaggerated motion like a pantomime villain.

Julia liked a man who could laugh at himself. She laughed along with him. She saw Sean glance away from his conversation with a woman on his other side at the sound of her laughter. He gave her a smile.

Christopher, who was bustling past with a new arrival, nodded approvingly and mouthed, 'You see?' in their direction.

'What could it be...?' David mused, drumming his fingers theatrically on the table. 'Are you in the music business?'

'Social worker, retired.'

'A noble calling. I don't suppose you live in Marylebone? We might be neighbours?'

'No, far from it, a little village called Berrywick.'

'Berrywick, that name rings a bell...'

'It's a lovely village in the Cotswolds. Have you been there?'

'No, but I recognise the name.' His frowning face broke into a sudden smile: 'Oh, I remember! I knew a band from there. Years ago. I was going to produce a record with them. Their name was the Red Berries, because they came from Berrywick. That takes me back!'

Julia could not believe her ears! What on earth were the chances of coming across one of the handful of people who knew about the Red Berries?

'You're not going to believe it,' she said, unable to hide her excitement. 'But I heard about the Red Berries just yesterday. I even saw a picture of them.'

'Seriously? Heavens, it must be forty years since... How did you come across them?'

'I was visiting a friend, my next-door neighbour, in fact. She had a photo album of her husband's, he...' Julia dug in her bag and pulled out her phone. 'Hang on a minute, I'll show you...'

The photograph Julia had taken at Hester's house was the most recent on her camera roll. She pushed the phone across the table to David.

'I can't believe it. That's them. And hang on, that's me!' he said, pointing to a lanky fellow in the back right of the photo dressed in black, with black-rimmed glasses, sporting a preposterous moustache. An enduring look, it seemed. He held the phone close to his face, pinched at the screen to enlarge the photo, and looked at it in disbelief. 'That's me. Goodness, what a long time ago this was. This is bizarre! So it turns out Christopher was right about us having something in common, although he wouldn't have known about this crazy coincidence.'

'It's completely mad! What are the chances? So, David, speaking of the band, there's something...'

Julia was interrupted by the *tink tink tink* of a fork on a wine glass. Peter stood between the two tables, beaming over the assembled gathering, and then turning his warm gaze to Christopher. Peter was a practised speaker, and he spoke amusingly and lovingly about the birthday boy, but Julia struggled to keep her attention on his enumeration of Christopher's many fine qualities. She was impatient to interrogate David about the Red Berries. To her shame, she was similarly distracted during Christopher's reply to Peter, but stood with the others and toasted his good health with her full heart, before turning her attention back to David. She had been about to tell him the sad news of the two men's recent deaths, but she stopped herself. Something told her that she would get more honest information if he didn't know. Although, now that she thought about it, it was odd that it was thought unseemly to speak ill of the dead, who were beyond caring what was said about them, but quite acceptable to talk badly about people who were actually living and breathing and capable of being hurt.

'David, do you remember when this picture was taken?'

'Actually, I do. I had heard the band at some club somewhere. I was always out and about in those days, scouting, looking for the next big thing. They were rough, musically inexperienced. Kids, really, but they had something. I brought them to London. I wanted to hear them in studio, and I'd got a record label lined up to hear them. This picture was taken the day they came up to London. We'd done good work in studio, the record label was keen and we were celebrating.'

'Do you remember Matthew, my next-door neighbour? He was one of the guitar players. Bass guitar.'

David shook his head. 'Only vaguely. It was a long time ago, and there were so many bands. Everyone with ten fingers was a guitar player. And some guys with nine or eight fingers.'

'And a guy called Lewis? This one.' She pointed at the man at the drums.

He shook his head, frowning, trying to make it all come back. 'I'm not great with names at the best of times. I remember the girl, though. The singer.' He tapped at the screen, looking at the girl on Matthew's lap. 'Wow, she was really something. The real deal. I wonder what happened to her. What was her name, now? Peggy... Milly... Sally, maybe?'

A waiter came by and put a small plate in front of each of them

'Egg?' Julia said.

'It's cheese, I think. Looks like burrata,' David said, poking at the food in front of him with his knife.

'I mean the girl's name. The word "Egg" was written underneath the picture. Maybe it's someone's nickname?'

'Egg! That was it! Can't blame me for not remembering that one! It was all the rage for musicians to have ridiculous one-word names – all thought that they were going to be Sting or Prince.' David picked up a piece of sourdough toast, spread the gooey cheese on it, and chewed, contemplatively. When he'd swallowed the rather large mouthful, he said, 'It was the girl who scuppered the whole record deal. The morning after this picture was taken, they were supposed to be in the studio again. The guys from the label had heard the tape I'd made, and they were there to work with them, with a view to signing them. Their song was set to be a Christmas hit. They were good to go, pens at the ready. The band arrived, hungover to the teeth and looking ropey as hell. As for the singer, she just didn't pitch at all. Without the girl, the band was just... average. The song was actually quite awful, but when she sang it, it somehow changed. And her being absent, it made them look unreliable. The record company pulled out.'

'How sad for them all. A golden opportunity, thrown away.' Julia decided not to mention that she had recently heard the song, and agreed that it was, indeed, terrible.

'It happens all the time. A lot of people have talent, but they don't have the temperament to make it work. Sometimes it's drugs, or booze. Sometimes it's burnout. Or the fame goes to their heads and it all falls apart. I've seen it a hundred times.'

'I can imagine. It's strange though, to think how different their lives might have turned out. Instead of being a taxi driver and a beekeeper, Lewis and Matthew might have been rock stars.'

'You know what, Julia? Chances are things worked out better for them, all in all.'

'That might well be true. I don't know how lives as rock stars would have panned out for them, but they both lived ordinary lives, quite happily as far as I can tell. Until recently, that is.'

'Lived? Recently?'

'Well... Sadly, in the last few weeks, they've died.'

'What, both of them? What happened?' David looked incredulous, like he thought he must have misunderstood.

Julia wasn't quite sure how to describe it. David waited.

'Hit-and-run. Run down in our little village of Berrywick.'

'How awful. Were they crossing the road together?'

Julia thought carefully about how much she should say. 'No. In fact they died separately, within a couple of weeks of each other.'

'Good God. That really is a weird coincidence, isn't it? Hard to believe, really.'

'Yes, yes indeed, David. It is very hard to believe. Very hard indeed.'

'Did they leave families?'

'Yes. That's actually why I'm asking you so much about the band. Their widows are anxious to know as much as they can about that part of their lives. You know how it is.'

To Julia's mind, what she had just said made absolutely no sense, but David seemed to accept it, and said exactly what she had been hoping for.

'Tell you what, let's exchange numbers. If I think of anything more, I'll let you know. And if the widows want to chat, please feel free to pass my number on.'

'Thank you, David, that's very kind of you,' said Julia with a smile.

18

The weather looked kindly on Julia and Sean's London jaunt. The day was bright and crisp and still, and the temperature mild for the time of year. Outside the window of their B&B, the sky was a clear, pale blue, broken by the almost-bare branches of trees and dotted with puffy white clouds.

'So, are you going to tell me where we're going?' Julia asked.

Sean had planned the day, the details of which he had not shared with his companion.

'You'll see soon enough,' he said.

'It's just that I'm trying to decide what to wear. Will we be walking? And will we be mostly inside or out?'

'It's London, my darling. Wear shoes you can walk in and bring something warm and waterproof in case there's rain or snow.'

'Yes, you're right. But can you at least tell me where we're going for lunch?'

'You're finding this difficult, aren't you?' he said with a teasing grin. 'Not knowing where we're going. Relinquishing control.'

'Not at all! I love surprises.'

This was sort of true. She liked the *idea* of surprises, but uncertainty made her mildly anxious.

He nodded. 'Good. Well, I hope you'll love this one.'

'It's just that I don't want to be underdressed. Or overdressed, for that matter.'

This, too, was sort of true, although she only had a small overnight suitcase, so it wasn't as if there was a huge amount of choice, as far as her wardrobe went.

'You look perfect,' he said, taking her hands, and looking into her eyes with a twinkle. He leaned in and kissed her, and said again, 'Perfect.'

She blushed. 'Good.'

'Although they'll probably make you take off those shoes when we do the skydiving,' he said.

She laughed with him, and batted his arm. She knew she was being silly. When he'd first mentioned the surprise day out, she'd been delighted at this thoughtfulness. It would be an adventure, and wouldn't it be nice not to have to make all the decisions and arrangements herself

She was determined to let go and allow the day to unfold. She leaned in for a hug. 'I'm really excited about the surprise day out. It's a lovely idea, and you are a dear to organise it. And you're right, I have found it a bit difficult. I realise that my inner control freak is freaking out just a little bit. I'm used to deciding where I'm going and what I'm doing. But I'm over that now; I'm in your hands. Let's go!'

Although she'd lived in London for years, Julia had never lost her delight in the city's iconic sights. They walked alongside the Thames, taking in the boats, the big wheel of the London Eye, the Waterloo Bridge, Cleopatra's Needle. They admired the Houses of Parliament with the huge Christmas tree in New Palace Yard, which Julia had always wanted to see in person, but had never quite managed to get to.

'I always feel like I'm in a movie when I walk this route,' she said, as they walked past Big Ben

'Yes. Gosh, I wonder how many times I've seen this view in movies.'

'Dozens. I think this is the point where Hugh Grant arrives with a bunch of roses.'

'I don't see him,' Sean said, peering into the flow of pedestrians coming towards them. 'You'll have to make do with present company.'

'I have no complaints about present company. No complaints at all.'

'This way,' said Sean, turning away from the river. Not being a Londoner, he had the map open on his phone. Julia, an old hand at the London streets, could probably have got them wherever they were going without access to technology, but she had now willingly given herself up to trotting along beside him while he played guide.

They stopped outside the National Portrait Gallery.

'Our first destination,' said Sean.

'Sean! This is one of my favourite places in the whole of London!' she exclaimed.

'You mentioned it once. I remembered.'

'Oh, clever you. Clever, thoughtful, you.'

They joined the flow of real people looking at the pictures of people. There was Shakespeare, there was Henry VIII, brushing shoulders with Joan Armatrading, with Adele. Julia imagined them all coming to life, and wondered what they'd all think of each other.

They took a selfie next to the portrait of Queen Elizabeth II in a yellow dress, holding a corgi. In the selfie, Julia looked happy, a manic smile on her face, and Sean, who was taking the photograph, looked worried. Selfies would do that to you. The Queen, however, looked calm and lovely.

Sean sent the picture to the children, his and hers, on a

combined family group that Julia had made a few months ago. It had seemed like some sort of significant milestone, the joint family group, but she had tried not to overthink it. And the group was quite useful for occasions like this.

Sean looked at his watch. 'Have you seen enough? I've booked a table for lunch.'

'You have? And might I ask...?'

'You might ask, but I won't tell you. Wait and see...'

An hour later they were seated at a restaurant in Chinatown, with a beer each, making their way through stacks of bamboo baskets of steamed buns filled with spicy pork, chilli crab and soft prawn. The smell of ginger, garlic and sesame filled the air. Life in the country had plenty to recommend it, but authentic dim sum restaurants were not generally listed amongst its charms. Julia had remarked, once or twice, on this minor failing of her adopted home, and her deep adoration of dumplings. Sean had clearly been listening.

'So, so good,' said Julia, for about the eighth time, leaning back in her chair with an air of deep satisfaction.

'Best in London, according to my research.'

'You are amazing! Thank you, Sean. It's been the perfect day.'

'Would you like something more? A last order of potstickers? Or a dessert, perhaps.'

'I don't think I'd be able to fit in a peppermint.'

'I'll get the bill.'

'Can I contribute?'

'No. This day is my treat.'

'It's been the most wonderful day. Just perfect.'

'I'm glad you're happy, Julia.' He took her hand and looked suddenly serious. 'I want you to know how much I appreciate you. And love you.'

'Oh Sean, I do know. Even before the dim sum extravaganza. And I love and appreciate you too.'

A waiter interrupted the moment, with offers of still more dumplings. They declined. Sean asked for the bill.

Back at the B&B, they took to the sofas, feet up, recovering from the miles of city walking, the visual stimulation, and the dumpling overload. Their phones pinged occasionally in almost-unison, as the various children in various time zones – Jess in Hong Kong, Mark in Vietnam and of course, Jono in Berrywick – responded to the photo on the family group. Unsurprisingly, the responses were brief and emoji-heavy – *Cool shot* and a string of hearts.

Julia's phone rang. She contemplated not answering – an unknown number which would probably turn out to be an annoying sales call. But these people always persist, thought Julia, so one might as well get this out of the way. And there was always the nagging feeling that she might be missing something important.

'Julia, it's David,' came the voice when she answered. 'We met last night. Christopher's cousin.'

'Oh, yes, of course, David. Lovely to hear from you.' Julia couldn't think what the man could be phoning her about, as pleasant as he had been.

'You really jogged my memory about those times with that band. I even dreamed about that studio last night. Dreamed I was back there, mixing an LP with David Bowie and a dog, one of those big sled dogs, a husky, and Bowie said... Never mind... Anyway, I remembered something. One of the band members got in touch with me a few times in subsequent years.'

'Was it Lewis or Matthew?'

'No. I found his name in an old diary – I kept a stack of them from back when they were paper – his name was Ken. And he came calling some years after the band split up.'

'What did Ken want?'

'What everyone wants in this business. Fame and fortune. He was upset about how things had gone down. Upset that they didn't get the recording contract. I actually met up with him once. He phoned and said he had something to pitch, a solo thing. He'd moved to Scotland, where his family was from, but he came down all the way to London to see me. When he got to the office, he had nothing to pitch. He just kept trying to convince me to get the band back together and give them another chance. Or to give him a shot at a solo career – absolutely no chance of that, I assure you. He couldn't let go of the thing, his one shot at the big time that had been ruined.'

'Poor guy. It must have been hard to get so close and then fail.'

'Well, he didn't make things better by pitching up at my office smelling of booze and shouting. He said some particularly rough things about the singer. Although frankly, the way he behaved, I felt I'd dodged a bullet. Imagine managing that lot.'

'Did you ever see him again?'

'No, he phoned me a few times, wanting to come down from Edinburgh, or send demos. And getting pissed off when I refused. After a couple of not very lucid and borderline threatening conversations, I told my secretary not to put his calls through any more. But I'm not sure if this is the sort of information their widows want?'

'Maybe not. I don't suppose you've also remembered the names of the other band members – the fourth guy and Egg's real name? I think that the widows would like to look them up.'

'I don't remember much about the other guy except that he was quite posh, and self-assured. Not like Ken at all. And he had a name, like… I'm thinking Tom, something like that? And the girl, I'm sorry, I only ever knew her as Egg.'

'Ah well, thank you, David. I really appreciate you phoning. And if anything else comes to mind…'

'I'll be sure to let you know. What a strange and sad loss.'

19

Whoever said 'home is where the heart is' must have had a Labrador. Julia's return to her house after a two-day absence (days in which Jake had been showered in pats and snacks and walks and love and Leo's company) was greeted with yelps and yowls of delight. It was lovely to be enthusiastically welcomed, although it could be perilous, too. She held on to the door frame for balance while Jake jumped up and down, and then watched as he set off in a manic zoom around the garden. She felt well and truly loved.

'As you can see, we kept him locked in the shed without food or water,' Jono said, solemnly.

'We didn't give him a walk or a pat the whole three months you were away,' said Laine.

'I'm sure he had a wonderful weekend with you two,' Julia said, patting the chocolate blur as it whizzed by. 'Yes, I'm happy to see you, too. Good boy. Settle down now, Jakey.'

'Bit rude, actually, if you ask me,' Jono said, sadly. 'I was his best friend until ten minutes ago. Hey Jake? Even after the late-night sausage snacks? The cuddles in bed... Oops, sorry Julia.'

Leo greeted Sean with a happy whine and a frantic wagging

of his tail, but didn't feel the need to knock over bits of furniture or bruise shins. Sean patted him and played with his silky ears, and opened the car door for him to jump in.

'I'm going to go straight off. I need to be getting home,' he said. 'Thank you for a lovely weekend.'

Julia gave him a quick hug and a peck of a kiss. 'And thank *you.*'

Sean turned to the young folks. 'And thanks for looking after all the animals.'

'No problem, it was fun,' said Laine, putting her arm through Jono's. 'Shall we get going too?'

Much as she loved them all, Julia was pleased to see everyone go. 'I've become such a homebody,' she said to Jake. 'I'm all peopled out. I am so looking forward to a quiet afternoon all to myself. And with you, of course. You and the other animals, but no humans. No talking.'

Having tossed some dirty clothes into the washing machine, she went out into the garden to let the chickens out for a scratch, and to see how the plants were doing. There was always something new to see, even after a couple of days, and even in winter. That was one of the lovely things about gardens. Chaplin followed her, trying to look as if he happened to be going for a walk which happened to be in the same direction as hers. 'Funny boy, come here, *ksksks...*' Julia sat on the low stone bench in the kitchen garden, watching the chickens peck about. The cat jumped up next to her, sitting close enough that she could feel the rumble in his ribs against her thigh. Much as she resisted it, her mind couldn't help but turn towards London. More specifically, to what David had said about Ken, the bitter, out-of-control band member.

Two people were dead, both killed in the same way. And both had been members of a band in their youth – the local band that had almost made it big time. And one of the surviving members was bitter. He would have been on the list of suspects, if the deaths had occurred forty years ago. Maybe even more recently, if he didn't live hundreds of miles away. But she was being silly – the fact of the matter was that the band had dissolved forty years ago, and angry Ken lived in Scotland, not down the road in Edgeley or the likes.

She closed her eyes, listening to the chickens' contented clucking and the cat's purring, and enjoying the peace.

'Oh, you're home!'

Julia opened her eyes to see Hester peering over the wall that separated the two gardens.

'Thank goodness. I want to talk to you about something. Can I come over?' asked Hester.

'Yes, of course, please do.' Julia sighed quietly to herself. She didn't feel like having a visitor, not at all. But Hester was a neighbour, and a new widow, and of course she could come over if she felt like some company. Hester's head disappeared from the wall, and reappeared – along with the rest of her – coming down the garden path towards Julia's house.

Julia shifted up, and patted the bench beside her. Hester sat down with a groan. 'How are you, Hester?' Julia asked, with genuine concern. Hester looked tired and pale, and about ten years older than the enthusiastic honey seller Julia remembered from the Christmas market just a few weeks earlier.

'Oh well, you know... Putting one foot in front of the other. I decided to make a start on some paperwork, try to get to grips with the dreaded admin. I thought it would make me feel better. I've been going through Matthew's papers.'

'Ah, well, that sounds like a good step forward. It can be hard, though, I'm sure. A lot to think about, and decisions to be made. And it's all so personal, somehow. Seeing his handwriting, all the everyday things...' Julia sighed, remembering how hard it had been when her much beloved mother had died.

'Yes, there's that. But, there's something more... Something... strange.'

Hester stopped. Just when Julia thought she'd changed her mind about speaking about whatever was bothering her, Hester continued: 'I don't know who to speak to about this. I don't want to make a drama, and lord knows I've got enough to worry about, but there's something... Can we keep this between us?'

'Of course.' Hester looked worried, and Julia tried to use her most reassuring social worker voice.

'There's less money than I thought. Our retirement money... It wasn't a fortune, but we'd saved up a bit here and there since we were young, and we didn't touch the interest, so it added up over time. But half the money is gone.'

'Gone? Did you check the transactions?'

'Yes, it turns out Matthew took it out about two months ago. I don't look at the account very often. We just leave it there, pop in what we can. The notifications go to Matthew's phone, so I didn't notice. But it's gone.' Hester looked like she might cry.

'And he didn't say anything?' asked Julia,

'No.'

'Who did he transfer it to?'

'The bank account is just letters. AAI. I have racked my brains as to who that might be, but I can't think of anyone. A name, a company.'

Hester shrugged. 'I have no idea.'

'Did the two of you talk about money?'

'We talked about everything! Well, I thought we did. If you'd asked me yesterday, I'd have said there were no secrets between us, but now... I'm driving myself mad thinking about what could be going on. Was he being blackmailed? Or was there another woman? Or an illegitimate child who just turned up out of the blue? It's just not like Matthew, not Matthew at all.' She paused and sighed. 'But I suppose everyone says that, don't they? When the terrible truth finally comes out.'

'Now, let's not jump to conclusions. It might have been an investment, or something to do with the business. Let's think about this logically and see what we can find out.'

'That's why I came to you, Julia. I know you're good at this sort of thing. Should we go to the bank?'

'We might have to do that, Hester. But we can likely find out for ourselves. Go and get his phone and laptop. Let's do some digging.'

Julia had thought that a simple search of 'AAI' on Matthew's email and phone might find her the solution, but this was not to be. On Matthew's phone, a search of AAI brought up his Dutch friend Willem Kraaij, who rather enjoyed sending Matthew articles about bees, but also wasps and mosquitos and spiders. Hester did not think that Willem was the answer to the riddle. Julia then looked at all the 'A' contacts on Matthew's phone and emails, but who could tell? Was AAI Anne Jones, or Anton Delaware, or perhaps George Adams? The list was endless – it could be anyone.

It was only when Julia widened the search to related keywords – 'money', 'invest', 'payment' and so on – that she had success. On the laptop, the search turned up an email trail with someone by the name of Anthony Ardmore, of the company Ardmore Accelerated Investments.

'AAI,' said Julia, triumphantly. 'Got ya!'

Julia opened the first email, with the subject line: *Investment opportunity*. 'Here we go,' she said, turning the laptop towards Hester. They had moved inside, as the afternoon temperature had plummeted, and they were now at the kitchen table. 'Do you recognise the name Anthony Ardmore?'

'No, I've never heard of him,' Hester said weakly.

'Well, let's see what he's got to say, shall we?'

The two women read on. The emails were enough to give

Julia a headache. It all sounded rather complicated. Anthony Ardmore – why did that name ring a bell? – was offering Matthew some kind of investment opportunity that was somehow related to the farming of medicinal plants. From what Julia could make out, Ardmore Accelerated Investments would invest in a number of different farming opportunities for medicinal plants such as turmeric, garlic and African potato. *What differentiates us from our competitors*, read an early email, *is that we have the inside track on cutting-edge drug development in the US. A number of innovative and revolutionary dread disease drugs have recently been passed by the FDA, with our targeted ingredients as the primary active ingredients. Big Pharm is keeping this silent – but now you are in on the opportunity!*

Julia read the emails with a sinking heart. In her life as a social worker, she had seen too many elderly people taken in by get-rich-quick schemes – some clearly daylight robbery, like the old lady who had been sending her Facebook friend, Harrison Ford, a thousand pounds a month to help him rescue squirrels. Others were murkier, ideas that on the surface sounded slightly credible, but when you unpacked them, came to nothing. She would never forget the desperate grandmother who had invested her small inheritance in a natural toothpaste. She hoped that Matthew had not been taken in by something like that, but she didn't know enough about developments in the world of medicine to say for sure.

'He really pushed the deal, didn't he?' said Hester, reading one of the emails from Anthony Ardmore over Julia's shoulder. 'You can see why my Matthew might have been taken in by it.'

Julia felt a deep sadness for the woman beside her, who loved her husband so much she was justifying his foolish choices even after his death. But it was true that Anthony Ardmore was a hard-sell kind of guy. Matthew was fortunate to be 'getting in on the ground floor', which would result in 'first-move advantage' and 'maximum returns on investment'. This was something Matthew seemed very excited about. He had thanked Ardmore profusely for the great opportunity, and assured him that the money would be transferred before the end of the day.

A lamb to the slaughter, was the phrase that came to mind.

'Have you finished reading this?' Julia asked Hester, grimly.

Hester nodded. She looked shaken.

Julia was about the close the document outlining the convoluted workings of the investment proposition when she noticed another name. Someone else had been cc'd in on one of the emails. Her heart skipped a beat when she saw who it was.

Lewis Band.

'Hester, you are going to have to take this to the police,' Julia said firmly.

'The police? Whyever...'

'Look here.' Julia pointed at the address field.

'Lewis Band?' said Hester, with a frown. 'Isn't that a strange coincidence? The police said that they think there could be a connection between their deaths, and now we find he was involved in the same investment. I wonder how that happened?'

'Hester, it's too much of a coincidence. Don't you think there might be a connection between the investment and the deaths?'

'How could this money thing be connected to the accidents?' Hester asked, as if this was an absurd notion. She was still using that term, 'accident', as if her husband had tripped on a kerb or dropped a vase on his foot.

'I don't know. That's why we need to speak to Hayley. This whole situation is... unusual.'

'No,' said Hester, shaking her head. 'I'm not going to the police. I don't want all sorts of people knowing our business. Poking around in our private affairs. Matthew wouldn't like it, that's for sure. I'm going to find this Anthony Ardmore fellow – in fact, his address is right here on the email. I'll pop in tomorrow.' She paused and then nodded to herself, approving her own plan. 'I'll tell him what happened to Matthew, find out what it was he invested in, and explain that I need the money back. I'm sure he'll understand. Who knows? The money might even have increased already in the time it's been there.'

Hester smiled in happy anticipation of this positive outcome. Julia was no financial genius, but it was clear to her that Hester and Matthew were absolute babes in the wood. Lewis, too, presumably. Julia did not have a good feeling about this. Not good at all. She suspected that Mr Ardmore had seen them coming. Or lured them in.

She gave it one more try: 'Hester, you asked me to help, so please listen to me. I really think this is something for the authorities.'

Hester seemed determined to ignore Julia's advice. 'Thank you, Julia. I really appreciate you helping me find out what happened to the money. It's such a relief. I'm sure Mr Ardmore will do the right thing. I will go over there tomorrow.'

Julia gave a resigned sort of sigh. She knew herself. She knew there was only one way this was going to go. 'All right, then... If you insist on visiting Mr Ardmore, then I'm coming with you.'

20

The day was full of surprises. The first surprise was the unexpected presence of Coral Band, coming down the garden path alongside Hester Shepherd to where Julia sat in her car. Coral always dressed with a certain old-fashioned formality, but today she was in full battle dress, which was to say a pink skirt suit that fitted like upholstery on an armchair, court shoes, a string of maybe-pearls, a full face of make-up and her blonde hair poofed up to its full height and width. Hester was in her usual attire – a variety of shapeless flowing items, in patterns that looked as if they'd been hand-printed by nursery school children, layered for warmth, accessorised with what looked like homemade beads and baubles. An odd couple indeed.

Hester got briskly into the passenger seat of Julia's car, while Coral manoeuvred herself more slowly into the back, taking care not to mess her hair, break a heel or split the skirt that seemed to have been bought when Coral was a size or two smaller.

'Coral knew *nothing*, poor thing!' Hester whispered quickly to Julia, as if Hester herself had been in the know all along. 'I told her what we'd found out about the investment, and invited her to come with us to Anthony Ardmore. The more the better, I thought.'

Julia wasn't convinced of the logic – more could often be more chaotic and less manageable, in her experience – but time would tell, in this case.

'Right you are then, all ready,' Coral said, pulling her seat belt firmly across her body and fastening it with a satisfying click. 'Let's go and see what Mr Ardmore has to say for himself, shall we?'

Julia had found Mr Ardmore's phone number on the emails in Matthew's inbox. She'd phoned his office early that morning and found that there was no answer. She had tried several times since, but the phone just rang and rang. Despite this, the women had decided that they would just arrive at the office, and insist on a meeting with Mr Ardmore.

Julia asked Coral now, 'So you don't know anything about Anthony Ardmore, either? Lewis never talked to you about him?'

'Not that I can recall. Lewis knows – knew – a lot of people, on account of his job. He liked to tell me about this passenger or the other, but I didn't always concentrate. I mean, not on the details. Like the names, or... He might have mentioned the man. Mr Ardmore might have been a client of Lewis's, I suppose. And he did get all sorts of information and tips from his passengers. Horse-racing tips, weather predictions, where to buy this or that.'

'Yes, they could have met that way,' Julia agreed 'Did he ever mention plants or medicines to you?'

'No. I've read about the amazing things that people can achieve with herbal remedies, of course, on Facebook. And I suppose that I can see that if one knew about a new drug developed from a plant, that could be a great opportunity. But I'm worried. It sounds like insider trading to me.'

Julia was glad that she was not the one to raise this, because she had indeed had the same thought, although she had to admit that she wasn't entirely sure that she understood exactly what it was that insider trading involved. She had googled the subject quite extensively, and found herself going down a rabbit hole about Martha Stewart, who seemed to have got caught up in something that worryingly involved the FDA and medicinal issues.

When their explanations of what insider training actually involved smashed against the rocks of improbability, flailed in the shallows of ignorance, then petered out entirely on the shores of resignation, Hester sighed and said, 'We'll just ask Mr Ardmore to explain why this is all legal.'

They pulled up at the address on the emails, and Julia's heart sank. Instead of an office development or a shop or even a house, the address was home to what looked like a deserted warehouse. One of the windows was boarded up, and there was no sign of life.

'I suppose they need somewhere to store the plants,' said Hester, looking at it.

'Or maybe they even make the medicines on the premises,' said Coral, hopefully.

'Maybe,' said Julia.

The three women climbed out of the car, and knocked on the large doors of the warehouse. Nothing happened. Tentatively, Julia tried the handle of the door, and to her surprise, it opened. The creak of the hinges as she pushed it open echoed around the space, and behind her she could feel Coral and Hester move towards each other.

Julia looked around. The space was, for the most part, empty. The weak winter sun fought its way through the dusty windows, which were set high in the wall. The result was a watery light.

'There are no plants here,' said Hester.

'Nor is there anyone to talk to,' said Coral.

'No. But there is that.' Julia pointed to a small desk in the corner of the room, to the right of the door. She looked at the wall next to her, and found, as she had hoped, a light switch. It had to be said that the difference between the light being on and the light being off was barely discernible. Julia had to wonder why anybody had ever bothered with the light at all. 'If you're going to do something, do it properly,' she muttered under her breath, rather uselessly, as the installer of the light-bulb was most likely long gone, and certainly not in the warehouse at this point.

The small desk was covered in papers, and Julia walked over to have a closer look.

'This is the right place,' she said, pointing to a pile of brochures with the words *Ardmore Accelerated Investments – grow your future* emblazoned across the front. Next to the brochures was a messy pile of post, many of the envelopes, when Julia sifted through, labelled *FINAL DEMAND* in official-looking red ink. 'This doesn't look good,' said Julia.

'Maybe they're just really bad at admin,' said Coral. 'Some people are, you know.'

'Not the sort of people that you want to be investing money with, though,' said Hester, who sounded like she might cry.

Julia was still sorting through the pile of post. 'There must be something here,' she said. 'Some clue as to where we can find the elusive Mr Ardmore.' A moment later, her optimism was rewarded. 'Got it!' She waved an envelope at the other two. 'This is addressed to Anthony Ardmore, not the company. And it's got another address: Ambleside Way. I bet this is his home!'

'Well, what are we waiting for?' said Coral.

'Let's go,' said Hester.

Julia glanced around the empty warehouse. She didn't like the feel of it at all. She would have much preferred to call Hayley, and hand this whole sorry matter over to the police. But she looked at the bright, expectant faces of the two widows, and sighed.

'Let's do it, then,' she said.

Number 4, Ambleside Way was a picturesque cottage. A large Christmas wreath surrounded the knocker on the front door, and there were two small pine trees on either side of the doorstep, decorated in cones. It could not have been more different to the warehouse if it actively tried.

Julia picked up the handle of the ornate knocker, and gave a sharp few raps. Nothing happened.

She waited a few moments, and then tried again.

'There's nobody here,' said Hester.

'They're hiding from us,' said Coral. 'I'm going to find them.'

Before Julia could stop her, Coral had set off, her walk determined, to peer into every window, her hands cupped around her eyes.

'I suppose the back door might be open,' said Julia.

'Of course it will be,' said Hester. 'Why would a person lock their back door? This is the Cotswolds, not...' Hester paused for a moment, obviously trying to think of the most dangerous place she could – somewhere where the inhabitants would lock and bolt themselves into their homes. Julia waited with curiosity, wondering which of the world's trouble spots Hester would choose. 'Not Bath!' Hester said, eventually, making both Julia and Coral laugh.

The back door was, however, not only locked, but padlocked.

'This is very suspicious,' said Hester, rattling the lock.

'Maybe they keep the medicines in the house,' said Coral, once again peering through the window.

'It's like they've disappeared without a trace,' said Julia. 'The warehouse and now this.'

'Only criminals padlock the back door,' said Hester. 'Why would a good citizen need to do that?'

The answer came from behind them, making all three women jump and clutch their chests.

'It's the beavers,' said the voice. A deep, male voice.

Julia, Hester and Coral turned around as if they were one person.

'The beavers?' echoed Julia.

'We have a pair of very inquisitive beavers living near the stream,' said the man, who was holding a fishing rod. 'They were reintroduced to the area about twenty years ago, and last year a pair moved onto our property. They come up to the house and push the door open. For a while, we could just close it, but then the ridiculous creatures worked out how the handle works. They would open the door, if you can credit it, and poop all over the kitchen.' The man smiled. 'But I'm guessing that you didn't come here to talk about beaver poop, ladies, did you?'

Julia stepped forward. 'I'm Julia Bird, and these are my friends, Coral Band and Hester Shepherd. We're looking for Anthony Ardmore.'

'Well,' said the man. 'I'm Anthony – you've found me. Why don't you come in, and we can talk about why it is that you're peering into my home and discussing how I might be a criminal.'

'Thank you,' said Julia, trying her very best not to blush. 'We have a few questions we'd like to ask you.'

Anthony Ardmore was, it had to be said, a fine-looking man, slim and broad-shouldered, with a smooth, open face, lightly tanned, as if by rays caught on a tennis court or perhaps a ski slope. He looked familiar. Julia had an odd feeling that she'd met him before, but couldn't place where or when.

He led them into the house, and the four of them sat down at his kitchen table. 'Now, did I hear correctly that one of you is Mrs Shepherd and one Mrs Band?' he asked, holding out his hand.

'I'm Mrs Shepherd,' Hester said, taking his proffered hand. 'Hester Shepherd.'

'You are most welcome in my home, and might I offer you my deepest condolences. I had the utmost affection and respect for Matthew. He was a fine, fine, man.'

'Thank you. He really was. And I'm sure if he came to you, he must have trusted you. He had such good instincts about people.' Hester appeared to have forgotten all her worries about Anthony Ardmore. Julia was always amazed how this could happen when a person was good-looking.

'How right you are, my dear.' Julia felt a prickle of irritation at Anthony's 'my dear', but didn't let it show. 'Matthew had excellent instincts, about people and about investments.' He turned to Coral. 'And you must be Mrs Band?'

'I'm Coral, and this is our friend Julia Bird.'

'So you must be Lewis's...?'

'I am Lewis's wife. Well, Lewis's widow. I'm sure you've heard...'

'Again, I am most sorry to hear about the accident. A terrible thing, and what a fine man.'

'Thank you,' Coral cut his condolences short. 'The thing is, we're here about the money our husbands invested with you. The medicinal plant farming. We'd like you to explain the investment, please.'

Julia found herself very much admiring Coral's no-nonsense approach. The woman might look like the main character from a soap opera, but she was behaving like a Wall Street businesswoman, undistracted by Anthony's good looks.

'Gladly, gladly.' Ardmore had that combination of suave confidence and excellent tailoring that came with a lifetime of money. It was clear that he simply told people what to do, and

they tended to do it. 'Fortunately for you, your husbands identified an exceptional opportunity.' He rested his elbows on the
table and made a pyramid of his hands. 'I'll explain everything,
and I'll put it as simply as I can...'

Coral narrowed her perfectly outlined eyes. 'Please do,
although I'm a trained bookkeeper, Mr Ardmore, and I worked
at a bank for years, so I should be able to keep up.'

Julia felt a flush of pride. It was clear that one underestimated Coral at one's peril. Anthony Ardmore was slick, and
could lay on the charm, but Julia hadn't forgotten that he was
one of the few links between the two dead men, and had only
recently got his hands on a good chunk of both of their life
savings. Nor could she get the empty warehouse and the final
demands out of her head. She didn't trust him one bit.

'Excellent news!' said Anthony, with rather too much
bonhomie. 'Well, I can see you're a sharp one, and I'm sure
you'll understand right away just what an excellent investment
you have on your hands. Before I start – Mrs Bird, is it?'

'Yes. Julia Bird. I feel like we might have met. Or perhaps
I've seen you somewhere, recently. Now, where could it have
been?'

His face fell. 'I can't say I remember, I'm afraid. That's
village life, though, isn't it? We've likely seen each other around
the place. In the high street. At the shops.'

'It was in the last few weeks, I think.' Julia made a show of
scratching her head and frowning. 'I know. I've been to a few of
the Christmas activities around the area. I do love a bit of
Christmas spirit, don't you? Could it have been at the switching
on of the Christmas lights? Or one of the Christmas markets?
Were you at any of those occasions?'

One of those occasions where the men had mysteriously
died, in other words, thought Julia.

'Sadly, I haven't been able to attend any of them this year,'
Anthony said. 'Too busy with work, I'm afraid. Now, might I

ask about your connection to this, Mrs Bird? Does your husband...?'

'I don't have a husband. I drove the ladies here, and I'm interested to hear all about this investment too.'

Mr Ardmore beamed at her, his white teeth stark against his tanned face. 'Ah, an independent woman with an eye for a good investment. That's what I like to see.' He really was the most patronising man. 'Now, let me explain your investment, ladies. I have no doubt you fine ladies understand that there are a number of medicines constantly being tested and reviewed, and that many rely on the rich world of plants. Now imagine if you knew ahead which plant would be the one that is going to be used in a cure for cancer. Imagine if you had already invested in licensing and growing that plant.'

'That would certainly be lucrative,' said Coral. Anthony Ardmore beamed and nodded. But too soon, as it turned out, because Coral wasn't finished. 'But with all due respect, Mr Ardmore, this seems a little too risky for me in my current situation. It also sounds a little bit like insider trading. With Lewis gone, I'd rather have my money in more traditional investments, like the bank, thank you.'

'Me too,' said Hester, jumping quickly onto Coral's coat-tails. 'I can't take any risks with our money. And I need access to the cash to live on.'

Mr Ardmore's tan seemed to fade a little, and his confident white-toothed smile faltered. But to give credit where credit was due, he recovered in moments. 'Of course, I understand completely. You certainly don't want risk in your current situation – your very sad situation. What you want is to get excellent returns and to grow your capital, which of course is also what your wise husbands wanted for you. Your financial security. Which is why they decided to invest their money with me in the first place.' He held his arms wide, and beamed a dazzling smile, as if he had solved all their problems. Then he switched to a more serious, earnest persona. 'Ladies, I can see you are three very sensible, clever women – of course, Mrs Band, Mrs Shepherd, your husbands had said as much, but to meet you in person is an honour. And I know they would agree with me when I tell you that now is not the time to get out. In fact, now is the time to get further in! If you have a life insurance payout, for instance, you could consider *increasing* your stake. If things go as planned, you could be set up for life! I'm talking about long-term financial security. I am not at liberty to give details, but something very exciting is about to happen with dandelions, and the fund is investing heavily.'

'In dandelions?' Julia couldn't quite keep the incredulity from her voice. Dandelions were weeds! The gardeners of Berrywick were constantly doing battle with dandelions. It did not seem to be something that a person should be investing in.

Anthony turned to Julia. 'You'd be surprised by the returns, too, Mrs Bird. In fact, you should invest. Ordinarily, at this late stage, it would be impossible to take on an additional investor, but I'll have a word with my partners, and I am pretty sure I could persuade them to get you in. What do you think of that?'

'I think that you have an empty warehouse and unpaid bills, that's what I think,' said Julia.

'An empty warehouse?'

'That's where we went. It's the address on all your correspondence. It did not inspire confidence, Mr Ardmore.'

For a moment, Anthony Ardmore looked nonplussed, but then he smiled. 'Ah, a simple misunderstanding! We've cancelled our lease on that property.'

'It looked like you just ran out,' said Hester.

'Not at all!' Anthony laughed. 'We realised that our funders did not need to be paying for such a large space, when the magic in fact happens without the need for space.'

'Except for the dandelions. They need space,' said Julia, earning her a scowl from Anthony Ardmore.

'Ladies, I can assure you, your money is in safe hands.' Anthony spread his hands out, palms up, as if to illustrate the point.

'That's all very well, Mr Ardmore,' said Coral, 'but personally, I need the money in cash. I want out. What is the procedure for liquidating Lewis's stake?'

Anthony Ardmore's face assumed an expression that approximated regret, as imagined by a person who had never, personally, experienced such an emotion. 'The thing is, Mrs Band, the contracts are watertight. The negotiation is based, of course, on current figures, of which your investment forms part, so we can't get the sum back to you right this moment. Plus, the three invested as a joint venture. So there are implications there for release from the contract. Standard practice, in fact. But as soon as we have dotted every i and crossed each t, you can claim your returns, providing all the investors in your group agree, although I strongly suspect you won't want to get out. You'll be too busy buying yourself fancy new shoes and handbags...'

He laughed at his own joke, which fell like a lead balloon. When he saw their stony faces, and realised he was the only one laughing, the sound died in his throat, but his mouth remained stretched in a rather over-enthusiastic smile.

Coral returned his Cheshire Cat grin with a steady look, and spoke calmly but firmly: 'If we could just have a cheque, that might be best.'

Even Mr Ardmore's radiant positivity was starting to wear a little thin. 'In terms of our contract with your late husband, that's not going to be possible. We can certainly look at that once the deal has been finalised.'

Hester sighed. 'When will that be?'

'I'll get an update from my partners, and let you know asap. Just hang in there, ladies, you won't be sorry.'

He saw them out, fussing about, helping them solicitously with jackets and bags, and shepherding them to the door. A silver Land Rover was now parked in the road, having been driven up by Anthony while the three ladies were inspecting the padlock at the back. Anthony took out his car keys and pressed a button. The vehicle's lights flashed in response. It really was very large and sturdy.

'That's a very smart car,' Julia said, running her eyes over it in an admiring manner. She was, in fact, inspecting it surreptitiously for signs of damage. Anthony Ardmore didn't seem like a killer, he seemed more of a chancer, but he was the strongest link she could find between Lewis and Matthew. The car was buffed to a high gloss, with not a mark on it, as far as Julia could see. 'It has a lovely shine – it looks brand new.'

'Ah yes, my new baby,' he said, patting its rump as if it was a favoured horse. 'If things go as planned, ladies, you'll be looking for new wheels yourselves. I'm sure you won't want to miss out, Mrs Bird.'

Julia unlocked her own, much more modest car, with a click of the remote. The three women reached for the door handles. Julia felt that funny tip-of-the-tongue feeling she got when her subconscious was trying to tell her something. What was it?

'Oh, one last thing, just as a matter of interest,' she said, turning back to Mr Ardmore. 'How did you meet Lewis and Matthew?'

'I know them through my brother,' he said. 'They go back a long way. They were in a band together back in the eighties, if you can believe it.'

'Your brother?' Coral frowned.

Julia was frowning too, on the inside at least. This was either an extraordinary coincidence, or something much worse.

'Yes, Dominic Ardmore.'

That was why she recognised him. Julia had come across Dominic Ardmore a year or two before, when she'd been caught up in another murder investigation. He and his brother looked very alike.

'I remember the name. Your brother is Dom, from the band the Red Berries?' Hester said.

He grinned. 'The very one. He was on the keyboard. Not any more, of course. Luckily he gave up that band nonsense, same as your husbands did. Dominic's an engineer now. Very successful. Yes, it was Dominic who introduced me to Lewis and Matthew. The band had a get-together a while back, a lunch. One of the chaps from out of town was here. It seemed like a good time to introduce them to this opportunity. Might as well spread the good fortune amongst friends, right?'

Hester didn't answer the rhetorical question, just shook her head in astonishment. 'Well, goodness me. This is a surprise. Who'd have thought...'

'A small world, isn't it, Mrs Shepherd?'

It was indeed.

Far too small for Julia Bird's liking.

21

The weather, which had been unseasonably – some might say suspiciously – mild, had had a sudden change of heart. In fact, it seemed to be making up for lost time, chucking everything it had at Berrywick. Julia had woken to the pleasant sound of rain pattering on the roof, but it had cleared by the time she'd fed the animals and had her breakfast, leaving a watery light and biting cold in its wake. Julia had been in the Cotswolds long enough not to trust a brief respite, and had decided to drive into the village, in the expectation of more rain or even snow.

Her expectations were more than met – they were exceeded – when the first flakes of the season started to drift down mid-morning. Fortunately, when it began, she and Jake were already holed up in the Buttered Scone waiting for their order – a hot chocolate for her, and a pork sausage for him – and waiting for Hayley Gibson.

'Good lord,' said Julia, as the snow grew from a gentle flutter to a strong downfall. A gust of wind hurled the flakes horizontally at the front window of the tea room. 'It feels like we're in a boat in a storm at sea.'

Jake had never experienced a storm at sea, but he wasn't

enjoying the weather, not at all. He looked nervously at the windows, and then back at Julia, the whites of his eyes showing as his gaze swivelled to and fro.

'It's okay, Jakey,' she said, patting his shoulder. 'Lie down, there's a good boy.'

Flo came over with a huge steaming drink, and the warm sausage, considerably improving Jake's state of mind.

'Ah, that looks good! I don't think I've ordered a hot chocolate in years.'

'Well, it's the weather for it. That or a hot toddy with a good lug of brandy.'

'Eleven is slightly early for that,' Julia laughed. She took a sip of her drink, which was silky smooth and rich with chocolate. The Buttered Scone might just be the local tea room in a little village in the Cotswolds, but Flo prided herself on using the best local ingredients, and doing everything just right. The hot chocolate was made with real chocolate and farm milk, with a raft of whipped cream and a grating of dark chocolate.

The door burst open, and a little group of people came in seeking shelter from the snow, Pippa Baker amongst them. They slammed the door behind them against the weather. There was a small commotion, laughter and exclamations, and the stamping of feet. They removed raincoats and shook out umbrellas, and hung up their dripping outerwear on a coat stand, before dispersing into the warm fug of the Buttered Scone.

Pippa stopped by Julia's table and gave a dramatic shiver. 'I see winter's decided to join us. It's icy out there. So bad that I left the puppies – it's not the weather for dogs.'

'Nice weather for the ducks though.' Julia delivered the cliché with a laugh. 'For humans, I recommend the hot chocolate. Do you want to sit?'

'Just for a mo. I'm meeting my brother – I'm a few minutes early.'

Flo appeared noiselessly at their table, pen and notebook poised. 'What can I get you, Pippa?'

'Oh, thanks Flo, but I'll wait for my brother. We're going to have lunch. I've been dreaming of your delicious lamb chops.'

'Have you now?' Flo smiled. She was susceptible to a bit of flattery. 'Well, they've come in just in time. Delivery from the butcher was late, what with poor Lydia. Isn't that a thing?'

Flo was susceptible to local gossip, too. She wasn't mean, but if there was news to be broken in Berrywick, she did like to be the one to break it.

'I haven't heard...' Pippa and Julia looked at her expectantly.

'Died in her sleep, she did, poor thing.'

'What, last night?' asked Pippa, in astonishment. 'I can't believe it. I was in the butcher's shop just the other day with my aunt Margaret. She can't drive anymore, so I took her out to do her shopping. Lydia was behind the counter serving the customers, fit as a fiddle. Well, apart from her bunions, which have been troubling her no end, as usual.'

'I shouldn't think that was what did it. No one ever died of bunions, as far as I'm aware,' said Flo, frowning. Julia wondered if she was perhaps worrying about her own bunions. She was on her feet all day, after all.

'Indeed, I think not,' Pippa agreed. 'My aunt Margaret has bunions too, so the two of them had a good old chat about them. Aunt Margaret even insisted on going back that afternoon and giving Lydia some of her medication that she said really helped with the pain, and Lydia gave her some bunion plasters that hadn't helped her, but she thought might help Margaret.'

'Ah, well, isn't that nice of them both? Either way, the bunions won't be troubling her now. Gone she is, poor Lydia, but at least she went peacefully in her sleep.'

Julia reflected on Lydia's calm death, compared to the tragic ends of Lewis and Matthew. I hope I go that way, she thought. A nice quick heart attack or stroke in my own bed. The thought wasn't morbid or frightening. In fact, it was rather soothing. Julia had seen enough of life to be pragmatic about death.

'Hello, everyone.' Hayley Gibson had come in unnoticed, and was standing at the table.

Pippa said hello, and then said her goodbyes, claiming a nearby table for herself. Flo handed Hayley a menu as the policewoman made herself comfortable across from Julia.

'What are you in the mood for, Detective? We've got lovely hot tomato and pepper soup; I made it specially when I saw the weather forecast. Comes with a slice of fresh sourdough.'

'I'll have that, thank you, Flo.' Hayley handed back the menu, unopened. She looked pleased to be relieved of the burden of choice.

'Nothing for me,' said Julia. 'That hot chocolate will keep me going until next week.'

'Oh go on... A little drink like that?' said Flo. 'No room for a toastie? I know you love a little toastie.'

Flo's toasties were not little, not by any stretch of the imagination. And her little drink hadn't been little either. Julia waved her away with a smile.

As soon as Flo was out of earshot, Hayley cut to the chase. 'So, what's this information you have for me?'

Julia told her everything she had discovered from the time Hester came round to share her worries about the absent funds. When she got to the part where she and Hester and Coral had gone to call on Anthony Ardmore, Hayley let out an exasperated, 'For heaven's sake, Julia.' For the rest, she let her speak, interrupting once or twice for a point of clarification.

When Julia was finished, Hayley sat silently for a good two minutes, her face impassive, while her brain whirred, processing what she'd heard. She leaned forward and summed it up. 'So two men died in the same way, within roughly two weeks of each other. And it turns out they were members of the same band years ago, and they recently became investors in the same investment scheme.'

'That's it, in a nutshell,' said Julia. 'I think we can safely say the deaths were no accident.'

Hayley waved her hand. 'I was pretty sure of that from the minute Matthew died.'

'As was I.'

'But the way you've described it, it looks like it could be some kind of hit.'

It was the first time Julia had thought of it in quite those terms. 'Hit' was a word that belonged in the movies, usually movies about organised crime, or gang warfare. It gave her the shivers.

'What was your impression of Anthony, Julia?'

'He's smooth. Too smooth for my liking. He got up my nose, the way he talked to us. Patronising. He's good-looking though, and well-groomed, so he probably gets away with it. And he's a sharp talker, the kind of man who's got an answer for everything. My impression is that he's probably leaning towards dodgy, but just how far he's leaning, it's hard to say.'

'You paint a very vivid picture. I know the type. The question is, is this plant medicine thing an out-and-out scam? Or is it genuine, but making use of insider trading? Or might it even be a legitimate business venture, just a rather unusual one?'

With impeccable timing, Flo arrived with a steaming bowl of soup, a massive slab of fresh bread, and a tub of golden farm butter. She had to manoeuvre carefully between the tables, every one of which was now full. It seemed half of Berrywick had decided to take refuge from the weather and enjoy something warm and delicious at the Buttered Scone.

'Enjoy,' said Flo. Her plimsolls squeaked as she turned to leave.

They waited a moment, inhaling the tangy, basil smell of the soup. Hayley scraped a delicate layer of the surface with her spoon, and held it in front of her mouth, waiting for it to cool before sipping it.

Julia spoke. 'It's also possible that it's somewhere in between – a highly speculative investment that he's flogging to people who don't fully understand the risks.'

'Also dubious, but not necessarily illegal,' Hayley said. 'It's a minefield, honestly. I went to a workshop on Fraud and Financial Crime in the Digital Age, or some such, a couple of months ago. Very interesting, and pretty scary. Makes you want to close all your bank accounts and carry around a roll of tenners in your bra. But I do know that there are plenty of very strange-sounding things that are perfectly legit. And some people are making tons of money on them.'

Julia nodded. 'I've come to terms with the fact that it will never be me making tons of money off weird things. I'm more of a savings account sort of investor. And Hester and Coral, too, I imagine. They hoped to get the money back when we visited Ardmore, but he was having none of it.'

'First things first, I'll ask the financial crimes unit to have a look into the investment and see if it's legit.'

'Hester has got the emails with all the details, the contract and so on.'

'Thanks, Julia, I'll get them from her and take things from here.' Hayley pulled a chunk of bread, dipped it into the soup, and popped it into her mouth.

'Whatever the verdict on the investment, that still leaves us with the two dead men. Two *murdered* men, by the looks of things,' said Julia. 'It's an odd way to kill someone, though, isn't it, Hayley? Well, maybe one person, if you were trying to make it look like an accident, but two people? Two similar accidents in the same area within a fortnight or so seems likely to trigger suspicion.'

'Yes, I was assuming that the perpetrator was not a top-level professional criminal, and this was more of an on-the-fly kind of plan,' said Hayley, who was hoovering up the soup like a person who hadn't eaten for a week. Knowing Hayley, that might well be the case, thought Julia.

Hayley continued thinking out loud. 'Someone who thought, it worked once, so why not try it again? But this whole investment aspect might make me rethink that. Either way, Julia, whoever's behind this is dangerous. You can't go poking around asking questions.'

'I really wasn't poking around, and I had no idea this was anything to do with the deaths,' Julia said. 'Hester asked me to go with her to find out about the investment. That's all.' Julia tried to ignore the nagging guilt that this was not an entirely accurate portrayal of what had actually happened. She didn't like misleading Hayley.

'Well, that's the end of it,' said Hayley. 'I'll take this to financial crimes, and your business here is done.'

'Yes, yes, of course.'

'I'm serious, Julia,' said Hayley sternly. 'Don't go near Anthony Ardmore. If this is a scam, or insider trading, and you threaten them, you're in serious danger. These people can be ruthless.'

'You have my word.' Julia said, wondering as she spoke whether this was something she could promise.

22

Getting out of the full tea room with a Labrador on a lead was quite an undertaking, especially as Julia knew someone at just about every table, and everyone wanted to have a chat, or at least say hello, and many were eager to give Jake a pat. She evaded most of them with a cheery wave, but at one table, she came to a sudden and surprised halt.

'Molly!' she said, greeting a slim, pretty woman with a pale porcelain complexion and ash blonde hair, dressed in layers of creamy cashmere. 'And hello, Dominic.'

The man smiled manically at her, his eyes darting anxiously over her features, as if he recognised her, but couldn't place her.

'Julia Bird! How lovely to see you,' said Molly, simultaneously greeting Julia and enlightening her husband, who flashed her a grateful smile. It was a graceful move. 'We haven't seen you since...'

The sentence petered out, but if it hadn't, it would have ended: ... *since you helped clear our pyromaniac son of murder*.

'How is Marty?' Julia asked quickly, dissipating the awkward moment.

'He's doing very well... Please sit for a minute,' said Molly, pulling out the chair next to her. Julia sat, and Jake flopped down next to her. He was in no hurry. 'We found a lovely new therapist for him, and with that and the medication he's taking, he's in a good space.'

Julia was pleased to hear that things were going better for Marty. He was a sweet young man, despite his fascination with flammables. While Molly talked, Julia couldn't help glancing over at Dominic, who looked so similar to – although in crucial ways, different from – his brother. He shared Anthony Ardmore's even features and smooth good looks, but lacked the thin sheen of oiliness that seemed to adhere to the younger brother's manner.

Flo stopped at their table, and looked at Julia in surprise. 'Couldn't drag yourself away?' she said in a teasing tone.

'I was on my way out the door, but I got waylaid for a chat.'

'It's a common problem. Especially when half of Berrywick is in here taking shelter from the storm. You could stay all day and not run out of tall stories to listen to. Sit down, let me bring you another hot chocolate!'

Julia laughed. 'Definitely not, thanks, Flo. I'm going to be on my way in a minute.'

'Anything else for you?' Flo asked the Ardmores, picking up their breakfast plates, both scraped clean. 'We've got a nice fresh carrot cake. Homemade, of course.'

'You do tempt us,' said Molly. 'But just the bill, please, when you're ready.'

Flo made her way back to the kitchen, and Molly turned to Julia. 'I've been going on about Marty, and haven't asked you a thing. Now, tell us how you have been, Julia. What's been going on?'

This was a golden opportunity to quiz them about Dominic's brother, and the two men who had invested with him. The trick would be to make her enquiries sound innocently off-the-cuff.

'I've been very well. It's so odd that I should bump into the two of you, because I was thinking of your family just yesterday.'

'You were?'

'Yes. I'm sure you've heard about what happened to poor Lewis Band and Matthew Shepherd?'

'Of course, yes. Tragic,' said Dominic. 'I knew them both from when we were youngsters.'

'Well, that's exactly why I was thinking of you. I was talking to their wives, and your name came up. Hester mentioned that Lewis and Matthew had been together just a few weeks before, at a reunion lunch with friends from those days, including you. And now here you are. Isn't life funny that way?'

'Yes, indeed,' said Dominic. 'And it was quite a strange thing that we met up at all. It's been decades since we've seen each other, other than to wave to. Even though we all live fairly close by, somehow we seemed to move in different circles.' He was being delicate. Julia had seen Dominic and Molly's house: a huge barn, renovated to a light-flooded modern home in soft tones, set in a large, gently landscaped garden. They'd done very well for themselves. Lewis and Matthew's circumstances were very modest by comparison. They would, indeed, live in different worlds.

Dominic continued: 'And then, about a month ago, another chap we knew from those days got in touch. He had moved back to Berrywick. I hadn't seen him in forty years. The four of us had lunch together – it was great to see them. Odd, how it is with old friends. Even though we'd all gone our separate ways, and our lives are quite different, there was a connection. Common ground. Well, for the most part...'

'You certainly had a lot to talk about,' said Molly, elbowing her husband. 'This one got home after supper! They had a fine old time, the four of them.'

'We did have a fine old time. And I'm so pleased we did,

because, as it turned out, within weeks Lewis and Matthew were both dead.' Dominic's eyes filled up with tears that he quickly wiped away. 'It might have been a long time since we had all been close, but it's been such a shock. Really, it has.'

Julia allowed him a moment to collect himself, and then said gently,' Your brother was at the lunch, too, I believe,' said Julia.

'Anthony?' There was a wariness to Dominic's voice. 'Well, yes. He wasn't part of that crowd, he was a few years younger, but he happened to come past the restaurant where we were having lunch, and he stopped to say hello.'

'They were talking about some investment scheme of his, something to do with plants, if I understood it correctly.' Julia kept her comments deliberately vague, and didn't own up to having met Anthony herself.

'Yes, he was going on about his business, as usual,' Dominic said grumpily. 'He's something of a wheeler-dealer, is Anthony. Always got something on the go, always trying to sell you something. It's become embarrassing, to be honest.'

'Heavens, yes,' said Molly, coolly. 'Imagine going around town saying, "Would you like to invest in my miracle cures?"' It's like an actual snake oil salesman.'

Dominic nodded. 'It is. Anyway, he bent our ears for a while. They listened politely but I'm pleased to say they didn't bite.'

Except that they had, thought Julia. She suspected Anthony had tracked them down after the lunch, and made a harder pitch than he had made in front of his brother.

Dominic continued: 'I think mostly they didn't invest because neither of them understood what on earth he was talking about.' He gave a bark of laughter.

'Or perhaps because they're not idiots,' Molly snorted.

'That's debatable. You might not say that if you could have seen some of the stuff we got up to back in the day. There was an incident with a potato and an exploding Bunsen burner in science class that I'd prefer not to think about.'

'They were all at school together,' Molly said, filling Julia in.

'We all grew up here, went to school together,' Dominic affirmed. 'Not much to do in the village in our teenage years. Mostly we hung out in the car park of the pub when we were too young to be allowed in, played football, tried to play guitar. And, you wouldn't think to look at us now, all middle-aged and all, but we had quite a tight little band back in the day. Keyboards, that was my instrument.'

'Dom was very cool. You should see the photographs,' Molly said, her blue-grey eyes sparkling.

Julia had, in fact, seen the photographs, not that she confessed to that. 'I can well imagine,' she said, with a laugh.

'Fun times. Didn't last, of course. If ever there was a band that didn't end in a flurry of recrimination and disappointment, I'd be surprised. But still, fun while it lasted. It was good to see them.'

Flo came by, slowing to deposit the bill in the middle of the table, and then sweeping off again to take care of the rest of the mass of customers.

Julia had one more burning question, which she asked with as much casualness as she could muster: 'Sounds like fun. Who was the other guy, the guy who had just moved back?'

'Chap called Ken. The guitarist.'

The name sent Julia's heart skittering about in her chest.

'He was a fair guitarist, back in the day,' Dominic continued, oblivious to Julia's heartrate. 'You wouldn't have come across him, though. He only came back to Berrywick a month or two ago. It seems things weren't going too well for him in Scotland, poor chap. He's back in town and hoping to make a fresh start.'

A fresh start? wondered Julia. Had Ken decided to begin by settling some old scores?

23

The snow continued gently but steadily overnight. Only when the weak winter sun rose lazily above the horizon did it pause, as if to give the other side a sporting chance.

Julia started the day with a flurry of messages from Kevin Moore. He liked Julia's slogans for the road safety campaign, but wanted to add some of his own. 'People will die in pain' was one example, and most of his ideas were on this theme. Julia reminded him that they were taking a more constructive approach, and that slogans like his might be very upsetting for the families of the recently deceased.

Having handled this, Julia fed Jake his breakfast and left him outside to run around while she showered and dressed for the day. The ground was sodden with melting snow, which meant that Jake's feet were muddy and wet after his morning constitutional. It was going to be chilly, and she didn't want to leave him outside while she worked a make-up shift at Second Chances, because she had missed her shift on Wednesday when she accompanied the widows on their search for Anthony Ardmore. If he was to stay in the kitchen, she would have to clean him up.

Ordinarily, this would mean using an old towel, or wet wipes, or getting him to walk about on yesterday's newspaper, or some other dog-cleaning operation that he and she both disliked. But today, Julia was excited – yes, excited! – to clean Jake's feet. She had purchased, online, something called the Perfect Paw Washer. The reviews were five star – 'My Choo Choo loves it!' and 'Pinky's paws have never been so clean!' – and now Julia would see it in action herself. The item had been delivered three days ago, just before this latest deluge, and it would be used for the first time today. It was a large silicone cup, lined with flexible silicone bristles. It came with a simple set of instructions:

Fill with warm water up to the mark as indicated.

Place the dogs' paw into the cup.

She tried not to be annoyed by the misplaced apostrophe.

Swirl around gently for 1–2 minutes.

Remove the paw.

Do the same on the other feet.

Julia filled the cup with warm water. It was raining again, so she couldn't do the operation outside, but she set up a chair and a towel next to the open kitchen door, and called Jake in the calmest of tones: 'Come here, Jakey boy.'

Jake looked at her warily. Had he identified something suspicious in her too-calm voice? She had taken the precaution of bringing a pocketful of dog treats. She held one out towards him.

He came towards her slowly. She drew her hand back a little so that he was close to her. 'Sit.'

He sat, and she stroked his ears and spoke soothingly. 'There's a good boy, now, let's wash those feet, shall we?' Julia lifted his front left paw gently, being careful not to get mud on her clean grey trousers. It struck her that she should probably have done this before getting dressed for work. But Jake was calm, and she would be careful not to get any stray drops of water on her clothes. She brought the cup up to enclose the filthy paw. It was quite a snug fit, but it didn't seem to bother Jake. She imagined it was rather pleasant, like when you have a footbath before a pedicure. He looked mildly surprised, rather than concerned, to find his paw enveloped in warm water.

Until Julia got to point 3 of the instructions: *Swirl around gently for 1–2 minutes.*

She took his foreleg firmly and gave it and the cup a few gentle rotations. As the water sloshed around, Jake's expression went from mildly surprised to alarmed. He pulled away. Somehow, his leg slipped from her clutches, but the Perfect Paw Washer was still firmly attached to his foot. He fell back on the kitchen floor in surprise, and then scrambled to his feet in a panic. When he stood, the cup, still attached to his foot, skidded and clattered against the flagstone tiles. Now *this*, he didn't really like.

'Jake, sit! Calm down,' said Julia, lunging for him. But he was too quick. He made an awkward run for it, with the Perfect Paw Washer still remarkably well-lodged on his right front paw. Jake made a clattering circuit of the kitchen table, showering the place – and his owner – liberally with muddy water, sliding and slipping as he went, before the device finally detached from his foot and skittered across the flagstones, dispersing the rest of the water across the entire area of the floor. Relieved of the dastardly device, Jake bolted for the garden, into the lovely mud and the rain that had started to fall.

Julia surveyed the wet, muddy room, and sighed deeply. What a bloody mess. She would have to clean up the kitchen, and then herself. The grey trousers were unsalvageable, streaked with mud and water. She would be late for her shift at Second Chances, and have to endure Wilma's pointed checking of her watch as she arrived.

Bending down, she picked up the stupid silicone cup lying empty and innocent under the table. She tossed it angrily into the sink, then fetched the mop, closing the broom cupboard with a satisfying slam.

Why did Jake have to be so unrelentingly clumsy, she wondered, grumpily. Why couldn't he be more like the docile Chihuahua of the five-star reviewer who *loved* the Perfect Paw Washer?

She sent Wilma a message saying she would be a little late, and set to work mopping up the mess. It was astonishing how far half a cup of muddy water could disperse. She had to get out the kitchen steps to climb up and wipe a splatter from about six feet up the wall. Once she got over her irritation and accepted the situation, however, the cleaning action soothed her, and her cross mood dissipated as order was restored.

Outside the kitchen window, Jake was lumbering happily about, sniffing the morning smells, tail wagging, having quite forgotten his earlier trauma, and caring not a jot for the devastation he'd left in the kitchen. She felt a rush of love for the silly chocolate chap. She couldn't blame him for the debacle. It was her fault, really. She knew Jake's ways, and should have known better than to attach a foreign object to his paw and expect him to sit quietly while she jiggled it about and sloshed water all over.

Despite her eventful morning, Julia was only twenty minutes late for her volunteer job at Second Chances. She was a meticulously punctual person, who hated to be late, especially if someone else was inconvenienced by her tardiness. Wilma had said that the Feel-Good Christmas campaign and the festive Christmas display was 'pulling in the punters', and it was 'all hands on deck' for the Christmas season. Julia knew that the shop was seldom unmanageably busy, especially in the first hour or so, so Wilma and Diane wouldn't be under excessive pressure. She decided she could afford the extra five minutes required to stop on the way to buy mince pies for her co-workers, as a gesture of goodwill. Spreading the Christmas spirit, and all that.

They had the desired effect, causing a chorus of 'ooooh's, and a discussion about whether to have the pies for elevenses, or save them for later. They had yet to reach consensus on the matter when the ringing of the bell above the door alerted them to the arrival of the first customer. The first of many. Julia had never seen the shop so busy as it became that day.

'I saw the story in the *Southern Times* about Feel-Good Christmas and I thought, what a good idea,' said Nicky. 'It's good that people are buying second-hand. Much better for the environment, isn't it? The landfills and all that.'

'That's the idea,' said Wilma brightly.

'I wouldn't buy second-hand clothes myself,' Nicky said, with a little shiver. 'I know all the young people are into vintage these days, but I just don't like the thought of it. Someone else's armpits.'

Wilma blinked at her, at a loss for words, and said weakly, 'Well, you could wash them first, if you're not sure.'

'Nah, not for me. But I'll see what you have for Sebastian,' said Nicky, wittering on in her usual stream of consciousness, heading towards the children's section. 'Toys and so on. You know what kids are like, half the time you buy the fancy new thing and they don't even look at it, too busy with a pinecone. Or a snail. Last week, it was a snail he brought into his bedroom, into his actual bed, lord love me.'

The bell rang with the arrival of another customer. 'Good morning,' said Diane cheerfully.

A mildly dishevelled-looking man of about sixty nodded in their direction and perused the shelves. Mostly, people who came into the shop wandered about in what seemed to be a purposeless manner, waiting for something to catch their eye, but he seemed to be going systematically, as if in search of something particular.

'Are you looking for anything specific?' Diane asked.

'Yes, I am, actually,' he said. 'A guitar.'

Wilma chipped in, from her position behind the till: 'You know, I think I might have seen a guitar when I was looking for items for our Feel-Good Christmas display. Or maybe it was a banjo. Would a banjo do?'

'No, I'm really looking for a guitar. A specific guitar. It would have been donated a while ago. I'm not sure if it was even to this charity shop. But it doesn't look like you've got it – or if you had it, it's been sold.'

'Not necessarily... We do keep some larger items in the storeroom at the back and we rotate the stock from time to time,' said Diane. 'I'll have a look out the back.'

'Okay, thanks. I'd be much obliged.'

'Look on the top shelf; it might be there,' Wilma called after her.

Diane disappeared into the storeroom. There were a few grunts, a thump and a twang, and she emerged triumphant with a guitar in hand. 'Is this what you're looking for?'

'It is! This here is my first guitar.' The man's face broke into a smile, revealing a snaggle of stained teeth. He took the instrument from Diane, and stroked it lovingly. 'I got it when I was thirteen. We had plenty of adventures together, I can tell you.'

Julia could believe it. The guitar looked as weathered as its owner, its body peppered with scrapes and dings, and old stickers peeling off.

'What a piece of luck! My cousin helped Mum clean out the attic when she got sick. He got rid of a lot of my mum's old things, said they'd gone to a charity shop. I reckoned my old guitar must have gone with them. It was a very long shot, but here it is.'

'You're lucky it's still here,' said Diane. 'Musical instruments are quite popular with the young. Guitars and drums, mostly. Everyone wants to be a rock star when they're twelve.'

'Lucky indeed.' He held the guitar in a loose embrace, with a tenderness that made Julia feel a little sad, and then played a chord. 'Needs new strings, of course. But I'll get the old girl back into shape. New beginnings, hey? A fresh start and a good dollop of luck, that's what we need.'

Wilma, who was still at the till, piped up: 'If you don't mind me asking, was your mum Mrs Payne?'

'She was.'

'My condolences. I knew her a little, she was a lovely lady.'

'She was. I didn't see her as much as I'd have liked these last years. I wish...' He shrugged, letting his wish linger unexpressed, and then sighed as if to express the hopelessness of wishes.

'Ah, well,' said Julia, trying to be comforting. 'It's not easy keeping in touch. Everyone is so busy, and everyone is spread all over the country. The world, even. My daughter's in Hong Kong.'

'I wasn't so far, but still, it's quite a journey and I was either working on a job, or waiting for a job. And the train tickets these days, they cost a fortune. And with one thing and another... You know how it is.'

It sounded as if he'd had a rather precarious life, poor chap. Julia nodded. 'I do know. It's not easy to find the time or the money. I'm sure you did your best.'

'Are you planning on staying in Berrywick, then?' asked Diane. She was rather nosy, which could be handy, because she unearthed a lot of information Julia was interested in, without Julia having to be nosy herself.

'I'll be here for a while. It's a pretty village, isn't it? Relaxing. Weather's better than Scotland, too.' Julia's ears pricked up at the word 'Scotland' as they all looked out the window, where the view didn't exactly support his point. It was raining again, and the occasional person scuttled by under an umbrella. 'I've got Mum's flat. It's a nice, comfortable spot. And her little car. I feel like I could make a fresh start here.'

'And do you have friends here, still?' asked Diane.

'I do, I looked up a couple of them, and it was good to reconnect, although sadly, two of them have passed away recently. You will have heard about the accidents, I'm sure.' He frowned at the thought.

'Lewis and Matthew were your friends? I'm so sorry for your loss, and so soon after your mum. Too terrible, what happened to them,' said Wilma.

'Terrible,' said Julia, distractedly. She had a strong suspicion that she knew exactly who it was that was standing in Second Chances. 'So sorry for your loss.'

'Thank you. Very sad. Our other mate's still around, doing well. His brother, too. In fact, he's got me in on the ground floor of a good investment.'

There was absolutely no doubt about it. This man was none other than Ken, the disappointed band member.

'This investment requires vision, and it's the early adopters who make the big returns,' he continued. That sentence sounded as if it had come straight out of Anthony Ardmore's mouth. Which presumably it had, when Anthony was punting his investment scheme. 'So things are looking up on that score, at least.'

'I hope it goes well for you,' said Julia, who was less than certain of a positive outcome. In fact, she felt sure that this investment was either completely bogus, or illegal. She was tempted to say so, but decided against it. That was the work of the police, once they had figured it all out. Instead, she said, 'I'm Julia, by the way. Julia Bird.'

'Ken. Ken Payne,' he said, confirming Julia's suspicions. 'How much is the guitar?'

'Ah, there's no charge,' said Wilma, from her spot behind the counter. 'After all, it's yours. You enjoy it, now, you hear? It's what your mum would've wanted.'

24

Julia went to bed early after a busy day at Second Chances, but she slept badly. Ken Payne visited her in her dreams, draped in tinsel and playing a banjo, which even while asleep she knew was not his instrument. She woke late feeling poorly rested, the twanging banjo ringing in her ears, and her mind mulling over the previous day's events and discoveries. She had an uneasy feeling about the circumstances around Ken Payne's appearance – or reappearance – in Berrywick.

Chaplin jumped onto the bed with a '*prow*' of a good morning, and rubbed his head against her. She stroked him, enjoying the feel of his warm, rumbling body under her hand. Chaplin's good morning head-butting was becoming more insistent as the minutes passed. Now, he wasn't so much saying good morning, as reminding her forcefully of her duties – of which cat feeding was top of the list, obviously.

'All right, all right, I'm getting up,' she said, pushing the cat gently aside, and swinging her legs to the floor. She had slept late, and she had things to do. The week had run away with her. Between the deaths and the Christmas season, she had been so busy and distracted that she'd hardly shopped or cooked. She'd have to get to the shops unless she wanted egg on toast for supper.

Julia got up and padded to the kitchen to let Jake out, closing the door behind him quickly against the chilly morning. While the kettle boiled, she poured biscuits into Chaplin's bowl. To the soundtrack of his determined crunching, she set the tea tray, the sequence of movements happening automatically, without her conscious thought. While her hands found the teapot and the cup and saucer, her brain ran through the list of what she knew about Ken.

He had only been in Berrywick for a couple of months or so, after an absence of many years, following the death of his mother. On his return, he had reconnected with his old friends Dominic, Matthew and Lewis over a long lunch. Dominic's brother, Anthony Ardmore, had gate-crashed the lunch to pitch his dubious investment scheme. Ken had come into some money and property when his mum had died, and had invested in the scheme, along with Matthew and Lewis.

The whistle of the kettle brought Julia back into the present. She poured the water over the tea leaves and took the tray back to her bed. When she had settled in comfortably, she added a few more items to the mental list of what she knew about Ken.

He had been angry about the band breaking up all those years ago. According to what she'd heard from David, whom she'd met at Christopher's birthday party, he had been quite aggressive, even threatening. And, of course, Lewis and Matthew, his fellow investors and his old friends, were both dead.

It all seemed like rather too many coincidences, frankly. Was Ken somehow responsible for the other deaths? He certainly didn't look like the murderous type, at least not based on their interaction in Second Chances. If anything, Ken had seemed defeated. A fellow who had had some hard knocks in life, starting with the almost-success, but ultimate failure of the band. The knocks seemed to have left him weakened and down-hearted rather than aggressively angry.

Of course, Julia had been witness to enough violence to know that looks could be deceiving. The mild-mannered could be murderous, and the openly furious could be harmless. But still, from the little she'd seen of Ken, she didn't peg him for the violent type.

In fact, she had another, contradictory, idea. If Ken wasn't *involved* in the men's death, might he be in danger himself? The men all had one thing in common – aside from a youthful friendship – and that was their connection with Anthony Ardmore and his investment. Were investors being bumped off? And if so, was Ken in the firing line? If it was a possibility, she should warn him.

The only way that line of reasoning would make sense was if someone – presumably Anthony Ardmore – stood to gain from their deaths. Ordinarily, an investor's heirs would inherit their stake in the business. She wondered what DI Hayley Gibson's financial fraud people had discovered about Ardmore Accelerated Investments. Were there any unusual clauses? Any new life insurance policies? If so, might he have killed the two men for financial gain?

There was only one way to find out.

Handily, Julia had a completely legitimate motive for drop-ping in on Hayley. Hayley was an ardent and speedy reader, so Julia was always on the lookout for books for her. She had spotted a book by one of Hayley's favourite authors at Second Chances, and had gone to purchase it as a gift for the detective inspector. In fact, Wilma, who had seemed to be having a generous day, had told her to take it, and bring in another book when she had one going spare.

Julia messaged Hayley now:

I've got a little something for you. I'm going out soon to do some errands. Can I drop it by the flat?

Ah! Intriguing! But I'll be at work.

On a Saturday?

Paperwork.

Ugh.

Can you pop it in the post box?

Easier to drop it off at the station. I'll be coming right past. I've got to do some shopping. See you later.

Cheers.

The road safety protesters were nowhere to be seen when Julia pulled up outside the police station some hours later. Maybe they had decided that the two deaths were attributable to something more than just bad driving. Perhaps the ominous clouds and the stiff breeze had put them off. Or perhaps they had taken Saturday off to get a move on with their Christmas shopping.

Hayley was delighted with the book. 'It's one of the few I haven't read! I'd better let Sylvia know there will be no sparkling conversation from me tonight.'

'Just the weather for a good read, isn't it? I heard on the radio that there's another storm coming in. I'm pleased you haven't read this one, although I could have taken it back to the shop if you had. Oh, and Hayley, speaking of the shop, there was a strange coincidence yesterday, something I think you might be interested in.'

'Really?' Hayley's cheerful pleasure in the book was replaced with a suspicious narrowing of the eyes. 'What "coincidence" exactly?'

Julia could hear the invisible inverted commas around the word 'coincidence' but pressed on regardless. 'A man came in, a chap by the name of Ken Payne. He's an old friend of Lewis and Matthew, who recently moved back to Berrywick. It seems he was also a potential investor in Ardmore Accelerated Investments.'

'Well, I hope he didn't put in his last ten quid, because I don't think he's going to be making his fortune in this scheme.'

'I hope not. He seems even more of a babe in the woods than the other two, poor chap. What did the special investigators say? Is it a scam?'

'Most likely, from what I know so far.'

'I was thinking...' Julia paused, trying to think exactly how to phrase it.

Hayley put the book she was holding down on her desk, and said, 'Go on, spit it out. I know you've come with a theory or gone on a fishing expedition. Let's cut to the chase.'

Julia blushed, but didn't deny it. 'Well, since you ask, with two of the men dead already, I am worried that Ken might be in danger. Or maybe even that he was somehow involved in the other men's deaths. I can't see how it all fits together, but Anthony Ardmore and his scheme are the common denominator between the other two men.'

'It's one of the things they have in common. They also lived in the same town, they were at school together, they played in the same band, they would have known many people in common. There are lots of areas of overlap I can think of, and maybe more that I haven't.'

'They were killed just after they invested in the scheme.'

'Granted,' Hayley nodded. 'The timing is interesting.'

'Is there any chance that Anthony killed them, to somehow get his hands on their money?'

'He already had the money. They invested it with him.'

'Well, it was still theirs. Maybe the shares reverted back to him if they died, or something. Or maybe there was an insurance policy, I don't know. Something that gives him a motive.'

'I'll speak to the financial forensic guys about that. But Anthony has an alibi for the night of Matthew's death. While he was at home alone when Lewis died, which we can't really verify one hundred per cent, he has a witness for the night that Matthew died.'

Julia must have looked sceptical, because Hayley added: 'He was with his girlfriend. Clarissa someone or other. Walter Farmer followed up with her.'

'Well, I suppose if his alibi for Matthew checked out, that's something.'

'It takes him out of the running. It's incredibly unlikely that different people killed Lewis and Matthew in exactly the same way.'

'I see that,' agreed Julia.

Julia saw the detective's eyes flick towards the stacks of files and papers that populated her desk like hills and vales on some topographical model. She was clearly impatient to get back to work. 'Well, I'd best be getting home. Enjoy the book, Hayley.'

'Saturday afternoon on the sofa with a new book. My reward for getting on top of this,' Hayley said, casting her eyes on a papery Mount Snowdon.

'Good luck.'

As Julia turned into her driveway, Hester was leaving her own house. Hunched against the gathering wind, she locked the front door and picked up a large cardboard box from the doormat. Julia, emerging from her car, could hear what sounded like the clinking of glass.

'Oh, hello, Julia,' Hester said, as Julia emerged from her car. 'Have you had a good day?'

'It's been a busy one What about you? Are you on your way out?'

It was a slightly awkward moment, the two women standing there, Hester with the big box of honey jars in her arms, braced against the wind. One or two fat raindrops plopped down on the pavement. The advance party in a big rainstorm, Julia suspected. Hester, who was wearing a long raincoat, hunched over the box to protect it from the rain. 'Oh, dear. The weather... I'm going to go out and deliver honey. There are quite a few back orders that need to be processed and delivered. I've had so much on my mind, what with Matthew... and, you know, the money... and the worries. I haven't been sleeping well, and I'm so, so tired. I'm afraid I've let things slide.'

'That's quite normal in the circumstances, Hester. I'm sure the customers will understand if they have to wait a day or two.'

'I want to fulfil Matthew's last promises to the customers. And some of the orders from the Christmas market are for Christmas gifts, so people will be worrying if they don't get them.' Hester looked down at the box. 'This is half of them. But now I'm thinking, did I pick up the right box?' She shifted the weight of the box to her hip, steadied it, and freed one arm to pull a sheet of paper from the box. 'Oh dear,' she said. 'I think this might be the box for Edgeley, not Berrywick. But there seem to be too few jars. I think I have got into a muddle. I'd better go back inside and check everything.'

A rumble of thunder cut her sentence short.

'Hester, are you sure you want to go out in this?' Julia asked. 'Why don't you do this tomorrow instead? I'll come and give you a hand sorting it out. It'll be easier with company.'

'That's very kind, but I don't know...'

The fat drops were coming faster.

'I'm going inside, Hester. I think you should do the same. The weather is really terrible. Put the fire on and have a quiet afternoon and an early night. I'll come by tomorrow morning, and we'll go through those orders together and check you've got everything right.'

A crack of lightning split the sky. The two women flinched.

'That is very kind. Thank you, Julia,' said Hester, quickly. 'I'll see you tomorrow.'

The two women walked briskly towards their respective homes as the storm gathered force behind them.

25

Clarissa.

Julia could hardly believe her eyes when she saw the name on one of Hester's list of honey orders. It was an unusual name – in fact, Julia couldn't remember ever meeting a Clarissa before – and oddly enough one she'd heard just yesterday, from the lips of DI Hayley Gibson. Clarissa was the name of Anthony Ardmore's girlfriend, the one he'd apparently been at home with when Lewis died.

The address on Hester's delivery list was in Berrywick. It seemed unlikely that there were two Clarissas in a small village. Much more likely that they were one and the same.

'I've got errands to do around the village, so I can drop off whatever needs to be delivered in Berrywick. And you can deliver to Edgeley. How does that sound?' Julia offered, her curiosity piqued.

'That would be so helpful, thank you, Julia,' Hester said, her voice wobbling a little. 'I just feel so overwhelmed.'

'Of course you do, you've experienced a traumatic loss,' said Julia. 'Your whole world has been turned upside down.'

Julia gave Hester a quick hug, which the other woman returned, saying, 'You're a kind friend and neighbour.'

Julia felt a little flash of guilt that her kindness wasn't entirely selfless. She reminded herself that she had offered to help before she'd seen Clarissa's name. She *had* been kind, and now she was the lucky beneficiary of a stroke of good fortune.

'It's no trouble,' Julia said. 'Now, let's check the Berrywick orders. There's Clarissa, she has four jars...'

It wasn't that she expected to unearth anything that Hayley Gibson and Walter Farmer hadn't already found out, Julia thought, as she drove to the address on the list Hester had given her. It wasn't in the very poshest area – the smartest houses were mostly owned by 'old' families who had lived in Berrywick for generations, or they were owned by rich solicitors down from London – but it was on a nice street on the edge of the village.

With each curve of the pretty road, the honey jars clinked musically in the back seat. Julia was pleased she had decided to leave Jake at home – the combination of large jars of sticky honey and a boisterous chocolate Labrador in a small Fiat would have made her nervous. She would take Jake for a nice walk in the afternoon.

Julia drew up at a low stone wall, checked the address, and got out with the four large jars of honey Clarissa had ordered, clinking in a sturdy paper bag. She walked up the garden path to a house that was more modest than she'd expected, having seen Anthony Ardmore's huge new car, but neat and trim.

The door was flung open before she reached the doorstep, and a woman appeared, walking and talking at speed. Hester had messaged to say that the honey would be delivered, and Clarissa had clearly been waiting. She was much younger than

Julia had been expecting – and certainly a great deal younger than Anthony Ardmore.

'It's so kind of you to come and deliver,' Clarissa said. 'I was so sorry to hear about poor... Gosh! Doesn't that honey look lovely? We're doing a Secret Santa at work, and when I saw the stand at the Christmas market, I thought, well, what's nicer than a big jar of honey? Anyone would be delighted with it. And then I thought, my boyfriend, Anthony might need gifts for his family, or for staff or, I don't know, clients perhaps, so I bought a few extra.'

'What a clever idea, it makes a lovely gift for anyone,' said Julia, when Clarissa paused for breath and she was able to get a word in. 'Where should I put them?'

'Follow me,' said Clarissa, turning back to the house. She spoke over her shoulder while leading the way. 'I didn't want to carry them all around the market all afternoon, so the honey man said he'd deliver. I wasn't sure if I would get the honey at all, when I heard what happened to the poor man. Terrible, wasn't it? Imagine that. Horrible. And he seemed so nice. I would have quite understood if the honey hadn't been delivered.'

Julia followed Clarissa, speaking to her back as she bustled down the passage. 'He was indeed very nice. A very decent fellow. His wife is making sure all their customers are getting their orders, as he would have wanted. I'm their neighbour. I'm giving her a hand with the deliveries.'

'Well, that's very kind.' They entered a drab little kitchen with yellowing wooden counters and a sooty patch behind the stove. 'Here's a funny thing – I mean, not *funny* funny, but quite a strange thing, really – it turns out that the honey man was a client of my partner's, I discovered afterwards. Imagine that?'

Julia, who had been wondering how she would manage to seamlessly bring the conversation round to the subject of

Anthony Ardmore, wondered no more. 'Well, there's a coincidence,' she said.

Clarissa nodded. 'Isn't it? In fact, him *and* the other man who died. Both clients of Anthony's. They were two of three who were in a group, like a syndicate of some sort. Would you like to have a cup of tea?'

'I won't have tea, but I'd appreciate a glass of water if you're not in a hurry.'

'Right you are. Have a seat.'

Julia put the honey jars on the table and sat down.

''Scuse the kitchen,' said Clarissa, holding a glass under the cold tap. 'We're going to be doing a full renovation of it next year, knock through to the scullery, open it all up. My boyfriend plans to sell his place and move in with me – he spends so much time here anyway. But we need to fix it up, if this is going to be our forever home.'

She handed the glass of water to Julia and sat down opposite her at the kitchen table. 'You know these businessman types, always waiting for a deal to go through or cheque to clear or what have you. Promises, promises. But finally, it's going to happen! Imagine that.'

A fancy new car *and* a new kitchen... Business must be good for Anthony Ardmore.

'That's very exciting for you. It's a nice big space, I'm sure with a bit of love and paint it will be lovely.'

'Oh, it will. I've got big plans. Although I can't get Anthony to look at the vision board, or the paint samples, let alone the taps. The taps are so important to the overall look, don't you think? Well, that's what they say on Pinterest. But Anthony hasn't got the time, he says.'

Julia took a sip of her water and asked, 'Busy at work, is he?'

'Yes. He's in investments. It's a lot of responsibility, dealing with people's money. He's been under a lot of stress. It's the personal side, I think, keeping the clients happy, that takes its toll. Now that's a challenge. I can just imagine.' She rolled her eyes.

'You mentioned something about a syndicate?'

'A syndicate?' Clarissa's brow furrowed. She was one of those stream-of-consciousness talkers whose words disappeared like footprints on the sand once they exited her mouth. 'Oh, yes, I was talking about Anthony's clients. It's an investment syndicate. You have to put in a certain amount of money to buy in, and it's a lot, so sometimes people go in together. In this case, three chaps sort of clubbed in together to come up with the money. You know what it's like with that sort of thing, this one wants one thing, and someone else wants another, and then this one is in and that wants out and then someone else changes his mind and it's on again. I didn't follow it properly, but the investors were dithering about – they had to all go in, the three of them, for the minimum stake, and they finally signed, but then someone said they weren't sure and they wanted to cancel. Imagine that. Big stress. Because everyone has to be on the same page in a syndicate. And then, two of them suddenly died, just like that. It's been very stressful and difficult for poor Anthony.'

Clarissa stopped to draw breath, and must have realised how inappropriate that last sentence had sounded, because she said quickly: 'Not as difficult as for the two men, obviously, or their wives. Those poor widows. I mean, poor old ducks, I can't even imagine.' She gave a shiver. 'But still, poor Anthony, he's got to sort it all out, and people can be very tricky when they're grieving, quite unreasonable, as Anthony says. And you know what old ladies can be like when they get their feathers ruffled – no offence.'

Julia didn't let on to the prickle of offence that she did in fact feel on behalf of 'old ladies' everywhere. Clarissa rambled on, 'And there's the kitchen to pay for, to say nothing of deciding on the taps and the paint colours, which obviously he's not in the headspace to discuss right now, and he's half here and half at his place.' She stopped, and her face brightened as if a great idea had struck her. 'Would *you* like to see the paint colours?'

'Me? Oh, well, I'm not much of an expert on that sort of thing, but... Yes, of course, I'd be happy to have a look.'

Clarissa looked delighted. She got to her feet and bounded over to a drawer, from which she removed a fat folder. Plonking it down on the table between them, she pulled out a picture torn from a magazine. 'I was thinking of something like this.' She pushed it across the table to Julia, who studied the kitchen in the picture. It looked beautiful, and spotless. Julia had a horrible flashback to the incident with the Perfect Paw Washer. Whoever owned *this* kitchen didn't appear to have a lunatic wet Labrador. In fact, the only living thing in the picture of the kitchen was a spider plant. Unless you counted the contents of the fruit bowl, which were three perfect lemons. Did a lemon count as a living thing, Julia wondered?

Clarissa picked up a clutch of paint swatches. 'But with the walls more of a teal colour, lighter than in the picture, more like this one. Imagine that.'

Julia was starting to wonder if there was anything that Clarissa didn't want her to imagine.

Clarissa spread the little rectangles of coloured paper into a fan with her thumb, identified the correct one, and held it out. 'It's called Singing the Blue. Don't they have funny names? There's one called Donkey Breath – can't say I fancy it. So do you like the teal? There's also this dark grey, Scandinavian Storm, it's called. It's very fashionable at the moment, and it's smart, but I like light and I worry it might be gloomy... What do you think?'

Julia gave the colours her full attention, and gave Clarissa her considered opinion – brighter was better in a kitchen, especially in winter, and the teal was lovely, but she wouldn't use it on every wall. They were getting on so easily that she felt she could slip in a question: 'So, how were the widows being tricky?'

'Oh, I don't mean to be unkind about your neighbour. I'm sure she's had an awful time, and I don't know the full story. I only know that they wanted to take the money back, which put Anthony into a proper mood, I can tell you.'

Julia worked slowly through samples for window blinds, and, without raising her head, said casually, 'That does sound tricky. What's he going to do about it?'

'Oh, he can't give the money back, obviously, even if he wanted to. There's contracts and everything, but it's all complicated. Anyway, it looks like the other investor, the not-dead one, obviously, is keen to stay in and make lots of money. All three – the widows who've inherited their husbands' investments, as well as the not-dead chap – need to agree for them to leave, so if he wants to stay in, they'll all stay in. It looks like the drama will all blow over, and then maybe Anthony can look at the paint samples.'

Clarissa flicked through the colour swatches with a rhythmic, contemplative air, like someone shuffling cards. She put them down on the table, leaned towards Julia and said in a conspiratorial whisper, 'Now, you might think I'm mad, but I think I can trust you not to freak out when I tell you...'

Julia felt a prickle of anticipation.

'Just between you and me, I've been thinking...'

What could Clarissa's revelation be? And what light might it shed on the murders?

Clarissa leaned forward and said under her breath, 'Yellow.'

'What?' Julia asked, confused.

'You hate it? You're probably right. It's very eighties. Forget I said anything about yellow. Teal. Teal it is.'

26

Julia dropped off the rest of the jars of honey at houses nearby. Berrywick being what it was, she was invited in for tea at two of the three stops – the third was a harassed-looking young mum with a baby on her hip and a toddler pulling on her skirt, so who could blame her for not offering tea? Julia didn't take up any of the offers of hospitality, but made her rounds quickly and efficiently without going in for even a glass of water. She had much on her mind. As well as puzzling over the rather disjointed revelations from Clarissa, she was deciding what pudding to make to take Sean's that evening. Apple crumble would be nice. Sean loved a crumble, and someone on the road had given all the neighbours a bag of apples each. Yes, that's what she'd make, apple crumble.

It was only when she got home, and saw a book, *Pop Songs for Guitar*, on the table by the front door, that she remembered the other – non-bee-related – delivery she had to make that day. Diane had come across the book on Friday while she was sorting through stock in the storeroom to replenish the shelves at Second Chances.

'It must be his. Look!' she had said, pointing to the name,

KEN, written in blue ink on the inside of the front cover, which was yellow with age. Each letter in the name was fat and rounded to look three-dimensional – bubble writing, it was called, and an enduring classic amongst teens. 'It must have been donated at the same time as the instrument. What a pity I didn't spot it earlier – we could have given it to him while he was here for the guitar.'

'Oh, this looks like something precious, we will have to get it back to him,' said Wilma eagerly. 'I wonder who would have his number?'

'I wonder.' Diane frowned. 'I'll ask around. Someone will know.'

'I know the house, of course,' said Wilma. 'He's staying in his mum's place, over on Grange Lane. I could go over there.'

'That's close to where I live,' Julia had said. 'I pass it all the time, on my way to the river path with Jake. Give the book to me; I'll drop it off to him over the weekend.'

Julia now ate a quick lunch of warmed-up pea soup and wholemeal toast – it was just the meal for the chilly weather – and got the crumble filling ready so she could top it and bake it on her return. She bundled up against the breeze, and then bundled up Jake. It was the first time she'd tried to put on his Christmas jersey, and after the experience with the Perfect Paw Washer, she'd been rather apprehensive. Jake, to her surprise, was a model of sensible behaviour. He stood calmly while she put it over him and fastened it under his tummy. 'Don't you look smart?' she said. She was pleased with her choice: the red and black tartan looked good against his glossy brown coat. She attached his lead, dropped the music book into a tote bag and hoisted it onto her shoulder. The two of them set off on their mission.

On a Sunday afternoon, the river path was nicely busy, with plenty of dogs for Jake to greet, and humans for him to charm. He trotted along at Julia's side, tail wagging happily, his nose twitching inquisitively at each new smell. His tail-wagging pace stepped up a notch when he spotted Pippa and her clutch of puppies, accompanied by an older lady with a walking stick. They were walking towards them. The puppies were similarly pleased to see Jake, squirming in delight, soft little blobs of happiness. Pippa let them off their leads so they could play freely on a nice bit of lawn next to the path, on the side away from the river. Jake, similarly liberated from his lead, was like an indulgent uncle, playing gently with the youngsters, letting them jump up at him and nibble his tail.

Pippa introduced her companion as her aunt Margaret. Julia had heard from Pippa about her aunt's health troubles, but she seemed quite serene and even happy, if rather tottery on her feet. Up close, Julia realised she was younger than she'd appeared from afar. Only a few years older than Julia herself, but rather frail, which was hardly surprising.

Aunt Margaret greeted Julia, and then asked Pippa, 'Are we going to the shops now?'

'No, not now,' Pippa said.

'Good, I will watch these little chaps play with the big brown fellow in his kilt.' Margaret sat down on the bench and turned her attention to the dogs. Jake was lying down and the puppies were clambering clumsily all over him. Aunt Margaret chuckled.

'We've actually just come from the shops,' Pippa said quietly to Julia. 'She's terribly forgetful, and forever losing things. Or she thinks she's lost them. A special pen, some jewellery, her favourite hand cream. But she's often completely normal and lucid.'

Julia watched Aunt Margaret chortle when one of the puppies attached himself to Jake's tail in some sort of tug-of-war, pulling and growling. 'That's hard, but at least she seems quite cheerful and not too anxious about it all,' she said to Pippa.

'I know! It's so lovely, to be honest. A silver lining. She was never a cheerful person. Honestly, she was sort of bitter, and could be mean, but since she got sick and moved back to Berrywick, she seems happier. The neurologist says that it could be the position of the tumour. Honestly, the brain is a mysterious thing. Oh gosh, speaking of batty old aunts...' Pippa looked over Julia's shoulder. Julia turned to follow her gaze. Aunt Edna was tottering down the path towards them. She was reed thin, and Julia feared for her in the wind. She imagined the old lady's nest of scarves and what looked like a velvet cape filling with air like a spinnaker, and carrying her away to who-knew-where.

'Good morning, Aunt Edna,' Pippa and Julia said in unison.

'Is there an echo?' Edna asked, looking around crossly.

'No,' said Pippa and Julia.

'How are you, Aunt Edna?' asked Julia, solo.

'Old.'

'I see. Well...' Julia, uncharacteristically, was at a loss as to how to respond.

'And whatever they say, you can teach an old dog new tricks,' Edna said, decisively.

'Edna!' said Margaret, looking up from the dogs. 'Is that you?'

'Who are you?'

'I'm Margaret.'

'Margaret? I don't think so.'

Julia and Pippa were watching this exchange in bemusement, heads swivelling from one lady to the other, as if they were watching a tennis match.

'Oh yes, definitely,' Margaret assured her, nodding solemnly.

'Aren't you dead?'

'No. They say I've got a tumour in my head, but I can't see anything there.' She reached up and parted the hair that lightly adorned her head.

Edna stepped closer and leaned down to peer into the soft,

snowy tufts. 'No, there's nothing there, you're fine,' she pronounced, straightening up with some difficulty, and an audible creak.

'That's what I tell them. Well, you have a good day, Edna.'

'Let sleeping dogs lie, Margaret.' Edna started to move away, and then turned to look directly into Julia's face. 'And as for you, you're barking up the wrong tree,' she said, and tottered off down the path.

Julia considered the mysterious comment, and her current concerns and assumptions, as she and Jake continued their walk along the river, in the direction of Ken's house. Edna might be quite batty, and talk a lot of nonsense, but Julia often got a funny feeling that Edna *knew* things. *Was* Julia barking up the wrong tree? And which tree, in particular? And if so, which was the correct tree up which to bark?

Her conversation with Clarissa had given her a lot to think about. Their investment with Anthony was one of the things that Lewis and Matthew had in common. Could their deaths be connected with that? Clarissa had said the two men had dithered, and, at some point, had wanted to change their minds and exit the investment. She'd also said that all three partners had to agree in order to withdraw the money. Might Anthony have killed Lewis and Matthew to keep the money in the scheme? And where did that leave Ken – because Ken was, of course, the third member of the syndicate,

Julia reached the house that had belonged to Ken's mum, and was now his. It was a sweet little place, tiny, with two square windows looking out at her like two eyes either side of the nose of a front door. The windows and doors were painted a sparkling white against the brick.

With Jake trotting happily beside her, she made her way up a short path through a carefully planted, well-established garden. The garden path was in need of the attention of a rake and a broom. Picking her way past the leaves and twigs that eddied in the chilly breeze circling her ankles, Julia wondered if perhaps Ken was not as meticulous as his mum had been in the upkeep and maintenance department. Judging by the rest of the garden, and the outside of the house, she had not been the sort to let the path go unswept.

Jake surged forward as they reached the doorstep, and made a lunge for a paper plate of muffins that had been left on the doormat. 'Oh no, you don't,' Julia said, tugging at his lead just in time. She was, in fact, rather tempted to eat one herself – they were beautifully golden and perfectly risen, each with a slice of banana baked into the top. She resisted the temptation, picked up the plate and rang the doorbell.

She waited no more than a minute before the door opened and Ken appeared with tousled hair and the uncertain expression of a man desperately trying to place a familiar person.

'It's Julia,' she said. 'We met on Friday at Second Chances. When you came in for the guitar?'

'Oh yes, of course!' He looked relieved.

'I brought you something,' she said.

He looked down and took the plate of muffins. 'Gosh, people have been so kind. How nice of you to make muffins.'

'Oh, no, I didn't make those. That wasn't... I brought you a book.' She reached for the tote bag over her shoulder.

'Please come in out of the cold,' he said, stepping backwards. 'The dog is welcome. The old cat died a week before Mum.'

He closed the door behind her. It was blessedly calm and a little warmer out of the wind. 'I'm sorry about the cat, and about your mum. I won't stay,' Julia said. 'I just wanted to give you a book that we found at the shop. I think it belongs to you.'

As she pulled the book from her bag and handed it to him, his face lit up in recognition and pleasure. 'I don't believe it! I learned every song in this book off by heart. Hours and hours, I spent with it.'

'We thought it must be yours. Your name's inside.'

He flipped it open and smiled at the bubble writing. 'Mum kept it all these years,' he said, in a soft tone. 'Thank you for bringing it to me, that's very kind of you. Would you like tea?'

'We have to be getting back home, but some other time, that would be nice, thank you.'

'Right you are.'

'Oh Ken, there is something else I wanted to ask you about. It's Anthony Ardmore, and his investment.'

'Ah yes, I'm in on it. It's going to be huge.'

'So he says. I went to see him about it. It certainly is... innovative.'

'Right. Exactly, so you understand. Are you going to buy in on the next round?'

'Not personally. I was there to support my friends. Hester and Coral, I'm sure you know them – in fact, they are your partners in the syndicate now.'

'Oh, them.' Ken did not sound enthusiastic. The 'them' was said with what could only be described as a sneer.

'The women were keen to get their money out, given the circumstances.'

'So they tell me. They were just here, the lawyers explained to them how the syndicate worked in terms of the contracts. I told them the same thing I told Matthew and Lewis, may they rest in peace. We three signed up with Anthony after a good lunch, and then the two of them got cold feet. It seems they just didn't have the stomach for investing at this kind of level. But I do.'

Ken said this as if he, himself, had extensive experience in such matters. 'No way was I pulling out,' he said. 'I'm sorry, but I finally got in on something big, the opportunity to make some proper money. I wasn't going to let them ruin my chances. Not this time. They messed things up with the band, all of them. All those years ago, we had success in the palm of our hands.' He held his hand out, fingers curled up, as if he were cradling something precious. 'You know what I could have been today? I've spent a lifetime thinking about that.'

He looked so sad and desperate, Julia felt sorry for him. Imagine, still smarting over a forty-year-old brush with fame.

There was a long moment's silence, and then Ken said calmly, 'They're not going to ruin this for me too. I'm sorry for what happened to Lewis and Matthew, I really am. But I need this break. I need it. And those widows aren't going to change my mind.'

'I can see you're quite determined, Ken.'

'I am. They'll thank me in the end, when they're rich.'

'Well, good luck with it,' Julia said, turning towards the front door. 'I hope it works out well for all of you.'

'Thank you,' Ken said, opening the door. Julia and Jake steeled themselves and launched determinedly into the wind and up the path.

'And thanks for bringing the book,' he called after them. 'And the muffins.'

27

When Julia, Tabitha and Jake arrived at Sean's in the early evening, it was already well dark, and cold. They were pleased to step inside the warm aromatic fug of the kitchen and unravel themselves from their coats and hats and scarves. It was a hive of activity. Sean had a chicken roasting in the oven, glowing golden through the glass. Laine and Jono were 'on vegetable detail' as Laine put it, their two dark heads bent over an iPhone propped up against a bottle of olive oil.

'Smash the garlic with the side of the knife and add to the sizzling butter...' Laine read out loud.

'That sounds promising already,' said Julia.

'You're so right. You can't go wrong with butter and garlic. What are you making?' asked Tabitha.

'We're trying a new spinach recipe,' Jono said, pounding the side of his fist down hard on the knife, and releasing a strong smell of garlic. 'Spinach with almonds, za'atar, red onion and lemon.'

'Gosh, that sounds good.'

'I'm putting the baby spuds on now,' said Laine to Jono. 'I think they'll take about twenty minutes.'

'OK, timing should be good with the chicken, right, Dad?'

Sean looked at his watch. 'That's right. Fifteen minutes or so and then it should sit for a while.'

'Do you want me to set a timer for the potatoes, Lainie?' Jono asked.

'Nah, I'll keep an eye on them.'

Julia caught Sean's eye, and they smiled gently. She knew that he, like her, was observing the easy back and forth between the two young people, the way they worked together and communicated gently, anticipated needs and passed utensils, and moved past and around each other at the stove in the little domestic ballet that was cooking together. And it made him happy to see.

'Can I help at all?' Julia asked.

'And me!' said Tabitha.

'We've got it,' said Jono cheerily. 'You relax.'

'All right then,' Julia said, putting the apple crumble on the sideboard. 'It's still warm, and we can pop it in for a minute or two before we eat.'

'Yum, apple crumble, that's my favourite,' said Sean.

'Really? Well, that's a lucky surprise, isn't it? I had no idea,' she said, giving him a friendly nudge in the ribs.

'Of course you did. Thank you. Shall we leave the chefs to the kitchen?'

Sean, Julia and Tabitha went through to the sitting room, where a fire was alight. Jake and Leo were already lying in front of it, tummies to the heat source. A bottle of Pinot Noir stood on the sideboard, opened, but not yet poured.

'Ah, well this is very nice and cosy,' said Tabitha, standing in front of the fire. She stretched her arms over the dogs, reaching her palms towards its warmth. 'Sunday night at mine is usually a boiled egg and an early night.'

'Mine too, actually. Sometimes I push the boat out and open

a tin of baked beans. But the kids wanted to cook, and the weeks are so busy with everyone working,' said Sean.

'The kids...' said Julia teasingly. Jono and Laine were both well into their twenties, as was Julia's Jess, but somehow, they were still 'the kids'.

The doorbell rang, and they heard the hubbub of young voices in the kitchen. The dogs raised their heads, but decided not to involve themselves in the welcome. 'Speaking of the kids, that'll be Dylan,' said Sean.

Dylan was Jess's ex or maybe-sort-of boyfriend. After their whirlwind romance on Jess's trip to Berrywick for her father's wedding, when Jess had gone home to Hong Kong, she and Dylan had decided that 'a long-distance thing would be crazy'. So said Jess, although Julia knew for a fact that the two of them kept in almost daily contact, and that Jess hadn't dated anyone since she'd got back home. It sounded very much like a 'long-distance thing' to Julia. She felt her heart clench slightly at the thought of her Jess, so far away. She'd like to have her daughter in the kitchen with the others, making the gravy, or tossing a salad.

Dylan's shaggy head appeared at the door. 'Hello, Dr O'Connor, hello, Julia, hello, Tabitha.' He was dressed, as usual, in a style that Julia thought of as urban lumberjack, in a green-and-black plaid shirt over a long-sleeved black sweater and black jeans. He wore a fleece-lined suede jacket over the top of it all against the cold. 'Thanks for the invitation, Dr O'Connor.'

'My pleasure, Dylan. Please call me Sean.'

Dylan laughed and shook his head. Sean O'Connor had been his family doctor forever. To call him by his first name was unthinkable, no matter how many times Sean invited him to do so.

'I'll go and see if I can help in the kitchen,' he said, and disappeared from view.

'He's a good chap,' said Sean, when the door closed behind Dylan. 'What's happening with him and Jess?'

'Unclear,' said Julia. 'They obviously have some meaningful connection. She's eager to get back to England for a visit, which makes me happy of course, but I think it's as much to do with seeing Dylan as it is with me.'

'It's Jake,' Tabitha said, deadpan. 'He's the favourite.'

'Well, she'll be here next year, around Easter it seems,' Julia said. 'And I have to say I think Dylan is a big drawcard.'

'Ah, young romance,' said Tabitha. 'My niece is getting married next year, did I tell you?'

'I don't think so.'

'My sister Luanne's eldest. I'll be going to Ghana for the wedding. It's been nearly five years since I was there.'

'What a lovely thing to look forward to, Tabitha.'

'It is. I'll have to up my game, though. Those women know how to *dress!*'

'Come on now, you can hold your own next to anyone. You always look great.'

It was true: Tabitha was stylish and striking, with her grey curls and bold accessories, and her youthful energy and kind manner.

Tabitha patted her stomach in a friendly way and said, 'There's the five pounds to lose still.'

Julia laughed at the mention of the five pounds, which had been an ongoing joke between them for decades, 'Oh go on, you're perfect as you are. Besides, those five pounds are very happy with their current situation.'

'They've certainly been there a long time,' Tabitha said.

'Sitting tenants, I'd say...'

'They've got squatter's rights...'

Laine appeared at the door, interrupting the women's laughter. 'Supper's ready,' she said. 'I checked the chicken, Sean

– it's perfectly cooked. And we popped the crumble into the oven, Julia.'

'It's nice having competent grown-up kids in the house, isn't it?' Julia whispered to Sean, as they followed Laine into the kitchen. The cooking mess had been cleared and the table set with the food in the middle. The chicken shone golden in the centre. The spinach dish looked like something from a magazine – or a website or app, Julia supposed, seeing as that was where everyone got their recipes from these days. Nuts and herbs and slices of red onion were scattered over its top, and the steam that rose from it carried the scent of exotic markets, where spices were piled in brass bowls.

It was a merry scene, hands passing plates and bowls around, murmurs of pleasure as the food was tasted, and snippets of conversations, updates on each other's lives and shared laughter.

Laine was working part time at a design studio. She liked it, but she wasn't sure if it was what she wanted to do forever; the new road signs that Julia and the road safety committee had arranged would be going up next week; Jono was spending less time at reception at the vet, and more time handling the animals – he had been given a small pay rise; a virus seemed to be doing the rounds; Dora from the sweet shop had twisted her ankle and was hobbling about on one of those moonboots, poor thing; Tabitha had signed up for an online poetry workshop – she was nervous, but excited; the secret to good gravy was to make it over a low heat, and whisk constantly...

And so the conversation flowed.

Before long, the chicken was reduced to a carcass, and the spinach bowl had been scraped clean. Not even a single baby potato had survived to tell the tale.

'Time for apple crumble,' said Julia, pushing herself up from the table.

'You sit,' said Jono, waving his hand. 'I'll get it.'

He got to his feet. Julia sat down, thinking – not for the first time this evening – how different Jono was from the young man she had met less than a year ago. That Jono had been lost, depressed, unmotivated and lonely, and now here he was with a job he enjoyed, a lovely girlfriend, and a plan to study further. Most gratifying of all, he and his father, who had drifted apart almost to the point of estrangement, were close and loving.

When they'd finished the crumble – accompanied by a lake of thick yellow cream – Tabitha stifled a yawn. 'Ooh, I'm so sorry. You know me, my candle flickers early.'

'No need to apologise,' said Sean. 'I think we are all in the same boat. Well, not the young, I suspect. But the rest of us.'

Julia got to her feet. 'Yes, it's been a lovely evening, but I think Tabitha and I should be on our way.'

'It is a Sunday night, after all. Work tomorrow. Another long day at the coal mines of the library, hey, Tabitha?' joked Sean.

'Yes indeed. But then I'm only working half a day on Tuesday, because I'm going to a funeral in the morning.'

'Who died?' asked Jono.

'A woman called Lydia, who worked at the butcher's,' said Tabitha, who was at the door, taking her outdoor clothes off the hook, and layering up. 'Poor thing died quite suddenly.'

'I'll be at the funeral too,' said Sean. 'She was a patient of mine.'

'Was she now?' Tabitha asked. 'She always looked hale and hearty when she came into the library – apart from bunions, which she complained about endlessly. But I suppose you never can tell what's going on inside. I heard she went to bed and just didn't wake up.'

Sean didn't say anything. There was an awkward moment when everyone remembered that of course, Sean couldn't comment, being Lydia's doctor.

'I didn't know her, really,' said Julia, breaking the odd

silence. 'But I was sorry to hear about her death. Such a shock when someone goes unexpectedly.'

'We really have to cherish every moment, don't we?' said Laine. 'Be kind, be loving, do our best for each other, because, I mean, who knows what might happen to us or to anyone else?' Her words came out with real sincerity, but were so unexpected that they were met with an awkward silence. 'Not to be weird or anything...' she said, with an embarrassed laugh. Her face was flushed.

'Not weird at all!' said Julia, patting the girl's hand. 'You are absolutely right. Life is unpredictable and uncertain. None of us knows what's coming our way.'

Julia, for one, could not have predicted how the next morning would go.

28

Julia gazed down at the phone in her hand. On its screen, a mildly perplexing message from DI Hayley Gibson.

I need to talk to you. Can I come over?

Yes of course. I plan to be here most of the day.

12?

That's fine. Everything okay?

See you later.

On the face of it, it was a simple exchange to make an arrangement for a visit. But a deeper look showed a number of oddities that bothered Julia.

For a start, DI Gibson was not given to consulting her out of the blue. What did the detective need to talk to her about? Julia wondered if it was related to a case. But what did Julia know that could be of any help? Unless it was a personal matter. Something to do with Hayley's new relationship, perhaps?

But why didn't the detective just phone? Hayley was a busy woman, with two active cases of unnatural deaths on her desk. And yet, here she was proposing to drive to Julia's house in the middle of a working day. It *must* be related to the cases.

The last and most concerning thing was that she hadn't answered Julia's question: 'Everything okay?'

Julia tried on the idea that she was reading too much into the exchange. Hayley tended to be brusque in her communication. The absence of a 'yes, fine' didn't necessarily imply that everything *wasn't* okay.

'This is ridiculous,' she told herself, firmly. 'Hayley will be here in a couple of hours and all will be revealed. It's probably nothing to get worked up about.'

The thing about giving oneself a lecture was that no matter how reasonable the lecturing self's position might be, the worrying self didn't always take it on board. What was required, thought Julia, was a distraction. Something that would occupy one's time and energy, and keep the worrying mind busy.

Julia had just the job.

The woodpile, which had been neatly stacked for winter, had collapsed on the one side. The logs that were lying about the place needed to be put back. It was a job that required concentration, the application of thought, as well some physical exertion. That should keep her mind off things!

Fortunately, it wasn't raining, nor was rain expected for the next hour or so. And the weather was a little warmer than it had been. Julia changed into a pair of corduroys that had belonged to Peter, her ex-husband. He had retired them a decade ago, and she'd adopted them for gardening. They were not what you'd call stylish, but they were warm and hardy. She put on thick socks and Wellington boots, a big pullover, and her leather gardening gloves.

She felt less anxious already. She always felt better with a task ahead of her, and even better with a task completed!

Jake had picked up on her energy and was following her around the house eagerly, trying to ascertain whether whatever was happening was in his best interests. Could it be a walk? A drive? A play in the garden? Might there be a snack component to the busyness?

'Come on then,' she said, opening the kitchen door. Jake shot out. Chaplin ambled to the door, and stood in the doorway, considering his options.

'Come on, kit-cat, inside or out?' she said.

He sat down, and attended to the grooming of his smart white bib, his little head bobbing up and down, his pink tongue flashing.

'I'm not leaving the door open,' she said after a minute or so. She stepped past him and pulled the door slowly towards her, calling his bluff. It was halfway closed when he made his choice, and dashed out. The animals were frisky in the cold morning air, and Julia watched them with pleasure as she made her way to the woodpile. She set about putting the fallen logs neatly back into the pile. It was, as she expected, a rather satisfying task, and required just enough attention to keep her mind from straying towards the detective's visit.

Voices drifted over the fence from Hester's house. Julia straightened up and peered over to see Hester and Coral by the beehives.

'Good morning,' she called.

Hester spotted her immediately. 'Hello, Julia! What are you up to?'

'Sorting out the woodpile. And you?'

'Checking on the bees, giving them sugar for a winter snack. Coral wants to learn the ropes of beekeeping.'

'It's so interesting. I would so love to get a beehive,' said

Coral, wistfully. She was wearing well-fitted jeans and a green pullover, with the collar of a floral shirt peeking out from under it. The wellies on her feet were red. The outfit was understated and positively outdoorsy compared to the hot pink suit she'd been in last time, although she still sported a touch of make-up and a bouncy hairdo. Her manner, in comparison to her hair, was subdued. She sighed, and said, 'It's probably too soon for me to make decisions, really. I might have to move house, and that wouldn't be fair on the bees. With Lewis gone and the money tied up, I can't afford to stay where I am. Everything's up in the air. And it's all so complicated.'

Hester patted Coral's shoulder. 'One step at a time. Let's wait and see what the lawyers say about the contract,' she said. 'I fully intend to get us that money back, you know.'

'You're talking to lawyers?' Julia asked.

'Yes. It doesn't hurt to get a professional opinion. I'm not just going to accept what Anthony Ardmore says. Or do what bloody Ken Payne wants. One way or another, we're sorting this out.' She turned to Coral. 'We know what we need to do, and we've done it.'

'You're right, Hester, I just get overwhelmed sometimes,' Coral said. 'And then this morning...'

'Do you want to tell Julia what you found?' Hester asked gently.

'Oh, I don't know... It's difficult... It's personal.'

'Julia's clever about things. You might ask her what she thinks.'

'I'll come over,' Julia said, her interest piqued by the strange conversation.

'Okay, I'll go and get it,' said Coral, trotting towards the house.

Suspecting that this was a conversation that might be easier without a garden fence between them, Julia made her way round the front of the houses, exiting her gate and coming in at Hester's. Coral was walking up the path, holding a card in her hand. 'I found this in the car, in the glove compartment,' she said, handing it to Julia.

Julia read the text, which was handwritten in capitals: *YOU THINK YOU CAN JUST DO WHAT YOU LIKE. I WON'T LET YOU RUIN MY LIFE. YOU WILL PAY.*

There was no postage stamp. It must have been hand delivered. It wasn't scuffed, and the edges were sharp. It didn't look as if it had been hanging around the car for very long.

'What do you think it means?' Julia asked calmly, although her heartrate had increased to a canter.

'I don't know. I wondered if it might be from one of Lewis's...' Coral straightened up and pulled her shoulders back in a posture of strength and dignity, and finished her sentence: 'Friends.'

Julia waited.

'The ladies always liked Lewis. They sometimes made advances. He was a good husband, but he wasn't a saint. Over the years, there have been occasional... misunderstandings. People get over-involved, they have expectations. There's disappointment. Anger.'

'I don't suppose you know when it arrived?'

'No.'

'Have you shown this to the police?'

'The police? No. You don't think Lewis was run over by a jealous girlfriend, do you?'

Julia turned over the postcard. The picture on the back was of a rough and windswept landscape with a shaft of sunlight breaking through a layer of thickly curdled clouds. It was a generically beautiful moorland scene that could have been anywhere.

'No,' she said, in answer to Coral's question. 'No, I think that's unlikely.'

She turned the postcard over again, and read the small printed description below the angry capital letters.

Edinburgh Castle Gardens.

'You need to take this to the police,' Julia said, holding it carefully at the edges, although she suspected it was too late to save any fingerprints that might have been there. 'It might be useful in the investigation. It might be a clue.'

'I agree with Julia,' said Hester. 'The police should see it.'

'Oh, I don't know,' said Coral. 'Digging up old hard feelings, answering personal questions. Tarnishing Lewis's good name. And it's probably not even relevant.'

'Come on,' said Hester. 'I'll come with you to the police, and I'll throw in lunch at the Buttered Scone. How does that sound?

'It sounds good,' Coral sighed. 'You're probably right, both of you. I'll take it to the police.'

'I'll go in and get my car keys and I'll drive you,' said Hester kindly.

Julia was about to explain to the widows that there was no need to go to the police as the police were coming to her, when she spotted DI Hayley Gibson coming down the path. And she looked like she meant business.

The detective sat opposite Julia at her kitchen table, the postcard between them. Hayley had placed it in a clear plastic evidence bag – rather belatedly, seeing as it had already been passed from hand to hand by the other three women. She stared fixedly at it, and drummed her fingers lightly on the table, as if it might at any moment give up its secrets.

Julia waited. The kettle heated noisily on the stove behind her.

'What do you think?' Hayley said finally, gesturing towards the postcard.

'Well, as you heard, Coral thinks it might be from a woman. She said the ladies liked Lewis, although I suspect it was a case of Lewis rather liking the ladies.' Julia paused for a moment. Hayley didn't usually like her speculating, but she had asked a direct question this time. 'I had another thought. The picture is of a place in Scotland, and Ken lived in Scotland, so naturally, I'm thinking it might be from Ken. And although he comes across as rather placid, even rather down-at-heart, at least when I've seen him, he's a guy with a history of anger. There's a lot of bitterness in him, especially towards Lewis and Matthew. It goes back to their younger days in the band. And then there was conflict over the investment syndicate at some point, when Matthew and Lewis got cold feet. So, I don't know. Maybe Ken was threatening Lewis.'

Hayley nodded, slowly, and scratched at a drop of candle wax on the kitchen table. She seemed distracted, as if there was something else on her mind.

The kettle reached a boil. Julia got up and switched it off, but sat down without making tea.

'Hayley, why are you here? You didn't come to talk about the postcard, and Ken.'

'As it happens, I *am* here to talk about Ken,' said Hayley. 'I hear you visited him yesterday.'

Julia was taken aback. 'Yes, I did. I dropped something off for him.'

'Muffins.'

'Muffins? No. A book. There was an old book of his that had been donated to Second Chances, which Wilma thought he might want. I offered to deliver it. What's all this about?'

'Ken was admitted to hospital. Suspected poisoning.'

'Gosh, how awful!' Julia looked at Hayley, who was staring at her intensely, a small frown between her eyebrows. 'Wait, do you think it was deliberate?'

'Julia, I have to tell you that this is an official police investigation. If you want to have a lawyer present, that is your right.'

'A lawyer? Hayley, what are you talking about? No, I don't want a lawyer. Why would I need a lawyer?'

'Initial tests indicate that the source of the poison is the muffins you brought to Ken. They're doing a full assessment of the poison used now. Fortunately, he thought they tasted odd, so he only ate about a quarter of one. He started to feel dizzy, and had stomach pains. Luckily, he went to the emergency room. If he'd eaten the whole thing, he might have died.'

'Good heavens. That's appalling. But I had nothing to do with it.' Julia thought for a moment, remembering the tray of muffins that she had picked up outside Ken's home, thinking that she was doing him a favour. In her mind she heard her mother's voice saying, 'The road to hell is paved with good intentions.' Julia had to make Hayley understand what had really happened. 'Hayley, I didn't bake the muffins.'

'Ken said you brought them.'

'I didn't *bring* the muffins, I brought them *in*. They were there when I got to Ken's house. They'd been left on the doorstep. I simply picked them up and handed them over. He was so busy gushing about the book, he didn't listen to me when I said I'd found the muffins on the doorstep. Hayley, you know I...' Julia stopped speaking, unable to finish her sentence she was so distressed.

'Julia, I know you well. Of course I *know* you didn't poison Ken Payne. At least not deliberately. But the big brass are all over the Berrywick police now. First the motor vehicle deaths, and now the attempted poisoning. I need to follow the rules, play everything by the book, dot every i, cross every t. It's out of courtesy to our friendship that we are having this conversation at your kitchen table and not in an interview room at the station.'

'At the station?' Julia could hardly believe what she was hearing.

'I knew you wouldn't poison anyone, Julia. But someone did. The question is, who? Who would deliver poisoned muffins to Ken Payne, and why?'

'Well, baking, poisoning... not to be sexist, Hayley, but it does have rather a female feel to it, as murder methods go.'

'Not just a feel,' said Hayley. 'Poisoning is a preferred method amongst female killers – although females are in the minority of killers overall, of course.'

A horrible, niggling thought was trying to make its way into Julia's brain, even as she tried to push it aside.

Hayley interrupted her struggle with a question: 'Did you see anyone else about the place when you got to Ken's? Walking in the road? Driving away?'

'No. Not that I recall.'

'Well, the key question to ask is: why would someone try to poison Ken? Who would benefit from his death?'

'He's just a sad guy trying to get his life in...' Julia stopped short. 'Well there is someone. I mean, I'm sure they wouldn't *kill* anyone, not at all, but in terms of motive...'

'Who?'

'I'm not suggesting that they...'

'The name, Julia. Spit it out.'

She glanced in the direction of her neighbour's house, where Hester and Coral were likely pottering about with the bees, quite unaware that their names were about to be mentioned to the police. Feeling horribly guilty, she said: 'The widows. Hester and Coral...'

'Matthew and Lewis's widows?'

'They want to get their money out of the investment with Anthony Ardmore, and Ken is standing in the way. He's their co-investor, and all three have to agree if they are to withdraw the investment. Ken stood in the way when Lewis and Matthew got cold feet. He prevented them from pulling out, and now the widows want to get their money out. They need the money. They are not going to just back off. Hester said just now that they know what they need to do, and they've done it. And Ken mentioned that he had just seen them yesterday when I was there. Maybe they left the muffins after he failed to agree with them. Backup plan, so to speak.'

'You think the widows tried to poison Ken Payne?'

'I *don't* think so. Or I don't want to think so. They're both lovely.'

'Lovely people do terrible things,' said Hayley, standing up. 'I'm going to talk to them right now.'

'Please don't let them think that I'm accusing them, Hayley. I'm really not.'

'I will be clear that it is entirely my own idea.' Hayley frowned slightly. 'It does make a terrifying sort of sense.'

When Hayley came back some time later, she looked grim.

'We didn't have our tea,' Julia said, turning the flame under the kettle back on.

She waited for Hayley to say something. Her stomach growled in the silence; she realised she also hadn't had lunch. When she could bear it no longer, she asked outright.

'So, how did it go? They denied it, I assume?'

'Well, I didn't go and accuse them of attempting to murder the man,' Hayley said. 'I asked them what they knew about Ken Payne.'

'And?'

'The way they describe it, they barely knew him at all. He'd been away all those years, so they hadn't seen him, and apparently the husbands barely even mentioned him. They didn't talk about the old days much, or the band. It was ancient history as far as they were concerned.'

'When did the widows meet Ken?'

'Only yesterday, after they realised that he was a co-investor.'

'And they wanted him to agree to try and pull their money out of the scheme.'

The kettle whistled, and Julia got up to set a tea tray.

'Yes. He refused, as you know,' Hayley said. 'The way they tell it, they weren't pleased. In fact, Coral said she was furious and has sent him an email just this morning giving him a good piece of her mind.'

'She's quite a livewire, is Coral,' said Julia, pouring the boiling water into the teapot. 'But if she'd killed him, she probably wouldn't be telling you that, or leading you to the evidence of conflict.'

'I read the email. It wasn't threatening. And if she sent it this morning, she wasn't expecting him to be dead.' Hayley paused. 'Unless that's what she wants me to think.'

Despite the unfolding drama, Julia's mind kept returning to her stomach, which had that hot, empty feeling. She opened the breadbin, and took out half a loaf of seeded wholemeal. She held it up to Hayley with an inquisitive expression. 'Toast?'

'Yes please. Anyhow, they said that they saw him yesterday, and then set up a meeting with the lawyer. I expect that's what Hester could have meant when she told you that they had done what they needed to do.'

'Did you tell them about the poisoning?' Julia cut two slices of bread and put them in the toaster.

'Eventually. Once they'd told me all they knew about Ken. They seemed genuinely surprised and horrified to hear about it. And of course, they denied having anything to do with it.'

'Did you believe them?'

'They were pretty convincing. I could probably get a warrant to search their kitchens, and test for poisons and so on, but I doubt I'd find anything.'

'Well, that leaves you looking for a poisoner, doesn't it?' Julia said. She poured the tea, adding a drop of milk, as Hayley liked it, and handed her the cup. The toast popped up. 'Marmalade?'

'Thanks. And yes, I'm still looking for a poisoner with something to gain from Ken's death. This whole business is just so strange,' Hayley said. 'I feel as if I'm missing a great big piece of the puzzle, but I can't see what it is. Or where it fits.'

Julia brought the butter and marmalade to the table. 'I know what you mean, Hayley. There are lots of bits that might sort of fit, but it's not coming together. Let's go back to Lewis and Matthew's murders – if they are murders. What do the victims have in common with Ken?'

Hayley sighed, and said: 'They grew up in the village. They went to school together. They knew each other as young men, and played in a band. Most recently, all three of them invested together with Anthony Ardmore.'

The toast popped up. Julia put a piece on each side plate and handed one plate to Hayley. 'It's not poisoned, I promise.'

Hayley gave her a reluctant twitch that passed for a smile.

'And we know that with the brand-new car, and the kitchen still to pay for, Anthony Ardmore would do just about anything to keep that money invested...' Julia continued. 'But Hayley, would he stretch to murder?'

'That's a question one can never really answer,' said Hayley thoughtfully, spreading butter onto her toast. 'But he didn't do it. Walter Farmer checked his alibi for Matthew's death. He was home with his girlfriend, Clarissa.'

Julia felt a jolt of realisation so strong that it was almost like an electric shock: 'Oh my word, Hayley! I've just realised, his alibi doesn't hold. Clarissa bought honey that day.'

Hayley frowned at her in confusion, or perhaps irritation. 'What are you talking about? What's honey got to do with it?'

'Anthony said he was at home with Clarissa, and not at the

market, when Lewis died. But I know for a fact that he and Clarissa *were* at the Christmas market. Or at the very least, Clarissa was at the market, so Anthony wasn't at home with her. I know, because she ordered honey from Hester that day. I was helping Hester with the orders and I delivered it to Clarissa yesterday. Which means Anthony must be lying.'

Julia hadn't got to the end of the story before Hayley was on her phone: 'Walter,' she snapped. 'Anthony Ardmore...'

29

'Take your pick,' said Flo, waving across the tea room, where only two tables were occupied. 'As you see, it's very quiet, even for a Tuesday. Not that I'm complaining, I'll be run off my feet by the end of the day, I've no doubt.'

'Here's nice,' Julia said, and sat down at a table that gave her a clear view down the main road towards the centre of the village. She mused that she must have sat at every table in the place, in her time in Berrywick. For preference, though, she usually took a window table. It suited her inquisitive nature.

'You can keep an eye on the road from that window table. Watch the passing parade,' said Flo, who was not unobservant when it came to human nature. 'Shall I bring you a menu?'

'No need, Flo.' As well as sitting at every table, Julia reckoned she had probably tasted everything the menu had to offer. All of it good. 'Jake and I came out early and we have had a good long walk already. I think I'm going to treat myself to the full English. And a coffee, please.'

'Right you are,' said Flo. 'And I'll bring a little something for himself.' She nodded towards Jake, who was gazing upon her with limpid eyes and the level of adoration befitting the Queen of the Buttered Scone and Bestower of Bacon Largesse.

'That's very kind of you, Flo, I'm sure himself will be most appreciative.'

The fellow in question slapped his tail on the floor so enthusiastically that the table shuddered, and the little glass salt and pepper shakers clinked against each other rather prettily.

Julia had made a promising start on the Sudoku in the morning newspaper when Flo came back with her coffee. 'I've realised why it's so quiet this morning, Julia. It's poor Lydia's funeral at eleven o'clock. The locals are all there, I reckon.'

'Oh yes, poor Lydia from the butcher's. I didn't know her well myself, but she was well-known and liked around the village.'

'She was indeed. Berrywick born, but she left for the bright lights of Bristol after school, like so many do. But Lydia came back a few years ago and got a job at the butcher's. And quite a character she was too.'

'A sad day for many in the village, I'm sure. And such a shock. She wasn't even unwell, from what I hear.'

'Fit as a fiddle, other than the bunions. Still, I must say, they've got a lovely day for the funeral. It's turned out nice, after the week we've had.' Flo smiled cheerily at the atmospheric good fortune, and returned to the kitchen.

It seemed an odd thing to say – 'lovely day for the funeral' – as if it were a picnic or a little summer party that was being planned, not a burial. Besides, some might say that a gloomy mood would be more fitting for the occasion than the bright, rain-washed day that sparkled outside the window. Julia was still thinking about funerals and weather when Flo returned with a large and brimming plate. 'Soft eggs, crispy bacon, just the way you like it,' she said, placing it in front of Julia. In her other hand was a smaller side plate with a doggy treat biscuit in the shape of a corgi, and an additional slice of bacon. 'And your breakfast, sir,' she said to Jake, putting the plate down on the table. Jake smiled his most charming smile, which was very charming, if you didn't mind the sight of drool.

Julia hadn't even speared the yolk of her runny fried egg when she saw Tabitha come in the door. She came over and sat down.

Julia smiled at her. 'This is a surprise. I thought you said you were going to Lydia's funeral this morning?'

'I was going to go, but it's been postponed.'

'Postponed? Whoever heard of a funeral being postponed? Why, was one of the family members ill-disposed?'

'I'm not sure, but it was all very sudden. They sent out a message this morning, and asked that it be passed on to everyone who might be coming. Some of us were already on our way to the church when we heard.'

Nicky Moore came into the tea room, and hung up her coat to reveal a subdued navy blue dress, tights, and black court shoes. It was a far cry from her bold everyday wardrobe choices, from which Julia surmised that she, too, had been dressed and headed for the funeral which had now been postponed.

'Well heavens, I must say this funeral business is all very mysterious,' said Nicky, sitting down at Julia's table without so much as an encouraging beckoning of the hand. 'There might be more to this than meets the eye.'

'There was a daughter in Perth,' said Tabitha, who tended towards more straightforward, less dramatic explanations than Nicky did. 'Perhaps she was coming for the funeral and her plane was delayed? That would explain the postponement.'

Nicky widened her eyes with the excited look of someone with high-value information to share. She paused to look furtively around the Buttered Scone to make sure she wasn't going to be overheard gossiping – as if there was anyone in Berrywick who didn't know that Nicky was one of the biggest chatterboxes in the village, perhaps in the district. Although not a malicious one. Seemingly satisfied that she wasn't going to be overheard, she leaned in. Julia and Tabitha couldn't help but lean in too.

'Apparently,' she said quietly, 'when they organised the funeral, nobody thought there would be a problem. But late yesterday the post-mortem results came out and the police said that the funeral can't go ahead yet, not if they want to have the body in attendance.'

'I didn't realise that there'd been a post-mortem,' said Julia. 'Why was that?'

'Well, the death was very sudden and unexpected. Right as rain she was, until she felt ever so faint and dizzy, went for a lie-down, and never got up. You need to know what the cause of death was, don't you. For the doctors, in case they missed something. Or maybe, I don't know, maybe they think it could be something genetic that killed her. Like a wonky heart valve or something. A girl I was at school with had that, her whole family did. There was a wonky heart valve gene, and you wouldn't know there was a thing wrong with you and then one day – poof! – the wonky heart valve would give up the ghost and you'd just keel over, dead. She got hers fixed – the valve, I mean, not the gene – and she's right as rain. Just had a baby, in fact, eight and a half pounds, Lord help her. What a size! I hope they check the baby's heart valve too, after that difficult birth.'

Tabitha and Julia sat quietly for a moment, processing Nicky's story, which had started with a sudden death and somehow ended in a challenging childbirth. Two more women came in, both in funeral attire, and took a table near the counter. Next came DC Walter Farmer, looking very smart in uniform, his shoes shined, and comb marks visible in his hair. He stopped to greet them.

'You all dressed up for the funeral, are you?' said Nicky. 'Ah, strange times, poor things. Well, I'd best be getting my own table, Kevin said he'd meet me for a quick cuppa. Give my love to Amaryllis, will you, Walter? Tell her I said to put her feet up while she can. Once that baby comes, there'll be no sitting about reading a magazine.' Nicky cackled heartily at her own wit, and decamped to a table a few over.

'Goodness, look at the time. I'd better be going too. I cancelled the locum librarian when I heard the funeral was postponed and it's only ten minutes until I have to open the doors of the Berrywick Library to mobs of eager readers.' Tabitha stood up too.

Julia laughed and stood up to hug her friend goodbye.

'So, how is Amaryllis doing, Walter?' Julia asked, sitting back down. 'And how are you doing?'

'Ah, all good, Mrs B. We had an ultrasound scan yesterday. We saw the baby. Would you like to see...?' Walter blushed. 'I mean, only if you have the time.'

'Of course! I'd love to see a picture, Walter.'

Walter sat down and pulled a square of shiny grey paper from his top pocket, where, she suspected, he had stashed it for ease of retrieval throughout the day. He wiped the table with a paper napkin and gently laid the paper on the surface, as if it were made of crystal. The dark and light grey smudges could have been anything or nothing, at first glance. But in a moment the splotches resolved into a pattern that Julia recognised. The bean-shaped pale area was a foetus, lying on its back. Walter pointed: 'That dot is a foot, and that there's the spine.'

'Oh, how marvellous, Walter. Your little baby.'

'The spine...' said Walter, wonderingly. 'I mean, the little vertebrae... Imagine how small they must be...' His voice tailed off, leaving just a bemused and somewhat terrified grin on his face.

Flo came up with her pencil poised over her notepad. 'What can I get you?'

'Ah, um,' Walter was so engrossed in the baby's spine that

he seemed unable to answer her simple question. 'Hot choco-late,' he said, finally. 'And a scone please, Flo.'

'Coming up.'

He popped the precious bit of paper tenderly back into his pocket.

'What a special time this is for you and Amaryllis. It's so good that the dads are involved in everything these days. It's a very good start to the bonding between you and your baby.'

'I almost didn't make the appointment yesterday. It's been so busy at work. The DI, she's got a lot on her plate, and she sends it my way too, of course.' As if to prove his point, DC Farmer's phone rang. 'Good morning, boss,' he said, smiling at Julia. It was indeed Hayley Gibson. Speak of the devil...

Some mumbled words could be heard from Hayley's side.

Walter nodded, and made affirmative noises, and when she'd finished speaking, said: 'So I checked the CCTV cameras this morning, and saw Anthony Ardmore's car leaving the market at 4.15 when Matthew was alive and well and selling his honey. I checked the number plate, and it was definitely the car, but from a different angle I saw that Clarissa was driving. No Anthony. He was at home, as he said.'

There was another long pause, during which some indis-tinct mumbling could be heard from DI Hayley Gibson. 'Good heavens... Do they know what... Really? Yes. Yes. I'll be right in. See you in ten.'

Julia had picked up enough of the conversation to say, 'Sorry about the wild goose chase with Anthony Ardmore, that was my fault. I told Hayley that Clarissa and Anthony had bought the honey that day.'

'Well, you were half right,' Walter said. 'She did. But they were both back at his place and watching *Agatha Raisin* on the telly when Matthew died. We also checked his phone records for the night that Lewis was killed, and he was on the phone with Clarissa for hours, at the relevant time. Put those two things together, and DI Gibson says we can safely rule him out. Now, I have to get to work.' He waved his arm to get Flo's attention. 'I'm sorry, but I can't stay and eat. Can I have my order as a takeaway, please?'

'Ah, police work is it?' asked Flo, with blatant curiosity. She didn't move.

'Yes. Soon as you can, if you wouldn't mind.'

This was unusually blunt for Walter. Flo nodded, and went on her way.

'Everything okay?' Julia asked.

'Well, not really. I'm sure you'll hear soon enough, but it seems Lydia's death wasn't from natural causes.'

'You don't mean...' Julia lowered her head and her voice. 'Was she killed?'

'Poison,' he muttered, behind his hand. Flo was so determinedly curious that she had been known to lip-read.

'Lydia *and* Ken?' Julia whispered back, barely moving her mouth.

'So it seems. But keep it under your hat, please. I shouldn't be telling you.'

'Of course, I won't say a word. But Lydia from the butcher's? I mean, why would anyone...?'

Flo appeared silently behind Walter with a steaming takeaway cup and a paper bag with a scone-sized lump in it. 'I popped in some butter and jam, and a few slices of cheese. Looks like you've got a long day ahead of you, Walter. You've got to keep your strength up!'

'Thank you, Flo, that's very kind.'

She hung around for a moment, looking hopeful, but when no information was forthcoming, she bade him goodbye and went about her business.

Walter got to his feet. 'Okay, Mrs B, I'm off. Lots to do at the station, what with this latest development.'

'Walter, wait,' said Julia, waylaying him with a hand on his arm. 'If Lydia and Ken have both been poisoned, presumably it's by the same person?'

'I would think so. I mean, what are the chances of there being two unrelated poisonings within days of each other, in a small village?'

'Close to zero, I would say. But why them? Why Lydia and Ken?'

'Off the top of my head, I can't think of a thing that could connect them. We'll ask Ken, but he's having a whole battery of medical checks today.' Walter turned towards the door, signalling the end of their conversation.

'Unless...' Julia said slowly.

He stopped.

'Unless what, Mrs B?'

'Unless Lydia was also an investor with Anthony Ardmore.'

30

Lydia was not an investor with Anthony Ardmore.

Julia was on her way home when her phone pinged in her pocket. She pulled it out and peered at the screen. She wasn't wearing her glasses, so she could see well enough to determine from the shape of the words that it was a message from DC Walter Farmer, but not well enough to read the text message itself. She patted her pockets for her glasses, without any success. She sighed in frustration, and for about the millionth time, thought to herself that poor eyesight – not being able to read a note, or the ingredient list on packaging, or the price tag or the size on an item of clothing – was possibly the most irritating thing about ageing.

'I think I'd rather have perfect eyesight again than my twenty-five-year-old figure,' she'd told Tabitha once.

'Not me,' Tabitha had said decisively. 'Give me that firm young body, and I'll happily search for those spectacles all day long.'

Sadly, this wasn't a choice that was available to them in the real world, in which one was stuck with an ageing body *and* poor eyesight.

Julia moved to the side of the pavement, stood under the awning for the hairdresser's, and fished around in her handbag. Her fingers made contact with the familiar shape and smoothness of her glasses. She pulled them out, put them on, and read the message:

> FYI. DI Gibson checked. Anthony A doesn't know Lydia, and she wasn't a client.

Ah well, that was a mystery for the police to solve, Julia thought, placing a thumbs-up next to DC Farmer's message, and putting the phone and the glasses in her handbag.

Her walk took her down the main road, underneath the Christmas lights which would be turned on in the late afternoon for the enjoyment of locals and tourists alike. She walked past the butcher's shop, which was closed. On the door was a notice advising customers that it would be closed all day because of the funeral of their dear staff member, Lydia Barrow. The notice featured a picture of Lydia behind the counter, as alive as anything, and laughing heartily. She was holding a meat cleaver up as if she were threatening the photographer, but the expression on her face confirmed that she'd been snapped in the middle of a joke. For reasons she couldn't determine, Julia took out her phone and took a picture of the notice

'Poor woman,' she muttered to herself, shaking her head.

'Yes, poor woman indeed,' came a voice from close behind her, causing Julia to shout, 'Good lord!' and startle so violently that she thought she might be the next person in the village to pass away suddenly and unexpectedly. She turned to see the wraithlike figure of Aunt Edna standing next to her, leaning perilously in the direction of the door to peer at the poster.

'No need to shout, young whippersnapper,' said the old lady, sternly, to Julia.

'Sorry, Aunt Edna!' Julia said, at normal volume, her heart

still pounding. 'I didn't hear you come up behind me. I was looking at the picture of Lydia.'

'Not a bad sort,' said Aunt Edna, in what passed for high praise. 'All sorts, Liquorice Allsorts. Good and bad. Same with people. I like the orange ones myself. But she's a good sort.'

'I didn't know her well, but so I hear.'

'So you hear? You hear her sing, you say? Singing in the choir like an angel. Not one of those little chubby ones, the singing angels with the wings.'

'Ah, well, that's good to know. She was a woman of many talents and good qualities, it seems. I'm sure she will be missed by many people. Anyway, I'll be on my way. Good to see you, Aunt Edna.'

'Is it?' the old woman said, sounding genuinely intrigued by the question.

Continuing down the main road and out of the village, Julia determinedly put all thoughts of dead people from her mind in order to enjoy the walk. She appreciated the absence of wind for the first time in weeks, and the ever-so-slight almost-warmth of the wan sun on her cheek. The leafless trees looked elegantly sculptural against the pale blue sky.

It was a fact of Julia's nature that she could only reflect on the beauty of the day for a minute or two, before her mind wandered back to more prosaic matters. In this case, Lydia Barrow. Lydia and Ken, Ken and Lydia. If they weren't co-investors with Anthony Ardmore, what else did they have in common? Of course, if Lydia had been born in Berrywick, she and Ken could have known each other in their youth. Like Lewis and Matthew. Like half the people in the village.

Julia felt the familiar prickle of a question or a vital piece of information trying to elbow its way into her consciousness. She knew from experience not to chase the elusive thought, but pretend she hadn't noticed it, and let it make its own way to her. Like a cat, she thought, bringing to mind Chaplin, who met her advances with a haughty air, but snuck onto her bed or her lap when her attention was elsewhere.

The band.

There it was, the little kitty of a thought, climbing into her head.

Edna! In a snap, her brain made another connection. Aunt Edna had mentioned that Lydia had a lovely voice, that she'd sung in the choir.

Had Lydia been in the band with Lewis and Matthew and Ken and Dominic? Could Lydia be the mysterious girl who was simply called Egg, in the caption of the band photo Julia had seen? It made sense. Both Egg and Lydia sang. Both Egg and Lydia grew up in Berrywick, but then disappeared. And both Egg and Lydia knew Ken. It seemed more and more likely to Julia that Egg and Lydia were one and the same. If only there was someone that Julia could ask.

Dominic Ardmore selected a smoky grey document box from a shelf of identical smoky grey document boxes neatly stacked in the attic, each with a label on the front, attesting to their contents. The label on the box Dominic pulled out read: *Old photographs – Dom*. When he opened it, the contents of the box belied the neat and organised exterior. Julia suspected that Molly had been behind the purchasing of the boxes, and Dominic had been responsible for filling this one with the mismatched envelopes and sleeves and folders, and the drift of loose prints at the bottom.

'I've been meaning to sort through these,' he said, somewhat shamefacedly scratching through the box. 'One day I'll file all the pictures, or digitise them. That would be a good plan.' It was unclear if he realised, as Julia did, that this would absolutely never happen.

He picked up a bulging folder marked *LONDON*, a rather

broad organisational category that didn't inspire great optimism in Julia. From amongst the yellowing A4 envelopes inside, he pulled a scrapbook with the Red Berries scrawled on the front. 'Ah, here's something that looks promising,' he said. 'Let's see if we can find one of Egg. Or Lydia, if that's her name.'

'It's just a hunch I have. She died recently, and I started wondering about her past. So you never recognised Lydia from the butcher's as Egg?'

'We don't go to that butcher much. Molly uses the free-range one out near Malmesbury. Buys in bulk.'

'And Lydia only seems to have come back to town recently,' said Julia. 'She'd probably changed a lot.'

'We've all aged,' said Dominic with a sigh, unaware that he had probably aged less than most and was still a very good-looking man.

'What about before the band? Did you know Egg from the village? Weren't you at school together?'

'If we were, I don't remember She was Matthew's girlfriend. Egg was younger than the rest of us. A couple of years is like a lifetime when you're eighteen.'

'True.'

'I can tell you that if her real name was Lydia, I never once heard it. Everyone in the band called her Egg. Even the promotional material used the name. It was, like, her stage name, too.'

'It's a funny nickname, I wonder how she got it. Egghead? Good egg? Scrambled egg? Peggy?'

He paged through the scrapbook. Many of the photographs looked to be from the same series Julia had seen earlier. Egg's face was one tiny pale oval amongst four other pale ovals. Much like, it had to be said, an egg.

Julia had an idea. She took out her phone and found the picture of the poster from the butcher's. She held it up next to the photograph.

'This is what Lydia looks... looked like... recently. Do you think there's any chance that she could be the same person?' asked Julia, looking at the photo of Egg next to the more recent one of Lydia.

Dominic frowned. 'It's hard to tell. It's possible. She's older and, um... rounder in the face. The nose seems like a different shape.'

'I understand,' said Julia, her eyes flickering from the lithe young woman in the photograph, to the cheerful butcher in the printed poster. They certainly bore little resemblance to each other. 'It's difficult to tell after all these years. People change so much. Even their noses.'

'I can't tell,' he said, and went back to flipping through the scrapbook. 'Maybe I can find a better one from back then.'

'What's that?' Julia asked, pointing to what looked like a newspaper clipping, pasted onto the page.

'Oh, it's an article they did on us in the local paper. The *Southern Times*. I remember it because my mum was so proud! That's me on the left of the photograph... God, what was I thinking with that hair? Not to mention the trousers. And there's Egg...'

He handed the paper to Julia. She studied the picture. Then she turned her attention to the text, scanning it for any mention of Egg. She found a short paragraph referring to the singer:

> *The girl singer, who goes only as 'Egg', says she was inspired to start singing by listening to the choir at the church next door to the home where she grew up. Well, Egg certainly sings like an angel!*

Julia cringed momentarily at the term 'girl singer', remembering those days when almost everything was the domain of men, and, in the unlikely event of a woman partaking, the word 'girl' or 'woman' or 'female' or – heaven help us – 'lady' was inserted as a sort of prefix. Lady doctor. Female lawyer. But now wasn't the time for nursing old irritations. Now was the time for clues and connections! Egg had lived next door to a church. There were only two churches in Berrywick. And funnily enough, Julia knew someone who lived right next door to one of them. At least it was a place to start.

First thing tomorrow, she would investigate.

31

Julia was greeted at the gate by a writhing furry blur, yellow, black and brown, emitting yelps of delight.

'Come in, chaps,' called Pippa from the front door. 'Give Julia some space.'

A black blur broke away from the mass of blur and ran back down the path towards the front door, followed by two golden blurs. Julia opened the gate. The three blurs resolved into three little dogs that sat at Pippa's feet, their tails wagging proudly, while the fourth, chocolate brown one, affected deafness and continued to hurl itself at Julia's legs.

'Oh, the dear boy, isn't he just like you, Jakey?' Julia said to Jake, who was leaning against her leg, looking slightly wary of the frenzy of puppies. The puppy was, like Jake, brown and cute and friendly and clumsy, and the least obedient of the lot. But she didn't say that, she just fondled the silky ears. Jake sniffed and nuzzled his miniature like a kindly uncle.

'Come on in, Julia, the kettle's on. And you can tell me about this mysterious mission of yours, and what you want to know.'

Julia followed Pippa into the house, with the dogs trailing

after them. She felt like the Pied Piper, but with dogs instead of rats, the furballs tumbling over each other and hanging onto Jake's tail. Pippa shooed the puppies and Jake straight outside to play in the back garden, which calmed things down considerably.

Over big mugs of Earl Grey tea, Julia gave Pippa an abridged version of her mission: 'I'm trying to find someone who might be able to solve a mystery. I'm looking for someone who used to live near here a long time ago, and I'm hoping you might be able to help me find her.'

'Oooh, that's very intriguing! Of course I'll help if I can. Who are you looking for?'

'I don't know her name.'

'Ah, well that complicates things,' Pippa said with a laugh. 'Should I just shout out random people who live in the street?'

'Her nickname was Egg. There's a possibility she was actually Lydia, from the butcher, but I'm not sure of that. But I do know that she lived next door to a church in Berrywick. There are only two churches, so that's not very many houses.'

Pippa frowned. 'Doesn't ring a bell, but I suppose it's possible.'

'To further complicate matters, Egg lived in the village some years ago. About forty. You've been here a long time, haven't you?'

'I've lived here about twenty years, but I've known the house all my life. My mum and her sister grew up here. Mum moved away when she and Dad married, but we lived nearby and we came at least once a week to see my gran. I spent most of my school holidays here too.'

'Did you know the other neighbours at all?'

'Oh yes, we knew everyone who lived around and about. There was no one called Egg, though, as far as I know.'

'It was a nickname, and unfortunately I don't know her real name, unless it was Lydia. All I know is that she played in a band. A local band with other youngsters. It was called the Red Berries. And she would have been quite a lot older than you.'

'The people next door's surname is Bacon, if that helps.'

Julia thought for a moment. 'That could make a lot of sense! If her maiden name was Bacon, then that could be why they called her Egg! Was there a Lydia Bacon?'

'The parents were James and Ingrid, I think. And then there were only boys in the family,' mused Pippa. 'Mum used to say that they were like a litter of pigs, chaotic and muddy and always into her and her sister's business. Anyway, now it's Craig Bacon and his three sons there. The other brothers moved away.'

'Sounds like it's not them,' said Julia. 'I guess it would still be amusing if Egg and Bacon were neighbours. Is there someone older than you still living around here who might remember something?'

'I could ask my aunt Margaret. She grew up in this house, although she moved away from Berrywick quite soon after she left school. She might remember Egg.'

Pippa must have seen the doubtful look on Julia's face, because she said, 'Her tumour doesn't affect her long-term memory, although she can't always express what she remembers. Sometimes she remembers the most remarkable things. The other day we saw a picture in a magazine, a woman in a blue dress, and Aunt Margaret told me that it looked rather like the dress her best friend wore to the school dance! And if you ask her about her class from her first year at school, she'll probably be able to name every one of them.'

'The human brain is mysterious. It can be like that with brain tumours and injuries – very selective and uneven damage.'

'The doctor says it's different for everyone, depending where the tumour is. Poor thing, she doesn't know what's going on half the time, and she's dangerously clumsy. She was a wonderful baker, but she can't even do that any more unless I'm here to help. And I've had to take her car keys away. I feel sad for her, but I can't have her driving.'

'You're quite right, taking the car is the responsible thing to do. But it must be hard for her, losing her independence.'

'She gets a bit violent sometimes, which is the hardest. She is quite cheerful most of the time, like I told you, but when she lashes out... It doesn't happen often, but it's not fun.'

'You're a good woman, Pippa. And it's not an easy task you've taken on.'

'I must say, it's harder than I expected. Between her and the guide dog puppies, it can be a proper mad house. The social worker has been so helpful, and of course Dr O'Connor has been wonderful.'

'I'm pleased to hear that my profession and my partner have been helpful,' Julia laughed. 'Honestly, though, Pippa. She is lucky to have you to help her manage things, and to do it all with such kindness and respect.'

Tears came to Pippa's eyes, in response to Julia's gentle words. She blinked them away with a sad smile, saying, 'Ah well, we all do our best, don't we? I'll go and find her, shall I?'

Julia listened to Pippa's footsteps on the wooden floor. Listening to her speaking indistinctly to Margaret in a quiet and kindly tone, she turned to the window to watch the dogs, who had calmed down now. Jake lay on the grass, rolling and swivelling this way and that to scratch his back, while the puppies played on and around him.

'Aunt Margaret, this is Julia Bird.' As a kindness to Aunt Margaret, Pippa made the introduction as if the two women hadn't already met. 'Julia wanted to ask you about some of the people who lived around here when you were younger. She hoped you might know them.'

'I knew everyone. We all knew each other,' said Margaret. 'I remember everyone from those days.'

'Did you know a girl who went by the nickname Egg? She played in a band called the Red Berries,' said Julia.

'He called me Egg...' Margaret said, her face clouding over. 'That was his name for me.'

Julia didn't know what to think. Margaret was Egg! On one hand, she was thrilled to have solved that little mystery, but if Margaret was Egg, then it was back to the drawing board on the mystery of what connected Lydia to Ken.

'*You* were called Egg?' Julia asked gently, trying to keep the surprise from her voice. 'I thought perhaps Lydia Barrow was Egg.'

'Lydia? From the butcher's?' said Margaret, her eyes narrowed. 'She was *not* Egg. Not at all. I was Egg!' She paused, and muttered, 'Never liked that Lydia.'

'Aunt Margaret!' said Pippa, appalled. 'You *liked* Lydia! You made us take her a bottle of your special medication for her bunions.'

'She gave me the bad chops. Nasty, skinny ones with gristle,' said Margaret, smiling somewhat incongruously. 'She shouldn't have done that, should she?'

Julia tried to move the conversation away from Lydia and the quality of chops, and back to the band. 'So you were in the band, Margaret? The Red Berries? You were Egg?'

'*He* called me Egg,' said Margaret. She sounded proud.

'Who called you Egg?'

'He's gone now.'

'Who's gone, Margaret?'

'Matthew. It was his nickname for me. Margaret. Peggy. Peg. Egg. That's how he got to it.'

'Matthew Shepherd?' Julia asked.

Margaret flapped her hands in front of her face, as if she wanted to wave the question away. Although she didn't answer, her agitation told Julia that the name was the right one. She tried another gentle tack.

'I heard that you had a wonderful voice, Margaret. David, the record producer from London, told me you were extraordinary.'

A small smile lit Margaret's face. 'David? I remember David. He said that? Oh, how I loved to sing.'

Much to Julia's surprise, Margaret started to sing quietly:

> *'As white as the snow*
> *The Christmas trees glow*
> *And now I must go*
> *Hoooooooommmeee.'*

It was the same song that Hester had sung – the big hit that had nearly achieved fame and fortune for the band, but in Margaret's voice, it somehow achieved a mysterious and sad beauty. The song that before had seemed like an extremely weak attempt at seasonal rhyming was now an aching melody about having to leave.

> *'As red as the holly*
> *The holly is jolly*
> *And now I must go*
> *Hooooooommmeeee.'*

Margaret stopped after the chorus, looking quietly pleased with her efforts.

Julia swallowed a lump in her throat.

Pippa got up to let in the dogs, who were scratching at the kitchen door. Julia suspected that she was similarly affected, and was taking a moment to deal with the lump in her own throat. Jake and the puppies came in, their nails clicking on the kitchen tiles, and their cheerful canine energy lightening the mood.

'How lovely to hear you sing, Aunt Margaret. You should

sing more often!' said Pippa, sitting down next to her aunt and taking her hand. 'Mum always said you got the singing genes for both of you.'

'Ah well, your poor mum couldn't hit a note, but I could. I can hold a tune.'

'David said you were the real talent in the Red Berries,' Julia added. 'In fact, what he said was, "She was something really special".'

Margaret's smile spread: 'Oh, it was wonderful, being in the band. Matthew and I, we were in love. We were going to be famous. It was a dream come true at first. Until...'

She fell silent.

Julia had been wrong about the Lydia connection. Where Lydia fitted in remained a mystery, but Julia held out hope that Margaret could shed some light on the connections between Matthew, Lewis, and Ken. Julia spoke softly, 'Margaret, can you tell me what happened to the band? What went wrong?'

'It all went wrong, it went horribly wrong. It was Lewis's fault. All of it. Lewis ruined it for us all. He was a bad man.'

Julia waited for Margaret to continue.

'He always fancied me, Lewis. Tried it on a few times, made passes, even after I said no. You know those men who think they're God's gift to women? Think they can have whoever they want?'

'I do, I'm sorry to say. I know the type.'

'What goes round comes round, though,' said Margaret calmly.

Julia felt a shiver of apprehension. She remembered how sweet Dora had also implied that Lewis wasn't the nice man that he seemed to be. Had someone from his past taken revenge into their own hands? But that didn't explain Matthew or the attempt to kill Ken. The connections between the two dead men, the band, and Margaret, were so many and so tangled. Julia grappled for a way of making it all make sense.

Julia remembered what David had said: *It was the girl who scuppered the whole record deal... They were supposed to be in the studio... She just didn't pitch... Disappeared...*

It seemed so unlikely that she would disappear, and jeopardise the thing she had dreamed of. There must have been another reason for her non-appearance.

'Margaret, can you tell me what happened in London? Do you remember what you were doing there?'

'Oh, I remember. We were playing our music,' she said, calm and lucid as her damaged brain reached back decades to pluck out a treasured memory. 'You know the dream where you find out you can fly?'

Julia and Pippa nodded.

'It was like that. But with singing. My voice was strong and pitch-perfect. It was the best feeling. The band sounded good, too. I knew we were going to get a record contract. I *knew* we were going to be famous. I came out of the studio walking on air.' She smiled at the recollection. 'Then after, there was a party with champagne. I'd never had champagne before, imagine that?'

Pippa and Julia smiled.

'I shouldn't have had it though... That's when he...' She looked down at her hands. 'He... touched me. Like *that*.'

'Oh God,' Pippa whispered under her breath.

'Margaret, are you talking about Lewis Band?' Julia asked, gently.

'Lewis, yes. Bastard.'

'Did he assault you, physically?'

Margaret nodded, and when she spoke, it was in an anguished voice, as if she was a girl again, a young woman berating herself for her poor decisions: 'It was the dress. I was wearing a tiny dress, I still remember it, silver, all slinky, it felt like water. I bought it in Carnaby Street that morning. Never had anything like it before. Mum would never have let me go out like that, she was very proper, and she warned me about... what can happen, you know, to girls who dress like that. I thought I looked sophisticated, like a cool girl from a band, not like a little village girl in dresses her mum made for her on her Singer sewing machine. And, well, it turned out that the thing Mum warned me about... It happened. Mum was right. I should have known. If I'd worn the clothes Mum made, if I'd been the girl Mum brought me up to be... And I never could hold my liquor. If I didn't have the champagne, and then a whisky... Maybe...'

Jake, who hated sadness or conflict, sidled nervously up to Julia and put a paw on her thigh.

Pippa got up and stood behind the older woman's chair, her hands stroking her thin shoulders. 'Aunt Margaret, I'm so sorry for what happened to you. It's unimaginably horrible. But you must know that what that man did to you... It was not your fault. No matter what you wore or what you drank.'

Margaret seemed to snap back into the present. 'I know that *now*, Pippa dear. But I was young. And it wasn't like now. Women's Lib and Me Too and all that. I couldn't face him, or any of the band. The shame. The fear. I had a bath and got dressed. I threw that silver dress in the bin, and before anyone woke up, I ran away.'

'You went back to Berrywick?' Julia asked.

'I had to. I had nowhere else to go. I didn't know anyone outside the village. I had lived there all my life.'

'Oh, Margaret, I'm so sorry.'

'The band didn't last without me. Everyone was angry with me for ruining their big break. I couldn't tell them why. Lewis would deny it. There was no evidence. To be honest, I was angry with myself, too.'

'What about Matthew?' Julia asked. 'Didn't he help you? He must have been furious with Lewis.'

'I didn't tell him what Lewis did to me. I couldn't talk about it. I was sad and lonely. And angry with Lewis, with Matthew, with myself. I hardly went out. Lewis was living in the village, walking around cheerful as you please, as if nothing had ever happened. I didn't want to see him. I couldn't be a normal person any more. Matthew didn't understand. He never even asked me about that night. He should have known that something was wrong. Soon after we got home, he broke up with me. He said I had changed, and asked me why. But I couldn't tell him. I made him cry. But he should have *known*. He should have *asked*. He should have *realised*.'

'Oh no, I'm so sorry,' said Pippa, hugging her aunt.

Julia took the old woman's hand. 'You had an awful time, and no one helped you.'

'I did, I did... It was awful. I had no one to talk to... I couldn't tell anyone...' Margaret seemed to regress again, gabbling tearfully, 'Matthew said he loved me. But he left me. He left me all alone.'

32

The main road into Berrywick was lined with big white posters, attached to street lights, each with a single sentence.

Slow down, tortoises live here too!

Drive slowly, children bike on this road!

Slow down, dogs abound!

Be aware, children everywhere!

Julia felt a strange feeling of confusion and recognition. She recognised the words – after all, she had come up with the messages – but in all the drama with Aunt Margaret, she had completely forgotten that the posters were going to be put up that week. They must have gone up that very morning.

Julia was quietly delighted and slightly discombobulated by the fact that the words in the slogans had come out of her own brain. She drove on, in the direction of the police station, and saw the rest of her creations:

Drive slowly, our children walk to school.

Please drive carefully in our village.

Slow down, dog walkers ahead!

Tame driving keeps our wildlife safe!

They were pretty good, if she said so herself. Specific, official-sounding, but friendly. She was so busy reading her own road safety posters and congratulating herself on her copywriting that she failed to concentrate on the road. She looked up to see a pigeon standing in the middle of the road. Yanking the wheel to give the bird a wide berth, she almost scraped her tyre on the pavement.

'Mind where you're going,' shouted the old gent who was standing at the roadside, preparing to cross.

She jammed on brakes and mouthed: 'Sorry,' through the windscreen.

'Read the signs!' he said, jabbing an angry finger diagonally upwards towards the closest one.

She smiled to herself at the irony of it all.

'It's no laughing matter,' he said huffily. The pigeon eyed them both from the centre of the road.

Hayley Gibson was in her office with an expectant look on her face. 'So, what is it that can't wait until tomorrow?'

'Do you know Pippa Baker's Aunt Margaret?'

'The one who's ill?'

'Yes, she has a brain tumour, poor woman. It's been very hard on Pippa.'

Hayley frowned. 'You needed me to urgently know that things have been hard for Pippa Baker?'

Julia smiled. 'No, Hayley. Bear with me. Margaret, as it turns out, has a history with Lewis Band. Not a good one.' Julia relayed the story of the band and its young singer, fresh from a Cotswold village, and how she'd suffered at the hands of one of her fellow band members.

'If that Lewis Band was still alive, I swear, I would see him in prison, no matter how long ago the crime was committed,' said the detective, with quiet, cold fury. She steadied herself with a long, deep breath and said, in a more even tone, 'But I'm not sure that there is anything I can do now.'

'I just can't help feeling there's something more here, Hayley. That if we ask Margaret the right questions, she might lead us to the solution.'

'And you want me to ask those questions?'

'Yes,' said Julia. 'I know people. But you know crimes. You'll know what to ask.'

Hayley thought for a moment and then got to her feet. 'Let's go,' she said, pulling the jacket off the back of her chair, and swinging it over her shoulders in one swift, fluid movement. She was at the door before Julia had gathered her handbag and stood up. 'Come on,' Hayley said. 'Leave your car here. I'll drive us. We can talk on the way. I'll phone and tell Pippa we're coming. I need to speak to Margaret.'

'So after what Lewis did to her, Margaret left London and the whole record deal fell through?' Hayley asked as she drove.

'Yes, that's what it sounds like. And she went without talking to anyone, not even Matthew. So no one knew *why* she left. There was a lot of anger and disappointment.'

'I'm sure there was. And what about Lydia? Did Margaret tell you if she had anything to do with the band? She seems to have nothing in common with the others.'

'No connection to the band. Margaret knows her from the butcher's, of course. Grumbled about the quality of the chops she sold her. But she didn't know her from the old days, or from the band, as far as I know.'

'Mysterious.'

Pippa showed them through to the sitting room, which was bedecked with Christmas decorations. A fire was alight in the grate. It all looked quite festive. Even so, Julia's mood was sombre.

Hayley sat down and indicated that Pippa should do the same. Once Pippa was perched on the edge of her chair, Hayley said, 'I have some questions for you, and for your aunt, if that's okay.'

'I'll bring Margaret,' Pippa said, 'although I'm not sure how she can help you in your investigation, Detective. Whatever happened, it was so long ago. I can't see how it has any bearing on what happened to poor Lewis and Matthew.'

'It might be nothing, but I'd like to hear first-hand what she remembers,' Hayley said.

'She's not a robust person and the conversation about the assault really shook her up. She did some baking, which always calms her, and she had a little lie-down. I don't want her upset. You'll be gentle, won't you, Hayley?'

'Of course. I won't press her on the details of the assault. I'm more interested in the relationship dynamics at the time. And what happened after.'

'All right,' Pippa said, with some reluctance, and went to fetch her aunt. Once Margaret, Pippa and the pack of puppies were back and settled, Hayley got down to business.

'Margaret, Julia told me about the band, and what a good singer you were. She told me about your trip to London.'

'Long time ago.'

'Yes. Margaret, I know Lewis treated you badly,' Hayley said. 'And I'm sorry you went through such a terrible experience. If he was still alive, I would help you press charges against him, and make sure you get justice for what he did all those years ago.'

Margaret gave a humourless, monosyllabic almost-laugh: 'Hah!' Her eyes narrowed as she said, 'He paid the price in the end. He got his comeuppance.'

Julia and Hayley glanced at each other.

Hayley continued her questioning: 'Margaret, can you tell me about Matthew? He was your boyfriend, wasn't he?'

'We were in love. Sweet young love. Until... I ran away that night. He should have *known*. He should have helped me. I was so lonely.' Her voice wavered pitifully. 'I never forgave him for how he treated me.'

Pippa shot Hayley a warning glance.

The detective spoke gently: 'Have you seen Lewis and Matthew since you came back to Berrywick, Margaret? Did you see them before they both died?'

'Yes, I saw them.' Margaret's tearful moment was gone, replaced by rage. She spat out the words. 'All of them, laughing. Bunch of good-for-nothings.'

'Who are you talking about? Who did you see?'

'All of them. The people from the band. The boys' club. Together. Bastards.'

'Ken Payne?'

'Yes, him. And the other one. Dom. I saw them all,' Margaret said. 'I saw them all together. But they didn't see me. Too busy with their lunch. Laughing about the poor stupid girl I was in those days. Lewis was likely telling them the story. I could tell. They didn't see me. Not then, and not the other times. Never knew. Never saw it coming. Who's laughing now? Who?' A humourless shout of laughter exploded from her frail chest.

'Aunt Margaret, gosh, you are getting worked up. I think we could all do with a cup of tea and something sweet. I'll put the kettle on and get us a little something to eat,' Pippa said, standing up from the sofa. 'I think we should talk about something else. It's not good for Aunt Margaret to get so emotional. Perhaps you can speak to her another day.'

Pippa standing up disturbed the puppies who had been lying quietly at her feet. In the way of small Labradors, they went from snoozy balls of softness to wild zooming creatures in a matter of seconds. They went racing around the room as Pippa shouted, trying to get them to calm down, knocking into

Hayley, Julia and Margaret until the small brown puppy that had reminded Julia of Jake got entangled in Julia's handbag strap. In the process of trying to get aways, he pulled at the bag, still attached to the chair. As Julia leapt to her feet to untangle him, the chair fell backwards. The brown puppy pulled away, still entangled in the bag. The contents spilled out – a somewhat embarrassing mix of loose coins, a lipstick, a crumpled shopping list. The puppies gathered round to investigate, hampering Julia's attempt to scoop up the handbag detritus.

All eyes were on the scattered items, which had distributed themselves over a remarkably large area. Even Margaret surveyed the scene with a dazed expression.

'There it is!' she said, pointing at the floor with a quavering finger.

Julia grabbed a half roll of mints and a lip balm and put them onto the table.

'There it is. That's my St Christopher!' Margaret chirped.

'This?' Julia said, picking up the silver disc attached to a broken chain.

'Aunt Margaret has been looking for that medallion for ages. I thought it must have been lost, or just misplaced around the house,' said Pippa. 'How on earth did *you* get hold of it?'

Julia looked down at the St Christopher that she was holding. 'I found it on the road,' she said slowly, handing it to Margaret.

'I've no idea how it got there, but what a piece of luck that you found it!' said Pippa. 'How did you know it was hers?'

'I didn't know who it belonged to,' said Julia. 'But I thought someone might miss it, so I put it on the Berrywick Facebook page. There was no response and I forgot all about it. What a coincidence that it should belong to Aunt Margaret.'

Pipp smiled happily. 'Let me get that tea.'

As soon as Pippa left the room, Julia turned to Hayley and whispered, 'I found it near Lewis's body, Hayley.'

'At the crime scene?' Hayley hissed, her eyes narrowing. 'You found a piece of potential evidence at the crime scene? And you didn't hand it in?'

'It was a couple of days after the incident, and a little way away from exactly where it happened, and to be honest, I forgot about it.'

'You forgot.' Hayley sounded sceptical.

'Forensics had been and gone. The police tape was cleared away. It didn't seem important. I just popped it in my bag because I thought someone might be missing it, and I could return it. But I forgot it was even there.'

A small silent storm played over Hayley's face. Her team had missed a potentially useful piece of evidence. Julia had found it, but forgotten all about it. And she, Hayley Gibson, was angry with everyone, including herself.

Hayley turned to Margaret, who had sunk back in her seat and seemed to be having a small nap. 'Margaret,' she said loudly.

Margaret opened her eyes. 'No need to shout,' she said. 'I'm right here.'

'Is this St Christopher definitely yours?' she asked.

'Oh, yes. It was a present from my mum. It's got the saint on it, and also there's the chain. It must have broken.'

When it came to the questions of when and how she'd lost it, Margaret became vague. 'I suppose I dropped it. At the shops, maybe? Or on a walk. Or someone might have stolen it. Pippa never locks her door. I told her, you can't trust people. Maybe someone took it.'

Dusk was falling and the room was dim and grey. No one had thought to turn on a light. The fire had burned down, and needed another log. Instead of adding the bright and festive touch they had earlier, the Christmas bells and baubles now somehow managed to have the opposite effect, drawing attention to the gloom.

Pippa came back with a plate of muffins, which she put on the coffee table in front of Hayley and Julia.

The sight of Pippa looking so tired and pale reminded Julia of something.

'Pippa, you mentioned that Margaret stopped driving recently.'

Pippa looked slightly confused by the turn the conversation had taken. 'Well, I had to take her keys away, didn't I? She kept coming home with dents in the car and couldn't remember what she had driven into, poor thing.' Pippa gave a small laugh. 'I keep expecting a neighbour to claim for a postbox!'

Hayley and Julia exchanged a quick glance.

Pippa smiled and indicated the muffins. 'Help yourself. Back in a mo with the tea.'

Julia salivated at the sight of the muffins, and her tummy gave a low anticipatory growl. They looked delicious, deep golden brown, perfectly risen, and she'd had a very busy day with nothing to eat since breakfast. She reached for the plate, and then pulled her hand back, as if she'd been shocked. The little slice of banana pushed into the top of each one – she had seen those exact muffins before. In fact, she'd handed a plate of muffins just like that to...

'Ken Payne!' she said.

Hayley Gibson looked at her in surprise.

'The muffins!' Julia said, pointing. 'They look...'

Hayley caught on immediately. 'Has anyone eaten one of those muffins?'

Pippa came back in with the tea tray, the puppies trailing behind her. They looked delighted to see a room full of new humans, even if the humans seemed tense and distracted.

'What's going on?' Pippa asked.

Hayley didn't answer her question, but instead took a handkerchief from her bag, and picked up the plate of muffins, which she moved to a side table. 'Who made the muffins?' she asked.

'Aunt Margaret, of course. She's always been a wonderful baker, but she can only do simple things now. Scones and muffins. It's one of the few things she can still enjoy. It calms her down when she's agitated.'

'Nobody eat or drink anything,' said Hayley, reaching into her bag for her phone. 'Everyone sit down. We're going to be here a while.'

'What on earth are you talking about?' Pippa asked.

The puppies were looking for attention, jumping up at their legs, and trying to climb onto their laps. No one paid them any attention, let alone tried to wrangle them to order.

'Ken Payne was poisoned by a plate of muffins left on his doorstep,' said Julia.

'Luckily, he only had a bite or two and left it because it tasted funny,' said Hayley. 'He got very sick – vomiting and loss of motor function. The doctor in the emergency room found it peculiar, and did some blood tests. Poison, and strong pain medication. If he'd eaten more, he would have died.' She glanced at Margaret when she said it.

'A man was poisoned? In Berrywick? Good lord. Who would do a thing like that?' said Pippa.

Julia and Hayley looked at her. 'Someone with a grudge,' said Hayley.

Pippa looked pleadingly from Julia to Hayley and back again, hoping for confirmation that the notion was absurd.

'Why would Margaret have anything against this Ken Payne person? I've never even heard his name before today.'

'Pippa, think about it. Ken was in the band. So were Matthew and Lewis. And it's clear that Margaret was furious with them for what happened in the past.'

'If Margaret's muffins were poisonous – which I must say, I find hard to believe – then it was entirely by mistake,' said Pippa decisively. 'She might have put rat poison in the mix instead of flour – the woman has a brain tumour, you realise. I put all the dangerous substances up on the highest shelf, but when she gets an idea in her head, she's very stubborn. She might have been remembering some time in the past when they kept flour up there, or something. And I can't watch her every minute.' Pippa's voice rose.

Julia's heart broke for poor Pippa, who had tried so hard to take good care of her ailing aunt. She took her hand, and shook her head. She said gently, 'Pippa, I found that St Christopher at the scene of Lewis's accident.'

'This suggests that Margaret herself was there,' Hayley said. 'And I think that the forensics will find damage to her car which is consistent with hitting a person. Hard. Two people, in fact. It appears that Matthew died the same way, likely at the hands of the same person.'

'This is madness,' Pippa exclaimed. She looked at Julia pleadingly: 'Julia, please, explain to the detective that it's not possible.'

'Pippa, I wish I could... But I think Hayley is right. Margaret ran over two men, and when you took her car keys away, she poisoned the third. Unless I'm very much mistaken, Dominic – the fourth person at that lunch – might have been next.'

Hayley turned to Margaret, who had been gazing out of the window, seemingly unconcerned by the fraught conversation going on around her. 'What size shoe do you wear, Margaret?'

Margaret smiled. 'Four. Feet like a child, my mum used to say.'

Hayley turned back to Pippa and Julia. 'Consistent with the forensics.'

'There is no way my sweet, sick aunt is a murderer,' said Pippa. 'Not a chance.'

'The thing about getting old,' said Margaret, conversationally, 'is that people often underestimate you. Lewis saw me driving towards him, you know. He *knew* what he did to me back then. But he just stood there. Thought I would stop. Thought I didn't have the balls. Ha! He was wrong, wasn't he? Ran him over, and then again, just to make sure. My only regret is that he didn't suffer like I suffered all those years.'

Rather chillingly, Margaret described Lewis's death as if she were relating a story about a church jumble sale.

'Aunt Margaret! I can't believe you would do that,' protested Pippa.

Margaret turned and looked at Pippa, her eyes cold. 'I'm tired of being underestimated, Pippa dear. Very tired indeed.' Then she gave a warm smile. 'That's why I made some special muffins, dear. Where have they got to? I think all of you should have one.'

33

'Isn't that your friend the detective inspector?' Jono asked.

The whole table – Sean and Julia and Tabitha and Jono and Laine – looked up from their table at the Topsy Turnip in astonishment. The person coming towards them, moving slowly across the crowded room, *looked* like Hayley Gibson, but it seemed impossible that it was indeed her. She was wearing a bright green jumper, featuring a goofy red-nosed reindeer. On her head – and this, honestly, Julia could not believe – was a headband with antlers.

Julia could only nod.

'She looks... different,' said Jono.

'I saw my dentist at the gym once,' Laine said. 'She was wearing a leotard. Couldn't believe my eyes. It was so confusing. I was like, where's your apron thingy and your mask, and why aren't you wearing those magnifying glasses? And why are you so *cheerful*?'

Tabitha cackled at this anecdote, and said, 'Ah, Laine, you are a card.'

Behind Hayley was Sylvia in a red dress speckled with star-shaped snowflakes. From a close-fitting bodice, it flared out prettily into a short skirt, under which she wore green and red striped wool tights, and little boots. Somehow, she looked completely appropriately attired, Christmassy and rather gorgeous, and also just like herself.

Hayley was at the table now, and they all did their very best to behave as if there was nothing remarkable about her attire, and as if this wasn't the first time in living memory that she had been seen in an outfit other than her uniform of dark trousers (occasionally jeans on weekends) and a rotation of plain and sensible shirts and jackets, varied only slightly, as the weather conditions demanded.

'Hello!' said Sean, rather too loudly. 'And Merry Christmas Eve to you both! Don't you look festive?'

'Sylvia loves Christmas,' said Hayley, somehow managing to look proud and pleased and mildly embarrassed all at the same time.

'Oh, I do!' said Sylvia.

'Which is how I find myself somewhat unexpectedly at the Topsy Turnip Christmas Eve Celebration and Singalong,' clarified Hayley.

'Hayley is very kind to indulge me.' Sylvia put her arm through Hayley's and squeezed her.

The detective blushed and grinned and said, 'Well, it is Christmas, after all.'

'Dentist,' muttered Laine out of the side of her mouth, to Jono.

'Hayley, look how nicely your outfit matches Leo's,' said Jono. And indeed it did. Leo was wearing the green jumper Julia had bought at the Christmas market. Its red edging matched Rudolf's nose. 'We should get a picture.'

Hayley's arched eyebrow was answer enough. She and Sylvia sat down, without photographic evidence of their good cheer.

'Well, isn't this festive? And it's filling up fast. We should probably order something to eat before the music starts.' Sean waved politely at the waitress, who smiled and nodded to indicate that she'd noticed.

'Shall we get nice bar snacks to share?' said Julia.

'Good idea. Everyone okay if I order a selection?'

'I'm happy to put my fate in your hands, Sean,' said Tabitha. 'Order away.'

The waitress came over, her piercings glinting in her nose and eyebrow as the coloured Christmas lights flashed on and off, her pen poised over her notepad. 'Well, if it isn't Laine King!' she exclaimed, lowering her pen and pad.

'Bonnie!' Laine got to her feet to hug her. 'Wow, it's been ages.'

'I was away for a few years. Came home a month or two ago. I heard you were wandering about the place with a goat,' Bonnie said, peering hopefully under the table, but locating only two dogs in Christmas gear. Leo looked up and wagged his tail in welcome.

'I do indeed, but she's not here. Most venues are very species-ist. Happy to let dogs come along with their humans, but arrive with a goat...'

'It's not fair, really. How are they ever going to hear live music with that attitude?'

The girls laughed, and Bonnie said briskly: 'Now, what are you having?'

'We're going to share...' said Sean, running his finger down the bar menu. 'I was thinking, maybe...'

'You'll want the Scotch eggs, they're just out the fryer, and my other favourite is the fried cod.'

'Happy to go with whatever you recommend, Bonnie. Enough for five.' Sean snapped the menu shut. 'Thanks, Bonnie.'

'I'll be round to see that goat,' she said to Laine as she left.

'Ken will be on any minute,' said Julia. 'I saw him earlier

and he said he's playing one or two songs, sort of a warm up for the Christmas Eve Celebration and Singalong. But he is obviously thrilled to be playing again.'

'Probably thrilled not to be dead from poisoning, too,' said Jono.

'Jono!'

'Just joking, Dad, didn't mean to be unkind. I know it's not a joking matter.'

'It probably does give you something to think about though, a near-death experience,' said Tabitha. 'Re-evaluate your life. Carpe diem and so on.'

'Well, poor Lewis and Matthew didn't get that chance,' said Hayley, looking a lot less festive than her jumper. 'Or Lydia, for that matter.'

'Why did she kill poor Lydia?' asked Tabitha, who Julia had filled in on the relationships in the band. 'What did Lydia have to do with the band and the assault?'

'Nothing. Margaret had got it into her head that Lydia was rude to her. And gave her sub-par lamb chops. Emboldened by her success in getting rid of the two men, she killed Lydia by giving her a handful of her industrial-strength prescription painkillers. Told her they were a homeopathic remedy for bunions, it seems. Then she used the same painkillers crushed up and mixed with rat poison in the muffins she gave Ken. The rat poison actually saved him because it tasted weird and made him vomit – if she'd stuck to the painkillers, Ken would probably be dead.' Hayley gave a little shrug, as if to convey the randomness of life, and death by poison.

'Is Margaret going to go to prison for murder?' asked Julia.

'That's for a judge to decide, but I doubt it. If her behaviour was caused by her medical condition, she won't be held culpable.'

'Have you seen anything like that before, Dad?' Jono asked Sean. 'Someone going off the deep end because of a tumour?'

'Never heard of a murder, but depending on where the tumour is in the brain, it can cause increased aggression, impulsive behaviour and even personality changes. In this case, with terrible consequences.'

'And then there was all that buried trauma that came out when she saw those men again,' said Julia, sadly. 'If she hadn't seen them all having that reunion lunch together, laughing and joking, it's possible that none of this would have happened. She'd have died peacefully in a few months, and they'd all have gone on with their lives.'

'What about Anthony Ardmore's business?' asked Sean. 'Did that turn out to be a scam, or legit?'

Hayley sighed. 'It's a grey area. The business itself is a complete scam. There are no miracle plant cures anywhere close to being released, and there was no inside track with the FDA or whatever it was he claimed.'

'That sounds pretty straightforward,' said Sean.

'The part that isn't clear is whether Anthony was part of the scam, or a victim himself. Whether he simply embezzled the money invested in his company, or actually invested it in these non-existent farming opportunities. The financial guys are working at getting to the root of it. But he gave the widows most of their money back, and he has promised Ken his share back when he sells his house.'

'That's something,' said Julia, who had seen Coral and Hester murmuring to the bees that very afternoon, and guessed it must be this they were telling them. 'And at least it was all solved before Christmas, even though it will still be a difficult one for them both.'

Everyone gave a deep sigh, as if they had planned and scripted it.

'What about the postcard that the widows found?' asked Tabitha. 'The one that made you suspect Ken?'

'It turns out that *was* from Ken,' said Hayley. 'But he'd put it in the car the day before – he wanted to try to scare the widows out of withdrawing their investment. He says he was panicking and regretted it almost immediately,'

Hayley sighed. 'If I had a pound for every time someone has told me that – but it's usually about something with more serious repercussions than that postcard.'

'Let's talk about more cheerful things,' said Julia. 'I'll start – Jess has decided to come home when her degree finishes next year. She wants to spend some time in Berrywick while she applies for jobs. I'm delighted.'

'I bet Dylan is too,' said Tabitha, with a laugh.

'Not to mention Jake.'

Jake looked up hopefully at the sound of his name. There seemed to be no food in the vicinity, and definitely no walk. He dropped his head onto his paws with a sigh.

Ken came out from behind the bar, carrying his old guitar from Second Chances. He caught Julia's eye and lifted the instrument up in her direction with a little smile and a nod of acknowledgement. He sat on the stool on the makeshift stage, and cleared his throat.

'Thank you for coming, ladies and gentlemen... and dogs.'

The ripple of laughter from the audience seemed to ease his nerves, and he spoke with more confidence:

'I'm going to sing you a little song about friendship and second chances. Feel free to sing along.'

Julia smiled. Her life in Berrywick was all about friendship and second chances. She glanced over at Sean – her greatest second chance of all – and saw that he was looking at her. He raised his glass to her, as the room filled with the voices of her friends.

A LETTER FROM KATIE GAYLE

Dear reader,

By now you might know that Katie Gayle is, in fact, two of us – Kate and Gail. As we publish Julia Bird's eighth adventure, and our eleventh book as Katie Gayle, we look back at this journey that we have taken with Julia and have to pinch ourselves – it started with us just having fun and turned into a world that so many of you enjoy. We hope that you have loved this latest visit to Berrywick!

We're hard at work on more adventures for Julia and Jake and the people of Berrywick. If you want to keep up to date with all Katie Gayle's latest releases, just sign up at the following link. Your email address will never be shared and you can unsubscribe at any time.

www.bookouture.com/katie-gayle

You can also follow us on Facebook for regular updates and pictures of the real-life Jake! We really love hearing from you – especially those of you who have found Julia a help during difficult times in your life.

The best thing that you can do for us is to write a review and post it on Amazon and Goodreads, so that other people can discover Julia and Jake too. Ratings and reviews really help writers!

You might also enjoy our Epiphany Bloom series – the first

three books are available for download now. We think that they are very funny.

You can find us in a few places and we'd love to hear from you.

You can follow us on Facebook as Katie Gayle Writer. Kate and Gail are also on Insta and Threads, as @kate.sidley and @therealgailschimmel. Our website is katiegaylebooks.com.

Thanks,

Katie Gayle

facebook.com/KatieGayleWriter

PUBLISHING TEAM

Turning a manuscript into a book requires the efforts of many people. Katie Gayle and the publishing team at Bookouture would like to acknowledge everyone who contributed to this publication.

Audio
Alba Proko
Melissa Tran
Sinead O'Connor

Commercial
Lauren Morrissette
Hannah Richmond
Imogen Allport

Cover design
The Brewster Project

Data and analysis
Mark Alder
Mohamed Bussuri

Editorial
Nina Winters
Sinead O'Connor

Copyeditor
Gabbie Chant

Proofreader
Anne O'Brien

Marketing
Alex Crow
Melanie Price
Occy Carr
Cíara Rosney
Martyna Młynarska

Operations and distribution
Marina Valles
Stephanie Straub
Joe Morris

Production
Hannah Snetsinger
Mandy Kullar
Ria Clare
Nadia Michael

Publicity
Kim Nash
Noelle Holten
Jess Readett
Sarah Hardy

Rights and contracts
Peta Nightingale
Richard King
Saidah Graham

Printed in Dunstable, United Kingdom